MISTAKES WE NEVER MADE

MISTAKES WE NEVER MADE

HANNAH BROWN

with EMILY LARRABEE

FOREVER

NEW YORK BOSTON

Forever
Hachette Book Group
1290 Avenue of the Americas, New York, NY 10104
read-forever.com
twitter.com/readforeverpub

First Edition: May 2024

Forever is an imprint of Grand Central Publishing. The Forever name and logo are trademarks of Hachette Book Group, Inc.

Print book interior design by Marie Mundaca

Library of Congress Cataloging-in-Publication Data
Names: Brown, Hannah (Hannah Kelsey), 1994– author. | Larrabee, Emily, author.
Title: Mistakes we never made / Hannah Brown ; with Emily Larrabee.
Description: First edition. | New York : Forever, 2024. |
Identifiers: LCCN 2023054968 | ISBN 9781538756775 (hardcover) | ISBN 9781538756799 (ebook)
Subjects: LCGFT: Romance fiction. | Novels.
Classification: LCC PS3602.R69774 M57 2024 | DDC 813/.6—dc23/eng/20231201
LC record available at https://lccn.loc.gov/2023054968

ISBNs: 978-1-5387-5677-5 (hardcover); 978-1-5387-6993-5 (signed edition); 987-1-5387-6995-9 (special signed edition); 978-1-5387-5679-9 (ebook)

Printed in the United States of America

LSC-C

Printing 1, 2024

To my mom, for the many nights snuggled up reading tales of princes and princesses. They're what made me first love stories—and believe I'd one day find my own happily ever after.

1

WEDNESDAY NIGHT

(Three days before the wedding)

THE GREAT THING ABOUT TEQUILA IS THAT IT'S NOT JUST A DRINK. IT'S AN *activity*.

Lick. Shoot. Suck.

Salt. Tequila. Lime.

And an activity is something we desperately need.

Earlier this afternoon Sybil and I dropped our bags in the cottage we're sharing, at least until she marries Jamie on Saturday—then I'll bunk with Nikki. Her eyes had gone wide when I fanned out four identical, laminated copies of our itinerary on the white oak coffee table.

"Emma, this is so…thorough." And it was.

Complimentary hotel golf carts arrive at 7:10 p.m. Disembark at the Pelican Club at 7:25 p.m. Enjoy sunset and take photos 7:30 p.m.–8:00 p.m. Seated for dinner at 8:15 p.m.

Some might call it anal, but I just call it being prepared.

We had been progressing right on schedule. Five-star dinner: check. Oceanfront views: check. But now, a lull seems to have settled over our party. Full bellies and weak drinks will do that to you. Nikki has been sipping the same glass of rosé for an hour, while Willow nurses a nonalcoholic black pepper mango spritz. And Sybil has barely touched the rosewater and pistachio martini the bartender spent ten minutes concocting.

I covertly glance at my phone. It's only nine forty-five. This is bordering on pathetic. We're four women in our prime. Well, that is, if you consider "prime" to mean heartbroken (Nikki), pregnant (Willow), and possibly about to be fired (me). But no one can deny that Sybil is a woman in her prime, and this night was supposed to be about her. The wedding had come together in such a whirlwind that we didn't have time for a *real* bachelorette, but I had at least hoped that the Core Four coming to Malibu a day early for the festivities would allow us one unforgettable night to toast away Sybil's singledom. After mentally flipping through my itinerary of activities for the evening to see if there was anything I could shuffle around to revive our flagging group, there was only one option.

"I'm going to get us tequila shots!" I stand and adjust the sweetheart neckline of my most recently purchased Reformation sundress, brushing at the wrinkles.

Nikki perks up a bit. "I would do a shot."

"We're all going to do one. It's tradition." We do shots whenever one of us has a big win or life event. We did them when Nikki got picked to go on the reality show *LovedBy*, when I got my first big design job, when Willow got married last year. I'd even scheduled it to make sure we didn't forget: *11:15 p.m. tequila shots*. We had to have shots for Sybil's wedding. She may have been engaged three times, but she's only going to get married once. "Sybil, you're drinking Willow's too. I'll be right back, and then we can play the game!"

Sybil's eyes narrow. "What game?"

"It was on the itinerary!" I call over my shoulder, already halfway to the bar. "You're gonna love it."

The bartender—a white guy in his early thirties—is fairly cute, if only in a this-bun-and-beard-make-up-most-of-my-identity kind of way. I flash the smile that's worked on bartenders since I was a freshman at the University of Texas trying to convince them that I actually *was* Carly Mulherin, twenty-two and from Elk City, Oklahoma, not Emma Townsend, an eighteen-year-old Pi Phi from Dallas with a $120 fake ID. It's been a decade since those desperate days, but we need to get this show on the road, so I crank the charm to eleven.

"My friend Willow says the spritz you made her is the best drink she's had since finding out she was pregnant," I tell him, even though what Willow *actually* said was that it tasted like air freshener and she'd kill for a moscato. Drying a wineglass, the bartender just nods, so I plow ahead. No use wasting charm on an unreceptive audience. "Four tequila shots, please." While I wait for the bartender to pour our drinks, I take a moment to look at the material of the bar. It's a bone-colored marble with a sleek waterfall edge that adds a much-needed tension with the more boho vibes of the rest of the decor. I'm surprised that it's still in such good shape after being outside in the elements. I don't usually recommend using marble outdoors to my clients since it's so soft. Maybe it's brand-new, otherwise I need to ask what sealant they used.

"Unfortunately, I can't serve shots."

I look up from the marble. "Pardon?"

"It's against the hotel's policy." He seems entirely too pleased to be telling me the hotel's policy on alcoholic portioning. I feel the flicker of a challenge, and I fixate on it. I haven't had a ton of wins lately, but I'm not going back to our table without these shots. We're going to celebrate Sybil whether this bartender wants to help or not.

"What about four tequilas, neat," I ask, and shift my smile from friendly to conspiratorial. He looks like he's about to refuse, so I follow with a kill shot. "That man at the table by the firepit has a glass of whiskey. Neat. It really wouldn't be fair for us not to have our tequilas neat. Would it?"

He gives me a look that says he isn't particularly impressed, but must decide it's not worth the fight.

"I can give you sipping tequila," he says tightly, turning to the collection of bottles behind him. Instead of pouring the alcohol into shot glasses, he lines up four tulip-shaped glasses.

"This is an aged añejo. On the nose, you'll find a soft bouquet of lemongrass, melon, and a touch of butterscotch." He unscrews the top. "The palate opens with a hint of charred grapefruit rind, harvest grasses, and a light scent of caramel." I nod along, as if I have any idea what "harvest grasses" are supposed to taste like. "It finishes with a strong pepper spice."

"Oh, I love some spice. Could we have four lime wedges?"

He looks at me like only an absolute heathen would shoot his sipping tequila and destroy the aftertaste of "pepper spice" with a wedge of lime.

"I don't have any limes."

"Okay, lemon will work."

"No lemons, either, ma'am." That gets my attention.

"You're—are you messing with me?" I plaster on a smile, hoping against hope that this is just a mixologist's attempt at humor.

"We only use in-season ingredients grown on the property, ma'am."

"It's Southern California. Everything is always in season."

"Limes are a winter fruit. It is June."

"And y'all couldn't have gotten some from the grocery store?"

"I take my work very seriously. Some of us care about quality control and our carbon footprints." It takes him a beat, but he tacks on, "Ma'am."

That initial flicker of a challenge now roars to life. I *have* to have a lime. It's tradition. And not just for the Core Four, but for humanity in general. *Salt. Tequila. Lime.* It's practically sacred. I think back to when we arrived at the restaurant, and an idea blossoms. "Isn't there a giant floral arrangement near the host stand filled with limes?"

A vein above the bartender's left eyebrow twitches. *Victory.*

"I have no control over the aesthetic choices of the hotel's design staff."

"Okay, well, I'm going to take these glasses of aged jalapeño—"

"Añejo."

"Aged añejo," I correct as I clink all four glasses together, "and sip them very slowly. If you could just add this to my tab."

I'm not about to be bested by some snobby bartender. I'm getting one of those limes.

I turn back toward the table, drinks in hand, to see Sybil perched precariously on the deck railing, chatting with a man who has made his way to our table, drawn like a moth to a flame. He leans in to whisper something in her ear. Sybil tosses her blond hair and shoots him a megawatt smile in response, but then shakes her head and holds up her left hand, the stunning four-carat diamond catching the glow from the bar's Edison string lights. The man throws a hand to his heart like he's gutted, and Sybil consoles him, placing her right hand on his shoulder. Which means she now has zero hands on the railing.

"Oh, no, no, no." My espadrilles are sturdy, but they aren't built for speed. It's fifteen feet down to the sand, and a broken-legged Sybil would probably constitute a massive failing of my maid-of-honor duties. The glasses rattle against the slick polished wood of the table as I rush to put them down and reach for Sybil right as she begins to wobble, pulling her back onto the deck.

Sybil's admirer hovers awkwardly, as if waiting to see if he and Sybil will continue their conversation.

"Great to meet you, Glen," she says genuinely. "But I've got to get back to girls' night." The man wanders back to his table, grinning as he reaches his buddies. I've seen that look a thousand times before: high off the adrenaline of having mustered up the courage to talk to Sybil in the first place, and feeling like they really hit it off. If only he had gotten to her first, they would have lived happily ever after. Of course, in reality, Sybil could do leagues better than this middle-aged guy with a guacamole stain on his polo, but that's just how Sybil makes people feel. Special. Chosen. Like her magical light might fall on you, too, if you just stick by her side.

SYBIL AND I MET in the cafeteria of Eisenhower Elementary. It was a few weeks after my dad left us, and I was the new girl at school—which was pretty much the worst thing you can be as an eight-year-old. On the first day, Mom sent me wearing a bandanna shirt and a pair of thrifted denim shorts that she had "updated" by sewing on a bright trim with dangling rainbow beads. I'd loved the way they rattled together every time I took a step, like just walking was something worth celebrating. But clutching my red plastic tray and looking around for somewhere to sit, I quickly began to regret my one-of-a-kind ensemble. The other girls all wore those cool scrunchy micro T-shirts and a brand of jeans I'd never heard of. They looked like they'd walked off the pages of a Limited Too catalog, while I looked like my mommy's arts and crafts project. I sat down alone at the end of a table, beads digging into the backs of my legs, and prayed that the next half hour would go by fast. But then, a bright-eyed blond girl plopped down in the empty seat beside me, snapped open her Lisa Frank lunch box, said, "I like your style. My mom never lets me wear anything cool," and handed me half of a grasshopper brownie. And that was that. It was like she took my insecurities and recast them into something exceptional. Suddenly, I wasn't a weirdo in handmade clothes,

I had *style*. I wasn't alone and friendless, I had Sybil. And ever since that day, I've kept her close.

WITH SYBIL FIRMLY BACK in her seat, I motion toward the tequila. "I almost had to commit a felony to get these from the bartender, so you better drink up."

Nikki looks up from her phone and gives the bartender a predatory once-over. "He's very pretty."

"Nikki, no." Nikki has been tearing through men after her recent breakup. "He's very insufferable. And besides, I told you, you've hit your man-bun quota for the month. Now don't touch these. I have to go grab a lime."

Willow gives me a salute. "I will guard them."

I head out of the bar and back through the restaurant, swiping a saltshaker from one of the tables as I go. Like a woman on a mission, I weave through the white linen tablecloths and rattan chairs, hoping that the Pelican Club patrons don't notice the slightly wild look of determination in my eyes. I hate it when I find myself typifying the "fiery redhead" cliché, but sometimes I just can't help it. When I commit to something, I *commit*. And right now, I'm committed to making sure Sybil's wedding weekend goes off without a hitch.

I can admit to myself that the maid of honor really should have been Willow. After all, she's known Sybil the longest—ever since their mothers took a mommy and me music-in-the-park class together twenty-eight years ago. And she's always so serene and unflappable. She wouldn't have let her need to best the bartender pull her away from her friends.

But the pregnancy hasn't been easy for her, and I know Sybil didn't want to add any more stress to her life.

Nikki would have been a great maid of honor, too, or at least pre-breakup Nikki would've been. She was there when Sybil first met Jamie and had a front-row seat for all the major milestones in their relationship. But despite the many perfectly posed and flawlessly filtered photos she posts, it's clear that she's still hurting from her nationally televised breakup. And still not over Aaron.

In the end, I guess it does make sense that Sybil asked me to be her maid of honor. Our friendship has always functioned on a similar dynamic—Sybil, the glowing star of the show; me, the best friend keeping things on track behind the scenes. I know it might sound like that makes things unbalanced between us, but it's not like that. She coaxes me out of my comfort zone, and I make sure she has a soft place to land after each wild adventure she embarks on. I take pride in knowing what's best for Sybil—and all my friends—and making sure she gets it. Right now, what she needs is a lime.

I reach the gorgeous floral arrangement in the entryway. It's an explosion of greens. Bells of Ireland are a subtle kelly, the magnolia leaves a dark glossy emerald, sprays of eucalyptus are a delicate blue-green pistachio. My mind wanders—*could my painter color-match the electric chartreuse of the orchids?*—before I remember my mission. There at the bottom of the arrangement, piled high and juicy: limes.

I dart a quick look at the host stand. The woman there smiles back, but the phone rings, and she turns to the tablet in front of her. It's now or never.

I zone in on a lime right in the middle so as not to affect

the symmetry of the arrangement. It's a bit of a reach to the center of the table, but I think I can make it. Teetering on the toes of my shoes, I realize too late that one pair of my laces has unknotted. Right as my hand closes on a lime, I lose my balance. I pitch myself backward so I don't topple over onto the arrangement, but before my ass makes contact with the Spanish tile, two warm hands steady my hips, pulling away as soon as I'm stable.

As I turn to thank my rescuer, the smile on my face ices over, but I can still feel the heat of his hands around my waist. Hands I know well. Hands that have skimmed up the bare skin of my calves toward my knee, and—

No. Stop. It's not like that anymore.

I shut my eyes, as if my lids have the power to change the reality before me.

But when I open them a second later, I'm staring straight into deep brown eyes—dark but flecked with amber so they look like light through a glass of whiskey.

The eyes of none other than Finn frickin' Hughes.

2

WEDNESDAY NIGHT

(Three days before the wedding)

SHAKING MYSELF OUT OF the unwanted memory, I slip my foot back into my shoe, darting a look from the lime to the ribbons of my left espadrille puddled on the floor.

"Allow me." Finn drops down to one knee, matter-of-factly reties the bow at my ankle, and stands. Despite my six-inch platform heels, he's towering over me. I decide any flutter I feel is annoyance at being loomed over by someone so unreasonably tall.

Finn Hughes, my former debate team partner turned unforgivable asshole.

Okay, that might be *slightly* harsher than he deserves. He wasn't that bad for most of high school. But then he shot up six more inches, filled out to his current man-shape, and started making his way through the female half of our entire senior class. Once his soft smiles and serious eyes were paired with broad shoulders and a chiseled jaw, girls suddenly found him irresistible. Even smart, slightly cynical, redheaded girls were not immune.

I can chart my history with Finn in a series of *almost*s. We *almost* dated in high school. We *almost* hooked up, that summer after freshman year of college. We *almost* left our significant others for each other after things went too far one magical night on a rooftop in New York. And we *would have* never spoken again after that big blowup fight at Katie Dalton's wedding a few years ago, if it were up to me. Our story is a sequence of mistakes almost made—times when I thought Finn and I might be something more than just friends—but thankfully I've managed to avoid making the one mistake I know would be fatal: falling for him. He's a heartbreaker and a mess, and I've learned that the hard way more than once.

"What are you doing here?" I straighten up as much as possible and place my hands on my hips, tucking the lime and saltshaker to my side.

"Hi, Emma, I'm good, how are you? Why yes, it *has* been a long time." His voice is tinged with sarcasm, but he seems the slightest bit uneasy. He slides his hands into his pockets, rocking back as if he's trying to take in all of me. Feeling his eyes linger, I can't help the flush that blooms across my skin. I wonder for a moment if his brain is flipping through the same highlight reel of PG-13- to R-rated memories. His hand slipping into mine on the back of the debate team bus, his lips closing around my—

He clears his throat, and I'm jerked back to the present. "Seriously, though, it's good to see you," he adds in a casual, friendly tone.

I stare at him, steely eyed, willing my blush away. If he can stand there and be completely unaffected, then I can too.

It's been exactly four and a half years since I last encountered Finn Hughes—and I'd happily have gone four and a half *lifetimes* without seeing him again, if it weren't for our mutual friendship with Sybil. I knew Finn would be coming to the wedding, but I'd hoped to avoid him by busying myself with maid-of-honor duties and keeping my distance with the help of the nearly two hundred guests Sybil and Jamie invited. But I hadn't planned for an ambush before the wedding weekend officially got underway at the welcome party tomorrow night.

"Why are you here, Finn?" I repeat.

"I drove down early for a meeting in LA this afternoon. Sybil told me to swing by." Finn invented a healthcare app and is now a Silicon Valley tech bro who apparently zips down to LA to attend meetings and crash bachelorette parties. He rubs a hand along the nape of his neck. "The real question"—he steps forward to block me and my pilfered lime from the host—"is why are you stealing produce from a five-star resort?"

I suppress a shiver and force myself to take a step away from him. "The bartender refused to give me a lime, so I had to take matters into my own hands. You can't have a tequila shot without lime."

"Oh, of course. I'm pretty sure that's in the Constitution," he says with mock solemnity.

I nearly rise to the bait, but then remind myself that Finn and I don't debate for fun anymore. Unlike our teenage verbal sparring, which was clearly just a pretense for the flirting we were too shy to attempt, our adult arguments have the potential to wound for real. *Your Honor, I submit for evidence the complete and utter shit show that went down the last time Mr. Hughes and I saw each other.* But we need to keep our drama to a minimum this weekend for Sybil's sake. So I take a deep breath and lead him back to the group. "Come on. We're sitting on the deck out back."

We make it back to the girls, and I motion at Finn. "The stripper I hired is here."

"*That's* not on the itinerary." Nikki raises her eyebrows.

"Itinerary?" Finn's lips quirk up into a half smile. "Is this a bachelorette party or a corporate retreat?"

My grip on the lime tightens, and I set the saltshaker down more forcefully than I mean to.

"Finn!" Sybil leaps up from her seat and barrels into him. "I'm so happy to see you! You know Willow, of course. And do you remember my college roommate, Nikki?"

Finn lifts his hand in a wave. "Of course I remember Nikki," he says with a smile.

I settle onto the rattan love seat across from Nikki and Sybil, as Nikki cranks her own smile up to dazzling. "So *this* is what took you so long, Emma. I was beginning to wonder if you had decided to get the bartender's number after all."

"Nope. No man buns for me."

Finn gives a wry chuckle and settles into the seat next to Willow.

"True." Nikki nods. "You've always had a thing for guys with shorter hair. Who was that actor you loved from *Grey's Anatomy*?"

"Jesse Williams," I supply easily, but I regret it the moment I see the catlike grin on Nikki's face.

"Right! Actually..." she says, as if the thought is just occurring to her, "Finn, you look a bit like him."

Yup. I walked right into it.

"Oh, really?" Finn raises an eyebrow, clearly enjoying this. "Is that so?"

Finn doesn't look anything like Jesse Williams, unless you count the fact that they're both biracial, and built, and generally hot as hell.

"So I guess your type is someone a bit more like Finn," Nikki says, her wide blue eyes the picture of innocence, "wouldn't you say, Emma?"

I don't know what game Nikki is playing at, but I'm putting an end to it.

"Finn could be the *actual* chief of plastic surgery at Grey Sloan Memorial Hospital, and he *still* wouldn't be my type. Never has been. Never will be."

The playfulness disappears from Finn's face, and he says, "Wow, okay. Noted."

Tension hangs in the air. I fumble for something to do, and suddenly realize that I have no way to turn my hard-won lime into lime wedges. "I forgot a knife. I'll be right back."

Leaning over from his chair beside the love seat, Finn gently removes the lime from my hand and produces a small pocketknife.

"Don't worry. I know you can be a little single-minded when you're on a mission," he says.

"Do you just carry knives with you everywhere you go?"

"It's helpful to have a tool on hand."

"Well, thank the Lord we found you," I say sweetly.

He rolls his eyes but lets the insult roll off him as he quickly halves the lime, then cuts it into quarters.

"Here you are. Can't have a tequila shot without lime." He repeats my words from earlier and flashes me a smile. The sea breeze ruffles his shirt in a way that makes my stomach clench.

Sybil, Nikki, and I take our glasses, and Finn reaches for the remaining fourth.

"That's Sybil's bonus shot," I nearly growl.

"Finn can have it," Sybil says.

"You two are going to play nicely this weekend, right?" Willow asks Finn and me, a crease of worry forming on her brow, as if she too is remembering the shouting match that occurred four and a half years ago.

"Of course," Finn says quickly.

"Sure," I grit out.

And I *can* play nice with Finn. We're grown adults, after all. I'll just treat him like a demanding client with exceptionally bad taste—politely, yet firmly, pointing out when they are dead wrong. Still, might be best to stick to just one more drink. Three-Drink Emma can't be trusted to remember the "polite" part, and we don't need a Katie Dalton wedding repeat.

Finn swirls the dark gold liquid and brings it to his nose. "You know, you should really be sipping this tequila—not shooting it." I'm not a particularly violent person by nature, but I look longingly at the still-open pocketknife sitting on the table and then at a vein pulsing in Finn's neck.

"Come on, are we doing this or not?" I lick the side of my hand, sprinkle on a little salt, and pass it to Nikki. When she's ready, I raise the glass, "To Sybil!" And we both take the shot.

Lick. Shoot. Make a weird coughing noise. Blink back tears. Fumble for the lime. And, finally, suck.

Sipping might have been the right move after all, but I would throw myself off this balcony and drag my broken body into the ocean before I'd admit that. My only consolation is that Nikki seems to have had as hard a time as I did.

Willow winces at us, rubbing her belly. "I don't think I could throw back a shot like that, even if I wasn't pregnant." She sighs. "Didn't I used to be cool, once? Now I'm just a circus tent," she says, gesturing down at her patterned sundress.

"You *are* cool," Nikki insists, running a hand through Willow's dark brunette waves. "I don't know anyone else who can pull off a red lip the way you can." It's true. Willow has that chic, effortless Parisian vibe mastered. Of course, it helps that she is, in fact, French, and grew up summering at her aunt's château in Provence.

"You're stunning," Sybil adds. "And on top of that, you're a badass goddess, growing human life inside you. What's cooler than that?"

"Totally," I say, reaching over to rub her hand reassuringly. "You're still the epitome of chic. Nothing like a circus tent." Then I move my hand to her belly. "Just maybe don't wear stripes for the next three months."

Willow lets out a laugh and swats my hand away. She looks longingly at two men leaning over the rail of the deck and smoking. "I just want a cigarette."

"Willow!" My wineglass clinks against the table. "I thought you quit."

"I did quit. For a while." At my incredulous look, she adds, "I'm obviously not smoking while I'm pregnant, Emma."

"You shouldn't smoke *ever*," I say firmly.

"What am I supposed to do after I have sex, Emma? Just lie there?"

"You should go to the bathroom so you don't get a UTI," Nikki says sagely.

I make eye contact with Finn and raise an eyebrow as if to say, *Still glad you crashed our girls' night?* But to his credit, Finn does not seem fazed by our talk of post-sex self-care.

"You could always try vaping," Sybil suggests.

"Vaping is for children." Willow waves away Sybil's suggestion and takes a long sip of her mocktail, making a face as she sets it back on the table. She places a hand on her stomach and rubs absentmindedly.

"I will say one thing in the pro column for pregnancy," Willow says, as if the thought just occurred to her. "More-intense orgasms."

"Oh my god, Willow," I groan as Finn lets out a choked noise. Looking over, I expect him to be blushing, but he just looks amused.

"I'm just saying, Emma! As the first to embark on this journey, I want to give you three all the facts. Don't you want to know?"

Nikki nods seriously. "Yes, tell me everything. I hate surprises."

Finn leans forward with both elbows on his knees, his empty tequila glass dangling from his hands. His eyes crinkle with curiosity. "I'm *definitely* all ears."

Willow brightens and opens her mouth to respond—

"Time for the Newlywed Game!" I interrupt, willing away the shrillness in my voice.

The game is relatively simple. There's a series of questions to see how well the couple knows each other. If Sybil guesses Jamie's answer correctly, the three of us—four since it looks like we're stuck with Finn—take a drink. If Sybil guesses Jamie's answer incorrectly, then she has to drink. I sent Jamie the questions early last week, and he sent me back a video with all his answers.

I prop my phone up against Nikki's still-mostly-full bottle of Whispering Angel so everyone can see, and press play. The floor-to-ceiling windows of Jamie's corner office come into frame as he sets his phone up against his desktop computer.

Jamie smiles at the camera and settles back into his chair. "First question I have is: When Sybil says, 'They're playing our song,' what song is she referring to?"

Sybil answers before I can reach my phone to pause it: "'Heart Beats Slow' by Angus and Julia Stone."

"Angus and Julia Stone's 'Heart Beats Slow,'" Jamie says, nearly in unison, so we all drink.

"You guys are so meant for each other," Willow coos.

We make it through five more questions, and each time Sybil rattles off Jamie's exact answer to the trivia question. The four of us throw back swig after swig, while Sybil's undrunk cocktail threatens to slosh onto her white romper with every cross and uncross of her legs and frustrated flip of her hair. Each time the liquid comes right to the edge of the glass, but never spills over. By this point, I would be a sticky mess of rosewater-infused gin, but the universe always seems to keep Sybil from suffering anything too dire. I can't begrudge her though. If I were the universe, I'd go out of my way to make Sybil's life easier too. She makes everything sparklier. Since she left New York for LA, the city has lost some of its shine. There's no one to force me away from answering work emails or to suggest sneaking up to rooftops. But right now, Sybil's looking decidedly less than sparkly. I should have thought through this game a bit more—with every *aww*-inducing perfect answer, we all get tipsier while Sybil remains sober. No wonder she almost seems like she *wants* Jamie to get a question wrong.

Jamie's voice buzzes out of the speaker of my phone against the table. "Okay, here's the last one: What is Sybil's guilty pleasure TV show?"

I pause the video. The answer is obviously *Secrets of the Bizarre*. In middle school Sybil was *obsessed* with this sci-fi show that explored weird theories like where bigfoot lives and how aliens built the pyramids. If you don't know Sybil well, it seems pretty off-brand. I'm actually not sure if Jamie will get this one. In my anticipation to find out, I hit play a second too early.

"*Secrets of the Bizarre*," Jaime says on my phone.

"*Happiest Place*," Sybil overlaps.

"Wait, what?" I'm looking at Sybil, but she's looking at Finn. The two of them have dissolved into fits of laughter.

"Remember Tony from season three?" Finn asks.

"With the"—Sybil gasps for air—"loose tooth?"

Finn nods, and Sybil bursts out a tinkling laugh that somehow becomes a snort.

Nikki and Willow look as confused as I feel.

"That reality show about the sex lives of theme park workers?" Willow asks.

"Oh, right," Nikki says. "I know a girl who auditioned for that."

Wiping tears of mirth from her eyes, Sybil goes to take her drink, but I reach out a hand to stop her.

"I'm sorry, what the hell are you talking about?" I'm growing indignant—on Jamie's behalf, of course. "You loved *Secrets of the Bizarre*!"

"Yeah, but I don't really think of that as a guilty pleasure." Sybil shrugs. "It was just a phase. *Happiest Place* is..."

"A way of life," Finn finishes.

Irritation prickles along my spine. Clearly this show is something Sybil and Finn bonded over during what I only half-jokingly call "the dark years"—the brief period when my friendship with Sybil faded into childhood friends who have years of shared memories, but who don't talk on a regular basis. In some ways it was a natural, normal drifting apart—Sybil started hanging with a cooler crowd senior year, I threw myself into academic pursuits—but nothing about it felt normal at the time. Maybe because that's also around the time Finn and Sybil became close—despite the fact that Finn and I had already suffered a disastrous junior prom incident the year before that all but obliterated our friendship, which Sybil well knew. In some ways, it felt like she was choosing him over me. And that stung.

But this isn't about Finn Hughes temporarily usurping my role as Sybil's best friend. This is about the fact that Sybil is objectively wrong about this trivia question, and I grab my phone to prove it.

"Dictionary.com says a guilty pleasure is 'something one enjoys despite feeling that it is not generally held in high regard,'" I read off the screen. "I'm sorry, Sybil, but *Secrets of the Bizarre* is not held in high regard by anyone except you and the tinfoil-hat makers."

"Well, actually," Finn interrupts with perhaps the two most obnoxious words in the English language, "according to their IMDb, *Secrets of the Bizarre* won two Janner Awards for television production, so you could argue that—"

"No." I'm standing now, like I'm at an invisible podium. "You have to define the terms within the context of the social sphere in which they're—"

"Oh, here we go." Finn rolls his eyes, but he's standing now, too, both of us assuming the debate team stance. Willow steps between us.

"All right, nerds, settle down," she says, holding her arms out like she, at six and a half months pregnant, is going to prevent a fistfight from breaking out. Willow heaves a small groan and rubs her lower back as she shuffles over to give Sybil a hug. "Sybs, I'm sorry, but I think I'm going to head to bed. Don't worry, as soon as the baby is born, you can give them hell for making me such a party pooper."

Without Willow standing between us, suddenly I'm mere inches away from Finn Hughes and his deep brown eyes. They bore into mine, burning with that familiar spark—annoyance, competition, and maybe, just a little bit of fun?

"I'll go with you." I snap my gaze away from Finn's, away from what can only be described as dangerous territory. Finn and I have had our chances, and they all imploded spectacularly again and again, across a series of stupid moments from forever ago that I am totally over. Except for when I'm forced to come face-to-face with Finn Hughes. On those rare occasions, I'm suddenly dropped back into a swirl of memories and go from confident, twenty-eight-year-old Emma to heartbroken, sixteen-year-old Emma—every single one of my insecurities wailing like a tornado siren.

"It's nearly two a.m. New York time. I'm exhausted." It's a lie. I'm totally wired. But I hug Nikki and Sybil goodnight. Finn I just nod to. "Is it okay if we take the golf cart? I can ask the concierge to send one back."

"I can drive Sybil and Nikki back," Finn assures me. Willow and I wave a final goodbye and head to our rooms.

IT FEELS LIKE I'VE just fallen asleep when I hear a loud crash and soft curse from the living room of our cottage. I lay there for a minute debating going to check, but a history of cleaning up the aftermath of Sybil's late-night whims has me dragging myself out of bed. Sybil has thrown the doors to the coat closet wide open and is struggling to unzip the garment bag housing her wedding dress. I am immediately wide awake.

"What's going on?" I ask cautiously.

"I need to try on my dress."

"Why don't we do it in the morning when there's more light?" And less chance of a drunk Sybil destroying a five-figure gown.

"No, I need it *now*. I need to make sure it still fits."

This doesn't seem like a battle I'm likely to win, so I cross the room and help Sybil into her dress. Once I'm done, we both take a moment to look at her in the door's full-length mirror.

"I always thought it would be pouffier," she says sadly.

"Pouffier?" I ask. She sniffles and nods. "But this dress is so beautiful. *You're* beautiful."

Her fair skin and silvery blond hair look stunning against the eggshell white of the gown.

She sighs tearily and runs her hands over her hips.

"There aren't any sparkles." There aren't. It's a classically understated dress.

"We can add more sparkles." I rack my brain for ways to add sparkle to Sybil's dress without starting from scratch. "We can get a belt, a bolero, a brooch...maybe a tiara?"

Sybil perks up a bit. "A tiara?"

My worry ebbs a bit, and I crack a smile. Drunk Sybil has always been the sweetest version of Sybil. Other drunk women come out of bathrooms having made one friend; Sybil comes out of the bathroom trailing half a sorority house and invitations to Thanksgiving dinner. She also always cries. Always. Happy tears. Sad tears. Angry tears. Hungry tears. And somehow, instead of looking like a sad raccoon with frizzled hair, she always ends up looking like a woebegone fairy princess from an eighties fantasy film.

"A giant tiara." I promise. "We can talk to the hairstylist tomorrow. Nothing is set in stone."

She wipes at her tears, and she exhales softly. "Nothing is set in stone." Sybil echoes back my words. Then she grabs the skirt of her dress and spins to face me. She clutches both my hands, and I'm surprised by the strength of her grip. "Emma. I'm...I'm not sure I can do this. I need you to keep me grounded this weekend. You're my rock."

"Of course, Sybs," I say softly. "You know I'd do anything

for you." I give her hands a squeeze. "I love you to the moon and back."

My words set off another round of tears from Sybil, and she pulls me into a hug. "I love you to the ends of the ever-expanding universe, Em," she sniffles. Releasing me and turning back to the mirror, she takes a deep breath. "I know Jamie's right for me. I know it." Her voices wobbles a bit as she adds, "I just don't know if I'm right for him."

"You and Jamie are perfect for each other." I rest my head on her shoulder and meet her eyes in the mirror. The gown drapes softly at her lower back with dozens of white buttons all the way to the end of the short train. It's perfectly tailored and fits just like it's supposed to—like it's made for her. Just like Jamie is. Jamie does for Sybil what she does for everyone else. The parts of Sybil that may seem like flaws, Jamie sees as her shiniest facets. Her flakiness is *spontaneity.* Her inability to commit to a career path is *insatiable curiosity.* Her tendency to focus exclusively on one person at a time at the expense of anyone—or anything—else is *deep empathy.* "I am so happy for you, Sybs. You have it figured out. You've found your person. The one person who knows you better than anyone else on earth. Who will always be there for you, no matter what. And you'll always be there for them. Do you know how rare that is?"

Sybil's wide hazel eyes meet mine in the mirror. She's looking at me like I've just imparted some life-changing wisdom, but I know she's already halfway to forgetting this entire dress-trying-on frenzy even happened. She'll wake up tomorrow with a craving for hash browns and a head full of hazy memories of the night before.

Maybe that's why I feel safe enough continue in a whisper, "I don't know if I'll ever find what you have." It shouldn't be so hard to admit, this aching fear deep in the pit of my stomach. After all, it's a simple fact of life. Not everyone finds their person. And even if you do, finding them is no guarantee that the person will actually stick around. The women in my family know that better than most. I look back into Sybil's beautiful fairy-princess face. A face that's indisputably bound for happily ever after. I give her shoulders a squeeze. "When you walk down that aisle three days from now, just know that I'm going to be living vicariously through you, as your eternal spinster of a best friend, okay? I love you, Sybs." I tell her again for good measure.

"I love you too, Em."

"Good. Now let's get you out of this dress."

3

THURSDAY MORNING

(Two days before the wedding)

As usual, I wake up before Sybil. Even on vacation I can't stop my body clock from snapping to life at a quarter to six. While I brush my teeth, I rattle through my makeup bag looking for a bottle of Advil. After her crying jag last night, there's no way Sybs isn't waking up with a stuffed-up face and headache. I finish my morning routine, then fill up a glass with water and pad across the living room of our suite, double-checking that Sybil's dress is safe and sound in the closet.

Sure enough, the garment bag is right where it should be. No evidence of last night's episode to be found. I close the closet door and head to Sybil's room. *Urgh.* I've no sooner stepped inside when Sybil's slimy stick-on bra attaches itself to my foot. Sybil's tolerance for mess is unmatched. Don't get me wrong, I know chaos. Growing up, our house was always a topsy-turvy, cluttered mess. But while I've spent two decades learning how to rein in the madness enough to give the appearance of someone with their shit together, Sybil seems to just lean into the whirlwind. I've never understood how someone could live in such squalor and walk out into the world looking so gorgeous.

Though, to be fair, Sybil does not look gorgeous right now. One of her fake eyelashes partially detached overnight, and it looks like she's crying fuzzy black caterpillar tears out of her left eye. My heart clenches with familiar fondness. Seeing Sybil like this always endears her to me even more. It's like a peek behind the curtain. A reminder that even this effervescent goddess is human and not immune to the effects of forgetting to take your eye makeup off before bed.

I put the cup of water and the bottle of Advil right beside Sybil's phone on the bedside table so she can't miss it. Then I drape her bra, sticky side up, on the back of the desk chair by the closet and close her bedroom door behind me, breathing a sigh of relief as I return to the tidy and orderly world that is our suite's living room. I glance at my phone. There's a bunch of work emails that I'll have to deal with eventually, but for now I throw on my sneakers and slip from the room, careful not to let the door slam behind me.

THE EARLY MORNING SUN gives the trails behind the resort a gentle glow. I'm used to running on a treadmill, but the mountains looked so beautiful, and I never can resist a challenge—even one that threatens to leave me with shin splints and a stitch in my side. A few minutes into my run, I hear footsteps behind me. I guess I shouldn't have expected the trails all to myself. It's the perfect morning to be outside. The sun hasn't been out long enough to burn off the morning fog, and the air is cool against my skin even as I start to sweat. I try to focus on my breathing and the music pulsing through my earbuds, but the footsteps are gaining on me, and their ever-encroaching presence is causing a major distraction.

I'm weighing how likely it is that I'll end up the subject of a future true crime podcast if I turn around and tell this jerk to get off my ass, when suddenly a deep voice rises up from behind me.

"Good morning."

Finn frickin' Hughes. Of course.

I hold in my groan, largely because I can't spare the oxygen, and give him a brief wave assuming that he'll continue past me at his nearly inhuman pace and leave me in peace. The word *rugged* edges into my mind, and I stomp it down. Finn Hughes is *not* rugged. But here on the trail, looking all sweaty with one night's growth of stubble, he doesn't look *un*rugged. Instead of passing me, he slows down to match my speed.

I'm a good runner—or I thought I was a good runner, but I'm breathing heavily, while Finn is totally unaffected by what feels like an eighty-nine-degree incline. I consider just dropping into a walk, but there's no way that I'm going to let Finn Hughes beat me. Especially when it doesn't seem to make a difference to him whether we're going up a hill or down a hill. He keeps an even pace with me as we run another mile or so.

I'm dying. I am dead. I've died.

"How…are you…doing this?"

"There are a lot of hills in SF," he says and shrugs. "Don't worry, I grabbed a copy of the trail map before I headed out. There should be a little rest stop with water after the next switchback."

Nerd. It's not like we're hiking in the untamed wilderness—this trail is just a loop that goes right back to the hotel. But secretly I'm glad to know salvation lies just up ahead. Sure enough, after the next turn, there's a bench and a small shed. I collapse on the bench, while Finn ducks inside the shed and returns with two water bottles with the hotel's logo printed along the label. He hands me one, but I shake my head and wave him away. I'm still struggling to get oxygen back into my body. Water is more than I can handle right now. He places it beside me on the bench and looks out on the view. It's obvious why the hotel set up a rest stop here; the view from the mountains down to the ocean is stunning. If Finn weren't here to ruin it, it would've been absolutely worth the effort to get up here.

We sit there, basking in the fresh air—well he's basking, I'm struggling to return my breathing to normal—when Finn's phone pings. He pulls it out of his armband while I pretend to study the crop of wildflowers growing on the edge of the trail. He shields his eyes to read the message, and I subtly arch my back, trying to catch a glimpse of his screen. Yes, it's totally nosy of me, but I'm curious. It's barely six thirty. Who would be texting him so early? Work…or a girl? Maybe he's already swiping through the women of Southern California in hopes of landing a hookup or two while he's in fresh territory. He types away a response on his phone, each letter audibly clacking as he goes.

"Ah yes, I love the sound of technology in the morning. Really helps me commune with nature."

I can't help myself. And seriously, who doesn't keep their phone on silent mode these days anyway?

Finn shoots me a look, then scrolls up a bit and hands the phone to me.

I have no idea what to expect, but what I see there on the screen is probably the very last thing I could have come up with: there are at least three dozen photos of baby otters. One of a baby curled up asleep on its mama's belly. Another of a pile of four babies tumbled all over each other. And one where a baby otter has bared its teeth, clearly trying to look menacing, but only succeeding in looking totally adorable. I don't even try to stop the smile that breaks through. "That one reminds me a little bit of you," he says, and a warm feeling washes over me, snuffing out that spark of competition.

I turn my grin to him. "So what is this? A secret fetish?"

"My mom—"

"Your *mom* is your secret fetish?" I interrupt with glee. We may be having a friendly-ish moment here, but come on, I can't let that pitch go by without a swing.

"*My mom*," he barrels on, ignoring my outburst, "sends me these. She has it stuck in her head that otters are my favorite animal, so whenever she comes across a picture of them, she sends it to me."

Okay, even I have to admit that's possibly the cutest thing I've ever heard. Maybe even cuter than the picture of the otter wearing overalls. It's close.

I've scrolled to the end of the otter photos, and my eye catches a screenshot of a foyer covered floor to ceiling in a midnight-garden-patterned wallpaper. Not just any floral, but a hand-drawn original made by a Brooklyn artisan who has recently gone global. The exact original wallpaper, in fact, I used in a design six years ago. "Is that—"

He takes the phone back from me quickly, and I finish my question. "My foyer?"

It's the entryway I designed for Nikki's older sister, Jacqueline, when I first moved to New York. It's by far my most successful piece of design work, and the room that got me hired at my current firm. It's the first image that comes up on Pinterest if you type in my name. It's also one of the last times that I felt like I really nailed what my client wanted while still staying true to myself as a designer. The last few years at work have seemed like compromise after compromise. But working with Jacqueline, I was able to get her to take a bit of a risk while still making sure she loved the room when we finished.

Raising the water bottle to his mouth again, Finn tries to take a sip, but has forgotten to unscrew the cap. I'm surprised at how flustered he seems. He gets the cap off and takes a long swig before replying, as if he's deciding whether or not to deny it.

"I try to keep up with all my old schoolmates." My mouth quirks at *schoolmates*—a vastly inadequate term to describe our complicated history. A small whirlpool has formed around the warm feeling in my rib cage. All the feedback I've gotten from work recently has been negative. It's nice to know that maybe there are people out there who appreciate my aesthetic. "Sybil sent me the link to an article with some of your work.

She knows I might need some help with a remodel down the road."

Ah, so back to Sybil. I've always wondered if Finn carries a bit of torch for her, if maybe she's the one girl he couldn't catch. Sybil was never one of Finn's romantic conquests (thank god), but while she and I drifted apart senior year, he seemed to take her in like a lost puppy—or more like they were two lost puppies leading each other straight into traffic. While I was busy cramming, the two of them were poster children for senioritis, hopping from back house to back house getting drunk on Coke and vanilla vodka and smoking pot.

Sybil and I eventually found our way back to each other thanks to a European backpacking trip the summer after freshman year of college—a trip that sparked the creation of the Core Four, with Nikki, Sybil, Willow, and me all traveling together for the first time. Still, it wasn't until after college when we both moved to New York that Sybil and I got back to the level of friendship we'd had for most of high school. For three years, we were as close as sisters, living in a tiny two-bedroom in the East Village. But eventually the West Coast called for Sybil once more, and she moved back to LA. Now, with a full continent between us, I can feel her slipping away again. I'd written it off as normal adulthood stuff. I mean, she's marrying Jamie. He's going to be her person. That's how it should be. But I can't help but feel the slightest bit abandoned—and more than slightly territorial. Especially after last night's stupid game, when Finn seemed to be flaunting that he knows more about Sybil than I do.

So, I do what I always do: go on the offensive. "That foyer seems like it might be more color than you're up for." I raise an eyebrow at his black shorts and a slate-gray top. Clearly this man cannot handle bold design choices. "Aren't entrepreneurs supposed to wear the same black turtleneck every day? Are you suddenly big into florals now?"

"I could be." Finn shifts his entire focus to me, and the warm whirlpool in my chest sinks lower in my body.

I'm about to toss back another taunt, but I swallow it down. Maybe it's my worry about losing Sybil again, or maybe the lack of oxygen has left me without my full mental capabilities, but something makes me extend an olive branch. "We used to be a great team. If you do decide you want to work with a designer, you should give me a call."

He gives me a surprised look, and I'm equally surprised by how much I mean it. We *were* a great team. Finn never misses anything, and he's incredibly thorough. For debate prep, he would research all contingencies, all perspectives. The only downside was that he could spend too much time in the weeds. He wouldn't go in for the kill. That's where I would come in. I could follow my instincts, because I always knew that he'd be there to follow through with the research. It was one of the only times in my life where I knew I could depend on someone to be there for me when I was completely myself. I could go out on whatever limb I needed to because I knew Finn would be there to catch me. Until one day he didn't.

"Well, I'm going to head back down for breakfast." I stand, leaving my untouched water bottle abandoned on the bench.

"I think I'll keep heading up," Finn says. "Catch you at the welcome party tonight?"

"Yeah, I'll see you then."

★ ★ ★

I TAKE IT SLOWLY back down the mountain. When I make it to the patio for breakfast, the only people I recognize are Sybil's parents. Mrs. Rain waves me over to sit with them.

"I don't want to make you sit next to me while I'm all sweaty."

"Oh, sweetie, don't worry about it." She pulls out the chair beside Mr. Rain.

"Yes, we'll just put you downwind!" Mr. Rain quips.

I've always loved Sybil's dad.

Mrs. Rain, while perfectly pleasant, always seemed less accessible. She was a different kind of mother than the one I grew up with. Playgroups, PTA fundraisers, garden club. There's no world in which my mom would've had time for any of that. Even before my dad left, she worked part-time as a real estate agent, and then after he was gone, she usually had at least two jobs going. Between gigs at the dental office and the day care at the Y, Mom would still list houses on the side. Instead of ballet class or soccer, I spent nearly every Sunday in middle school trying to keep my little sister Liz occupied while my mother talked to strangers about ceiling heights and original hardwoods. Meanwhile, Willow and Sybil drove out to Lake Athens to ride Jet Skis and build bonfires and eat Mrs. Rain's perfectly baked chocolate peanut butter cookies.

Mr. Rain puts down his coffee and turns to me. "Did you see that Porsche parked out front? It's a 964 reimagined by Singer." He is very into cars, and I think has always had a soft spot for me, since I am too.

"Really? That body style is one of my favorites." I reach for a menu and make a mental note to swing through the parking lot on our way to the spa. "I've never seen a Singer in person. Is it one of the wedding guests?"

"I assume it's one of Jamie's friends. He tends to run with a flashy crowd, doesn't he? *Californians*. You know," Mr. Rain finishes, as if that explains everything. And it kind of does. Sybil's family is well-to-do in Dallas, but the difference between being rich in Dallas and rich in LA is $50 million and a private jet. "I'd try to hunt down the owner right now, but we're off to play a round of golf after this."

He's about to continue, but the waiter stops at our table. "Would you like something to drink?"

"Could I have a Bloody Mary?" I ask. "And could you make it very spicy? Maybe not the-surface-of-the-sun hot, but very-close-to-getting-vaporized hot."

The waiter gives me a long look, and asks, "So, you want it warmed up?"

"I—no." I have to remember that not everyone is ready for banter at seven thirty in the morning. "I just want it spicy. Thanks."

The waiter nods and heads back to the kitchen, and I know that I'll be getting slightly salty tomato juice.

Mr. Rain shoots me a knowing look. "Californians."

I smile. "You know, Sybil is technically a Californian these days."

He presses his lips together and gives a reluctant half nod, as if he's not quite willing to accept that fact.

The waiter returns and sets my Bloody Mary beside me, but before I take a drink, Mrs. Rain asks, "Are you ready for your speech on Saturday, dear?" I nod, though in reality my maid-of-honor speech is still a bit theoretical at the moment. Snippets of stories and favorite anecdotes swim in my brain alongside an inspirational quote or two. It feels like such a big responsibility, I've been avoiding putting pen to paper. People assume because of my debate team days that I'm comfortable speaking in front of a crowd, but I actually hate giving toasts. They completely stress me out for some reason. Just last year at my mom's birthday I tried to say a few words about how much she means to me and ended up getting so flustered I just mumbled out "*Hook 'em!*" and threw up the horns hand sign—which would usually be enough to win over any Austin crowd, except for the fact that my mom doesn't even *like* football. Needless to say, the thought of giving a speech in Sybil's honor two days from now has me slightly freaked.

"He's been practicing his in the shower," Mrs. Rain says over her orange juice glass, nodding to her husband.

"Of course I need to practice. This is important. This is my baby." Mr. Rain clears his throat. "She made me a dad, you know."

He says it so matter-of-factly. As if all fathers take one look at their baby girl and are instantly and irrevocably wrapped around their finger, when I know that some fathers take one look at their baby girl and then, eight years later, they pick up and move to Arizona with Kimberly from marketing. Mr. Rain's speech is just one of many classic father-of-the-bride moments I'll have to witness this weekend. I can't let them get to me. I take a long sip of my drink so that I have a moment to compose myself. But unlike last night's tequila snob, *this* bartender clearly has no problem with directions. I let out a gasp.

The cayenne from the Bloody Mary has vaporized up my

throat and into my sinuses, and I blink back tears. *Perfect.* I chug back a few more gulps, then my phone buzzes with one of the many reminder alarms I've set for today.

"Our first spa appointment is at eight thirty," I say, and grab a muffin for the road. "I'm going to find Sybil."

I make my goodbyes and head back to the cottage.

Sybil's bedroom door is closed when I arrive, and I don't hear any signs of life coming from inside. "Sybs! You gotta get up! It's time for phase one of Sybil's Ultimate Pamper Sesh." Nothing. I roll my eyes and head for my own room to take a lightning-fast shower. Afterward, I put on a clean pair of running shorts and a white tank top with tiny black flowers.

Are you suddenly big into florals now?

I could be.

I shake my head, roughly towel drying my hair.

Stop it, Emma. You are not going down that road again.

Meanwhile, Sybil's door is still closed. "Come on, sleeping beauty," I say letting myself in. "Time to rise and sh—aghhh!" I trip over a fuchsia stiletto and barely catch myself on the pencil-reed credenza to the right of the door. The blast radius from Sybil's suitcase has extended out another six feet since last night.

But wait a minute.

Her suitcase. It's gone.

And all that remains of Sybil is one false eyelash, winking up at me from the empty bed.

4

THURSDAY MORNING

(Two days before the wedding)

NIKKI'S ROOM IS THE first place I look for Sybil. It's very possible, I tell myself while crunching along the pebbled path from our cottage to Nikki's, that Sybil just headed to the spa without me. It's not what was on the itinerary, which clearly read:

> Meet at Emma and Sybil's at 8:15 a.m. Walk to the spa for 8:30 a.m. appointments.

Sybil loves an Irish goodbye, but she wouldn't Irish goodbye her *wedding*. People don't do that.

Except I know for a fact they do. People walk out of their lives all the time. My dad did. I ignore the thick bubble of anxiety in my chest. Sybil is not my dad. But she has bailed on two other engagements before...

I knock on Nikki's door a little more forcefully than I mean to, but Nikki opens it with a smile. For a moment it feels like everything might be back to normal, and I'm sure that I'm overreacting about Sybil. "Is she with you?"

"Who?" The false optimism I've been clinging to with my fingernails drops away.

"Sybil."

"No, we're supposed to meet at y'all's place." She gives me a very serious look. "It says so on the schedule. I'm almost ready. If you wait a second, I'll walk with you." I follow Nikki inside as she fills a tote bag to take to the spa.

"Have you heard from her?" I ask. "She had a little bit of a meltdown when she got home last night, and now she's not in her room."

Nikki's movements slow, and she turns to face me. "I have to tell you something, and I need you not to freak out."

"I won't freak out," I lie.

"So last night, we went into a bar in town after you and Willow left, and she had a little more to drink."

"One sec." Through Nikki's window, I see Willow waddling down the path, and I wave her inside.

"Are we meeting here? The itinerary said 'Emma and Sybil's.'" Willow leverages herself into a white bouclé armchair, and I regret every second that I put into that itinerary.

"The itinerary is done. It's over. We're all on Sybil Time now." I realize that for a weekend all about Sybil, maybe I should have just planned to be on Sybil Time from the start. "What happened last night?"

"Well, Finn suggested we check out this cool tequila bar his friend owns. Apparently Finn invested in it."

"He *invests* in things?" I don't want to be impressed, but I am. I'm barely able to invest in rent and a monthly MTA card these days.

"Focus, Emma. When we got there, we lost Sybil for a little bit, and when she came back, she was pretty upset." Nikki sinks into the chair next to Willow.

"You *lost* her?" I ask through clenched teeth.

"Obviously, not permanently!" Nikki raises her hands in exasperation. "I thought she had just disappeared to the bathroom or something, but the rest of the night she seemed so rattled..."

There's a soft knock on the door, and I lunge to open it, hoping it may be Sybil.

"Oh, girls. I'm glad I caught you all." Mrs. Rain is standing there in full golf gear. "Sybil just texted me that she's headed down to San Diego for a facial this morning, but she'll be back by the welcome party tonight."

I let out a sigh of relief, but it's short-lived.

"But wait—we already had facials scheduled here."

"She said she had too much tequila last night." *Finn.* "And that she needed a lymphatic massage to get rid of all the puffiness. There's a woman at the Hotel Del Coronado who is 'life-changing.'" She makes scare quotes with her fingers, and shrugs. "You know Sybil. It's probably a sentimental thing. I'm off to hit some balls. You girls have fun at the spa today."

Something's not sitting right. Yes, Jamie proposed at the Del, so it could make sense for Sybil to go all the way down there just for a massage. But sentimental isn't how I would describe Sybil. She's always looking forward—not backward.

I can feel the stress zit that I doused with salicylic acid in the hopes that I'd be able to head it off before the wedding pulse with new life. It's classic Sybil. She never means to hurt anyone, but she also never considers any of the collateral damage she leaves in her wake.

"Why wouldn't she text any of us?" I ask, closing the door behind Mrs. Rain.

"Probably because we would have asked follow-up questions." Nikki resumes getting her things together for the spa. "Last night, at the bar..."

"What?" I demand.

Nikki clears her throat. "She and Finn kind of had a heart-to-heart or whatever, and he said that if she wasn't absolutely sure she wanted to get married, she shouldn't go through with it." At the look on my face, she quickly adds, "Which you know is good advice, Emma."

"I most certainly do *not* know that. She already decided she wanted to get married when Jamie proposed and she put the ring on her finger!"

"I don't know if that's how Sybil sees it, Em," Willow says. She and Nikki seem much more relaxed after Mrs. Rain's report, but one piece still isn't fitting.

"But why would she take her suitcase?" That seems to get their attention.

Anxiety spikes through me as I remember Sybil's words from last night. *I'm not sure if I can do this. I need you.*

"She bolted."

"She wouldn't bolt." Even Willow doesn't believe what she's saying, though, because she follows up with "Would she?"

"But Jamie's great," Nikki says. "She's been different with him."

"She absolutely bolted," I say with growing certainty. I think back to her sudden urge to try on her dress last night, *to make sure it still fits*. It makes so much more sense now. And with my growing certainty comes a growing anger at Finn. He led her to the edge, and pushed her over. Sybil needs me to pull her back. I need to fix this. She as much as asked me to last night.

"I'm going to San Diego to get her. Willow, you stay here and help the Rains greet the guests as they arrive. Nikki, you're coming with me."

A pained look crosses her face. "Em, I can't. Aaron is at Torrey Pines. He posted about it last night." I blink once not understanding. She continues, "The golf course. He's there for the US Open. I can't be in San Diego while he's there. I can't look desperate, like I'm following him around. Someone might get a photo of me. I hate that we're even on the same coast right now." The likelihood of Nikki running into her ex in a city the size of San Diego seems incredibly small, but she looks so miserable that I don't push it.

"Fine. But I need a car."

Nikki nods. "You can take mine."

I make a face. The autopilot on Nikki's top-of-the-line electric car gives me whiplash, but it's my only option, so we head to the valet stand to pick it up. "Just promise me you won't interact with Aaron while you're there, okay?" Nikki says as the valet pulls the car around.

I nod to placate her, but can't resist an instruction of my own. "And *you* just promise *me* that you'll unfollow him on social media. I told you to do that ages ago."

Nikki nods, taking the keys from the valet and popping her head inside the car. "Oh no...I forgot to charge it. Sorry, Em—"

"It's fine." I open up my Lyft app and search for the Hotel Del Coronado. After a minute of searching, the app says a car can be here in fourteen minutes, and the ride estimate is *$347.* Okay, that's not happening.

Damn it. Why did I leave Sybil and Nikki alone with Finn last night? I should have known the king of failed commitments would find some way to derail things. But even as my agitation grows, an idea is taking shape.

"Didn't Finn drive y'all to that bar?"

"Yeah, that's his car right there." She motions to a black Tahoe, and I get my first glimpse of the Porsche Mr. Rain mentioned, parked right next to it.

"You know what, Finn made this mess. He got her stupid drunk on tequila and then gave her terrible advice. He needs to help clean it up. Where's his room?"

"I think he's over on the west side of the resort in one of the presidential cottages. Maybe 455 or 456?" Nikki says. "But I don't know that Finn..." I'm already turning down the path to his room before Nikki can finish her sentence, and I run smack into—

"Jamie!" I pull up abruptly and try to look as unbothered as possible. "Where are you going?" I wince at how accusatory I sound, and try to gloss over it with a smile. "I mean, anything we can help with?" Nikki rolls her eyes as she returns her keys to the valet.

"Just headed in to say good morning to Sybil." He either misses my shortness or has the politeness to look past it. "I stopped by your room, but no one answered."

"Um, she's not here. She just texted that she's already at the spa." Which according to Mrs. Rain is not technically a lie.

"Oh, that's too bad. I was hoping we could have a little time alone before everyone got here." He looks genuinely bummed that he doesn't get to see Sybil, which makes the worry I'm feeling for Sybil bleed into irritation that she's pulled this disappearing act. She has a guy who is crazy about her, and she's about to throw it all away like it's nothing.

"Well, I'll tell her you were looking for her. Maybe y'all can get together this afternoon?"

"Thanks, Emma. See you." He heads into the main clubhouse of the resort, and I head toward the presidential suites.

Room number 455 or 456...I have a fifty-fifty shot. One's facing the mountains and one is overlooking the ocean. I take a guess and start banging on the door facing the ocean. "*Finnegan Michael Hughes!* Open this door right now!"

The door swings open, and I plow through only realizing after the fact that my arm brushes against warm, wet skin, not cool cotton. Droplets of water glitter from Finn's black hair, and a clump of suds slides down his neck and settles on his shoulder. He readjusts his towel, and tucks it firmly against sculpted abs.

"Are you okay?" he asks.

"I'm—yes, I'm okay." I am *not* okay seeing Finn in nothing but a towel. It's been just under five years since I last saw him half-naked, and somehow he seems to have grown even more chiseled in that time. I open my mouth, but nothing comes out.

"Emma, what? Is Sybil okay?"

I pull my eyes up to his face. "Sybil could be dead in a ditch."

"Oh my god." He whips open the duffel bag and grabs a T-shirt and pants. The movement dislodges the soapsuds, and they begin to travel down his chest. "Wait here."

He's halfway to the bathroom. "I mean, I don't think she is. She said she went to San Diego for some lymphatic drainage, and right now she's too puffy to make any type of public appearance."

He turns back to me, and the suds slip from his chest to his stomach. I've never really had opinions on men's chest hair, but watching the bubbles catch in Finn's, I decide that I could definitely argue the "pro" side of that debate. "Drainage?" Finn asks. "Is that serious? Something's wrong with her lymph nodes?"

"I—no." I finish weakly, "It's just a type of massage."

His eyes narrow. "You nearly dented my hotel room door and dragged me out of the shower because Sybil went to get a massage?"

"A massage in *San Diego*."

"That's just a couple hours away, Emma. She'll be fine."

I straighten my shoulders. "It doesn't matter how far away she is. It matters that she's not here."

"Sybil's an adult, Emma. You need to start treating her like one."

The suds continue down his stomach. I imagine my fingers following the trail of foam, and my hand twitches. A large bubble pops just above his belly button, and I remember why I'm here. "You told her not to get married!"

"I told her she owed it to herself and Jamie to be absolutely sure this is what she wants. Marriage is forever."

That's twice Finn has been wrong in the last thirty seconds. Marriage is *not* forever. Or, at least, forever isn't guaranteed. He heads back into the bathroom and comes out with another towel, wiping away the bubbles left on his skin. I can admit Finn's body is somewhat...attractive, but it's unfortunately attached to Finn's brain and mouth. In that moment, I make the mistake of looking at his mouth, with its full bottom lip and Cupid's bow top, and amend my thought. It really is just the brain that's the deal killer here.

"I need to borrow your car."

"Emma, there is no way I am letting you take my car. You almost destroyed Mr. Rain's Porsche junior year—"

"*Almost* being the key word. I would never have let something happen to a 959."

"And you drive like a psychopath."

"I do *not*!"

"You almost threw Willow out of the golf cart last night."

"It's not my fault one hundred percent of torque is immediately available in electric vehicles! And those tires are bald. I won't be held accountable for this hotel's poor vehicle maintenance."

He cocks his head at me as if I'm a cat that has just started explaining algebra. "Wow, your car obsession is on another level, you know that? It's kind of adorable," he says.

I cringe at his use of *adorable*. It's the word people have used to describe me my entire life. Sybil is always ethereal and enigmatic. Willow is sexy and striking. Nikki is gorgeous and all-American. But at five foot two with bright auburn hair and a spray of freckles across my nose, I get to be adorable. "Just give me the keys."

"Wait here." He ducks back into the bathroom with the clothes he grabbed, and the shower turns on. The suite is huge. Crossing my arms, I plop down on the bed. I immediately regret it. It smells amazing, like woodsmoke and lavender. Like Finn. His scent mingles with the citrusy smell of my own still-damp hair. Grapefruit and lavender. Sharp but sweet. Me and Finn. It's a heady combination. I stand up. The shower cuts off, and a moment later, Finn emerges from the bathroom fully dressed. "We'll be back before the welcome party?" he asks.

"*I* will be." I put my hand out for Finn's keys, but he just shakes his head with a smile.

"If my car's going, then I'm going."

He's being incredibly precious about a ten-year-old Tahoe, but Finn is my only option at this point. "Fine, yes. We'll be back before the welcome party. Now can we go?"

We don't speak as we make our way back to the valet stand, but Finn is in a fantastic mood for a man who's just been bullied into spending his day off chauffeuring a grumpy bridesmaid. We pass the valet stand, and my hand is on the Tahoe's door, but Finn keeps walking. There's a soft click as the doors to the 964 unlock.

My hand drops to my side, but I don't move. "The Singer is *yours*."

He can't keep the smile off his face. "Pretty cool, right?"

I walk toward the car slowly, as if it might disappear along with Sybil. "I'm driving."

Finn laughs. "No."

I circle the car. It's got the wide hips and lower stance of a car built for the racetrack. The passenger door is so light when I open it. "Is this carbon fiber?"

"The body is. The doors are aluminum." Finn pats the roof of the car twice, and I'm struck by the unfairness of the universe. I run my hand over the bespoke woven seat inserts before I climb into the car and let out a small sigh of pleasure. If I have to chase Sybil, at least I get to do it in a perfect car.

The engine rumbles to life, and Finn turns to me. "Let's go catch a runaway bride."

5

THURSDAY MORNING

(Two days before the wedding)

MY DAD ALWAYS SAID you could tell all you needed to know about someone from how they kept their car. Scraped-off bumper stickers means they're probably impulsive but can't commit to anything long term. Grime on the body will tell you they can't afford a carport—much less a garage. Though my dad always had a soft spot when he saw cars parked on the street with their side-view mirrors folded in. They might not have a lot, he said, but they took care of what they had.

In Texas, we measure our lives in hours of driving. Dallas is three hours from Austin. Austin is nine hours from El Paso. And El Paso is eight hours and two missed childhoods away from my shitty dad. Cars are an assurance that no matter how bad it gets, you can always get in and head into the unknown, which is probably why my dad loved them so much. But it turns out there are some things you can't leave behind no matter how much horsepower you have.

The Singer purrs beneath us as we weave down the Santa Monica Mountains and out to the coast. The view is spectacular. Manhattan may be an island, but these days the closest I get to the water is when the L train goes under the East River on my way to work.

I start to put down my window, but Finn hits what must be a child-lock button on his driver's-side door.

"The AC is on," he says by way of explanation.

"Well, I can't smell the ocean through the AC."

"Strong rebuttal, but I'm going to have to counterargue that you won't smell the ocean so much as the exhaust fumes from that eighteen-wheeler up ahead."

I roll my eyes at his debate team speak but concede the point. We may be on one of the most scenic highways in the country, but the fact remains that it *is* a highway and we're in near bumper-to-bumper traffic.

"So what time did you tell Jamie that we'd be back?"

"Jamie thinks we're at the spa at the hotel," I say, pulling my gaze from the ocean to see Finn's appalled face.

"Jamie doesn't know?" He reaches for his phone, but suddenly has to pull up short to shift gears as the car in front of us slows. "I'm calling him right now."

"You are *not.*" I pluck the phone out of his cup holder. "This'll all be fixed soon, and he never needs to know."

"If it was my fiancée, I would want to know." My skin tingles at the low rumble of Finn's tone. He reaches across the gearshift, his forearm grazing my bare thigh, but I manage to hold the phone out of reach.

"Well, clearly Sybil *didn't* want Jamie to know, or she would have told him her plans. You really want to rat her out?" His loyalty to Sybil gives him pause just long enough for me place the phone on the floorboard beside my feet, where he can't reach it without risking sending us crashing over the guardrail and into the waves below.

As I lean back into my seat, I notice an old CD in the pocket of the car door. I rotate it so I can see the spine. *Celtic Woman.*

I stifle a laugh. I used to have this exact album. Well, Mom did. She would blast the melodic wailing, reminding Liz and me that this was our heritage (as if my auburn hair wasn't constant reminder enough of our Irish roots). It's the type of CD that would immediately lose Finn cool points with his tech-bro friends, so naturally, I have to call him out on it. I'm racking my brain trying to remember any Gaelic song titles I can work into a sentence, when suddenly the phone at my feet buzzes.

Finn raises an eyebrow at me. "That could be important."

I lean forward to grab it. "More otter pics from your mom?"

"Emma…" he warns.

"Ooh, is it your girlfriend calling to check in?" The phone continues to buzz in my palm and I check the caller ID. It's an unsaved San Francisco number. "Wow, you don't even have her number saved to your contacts? That's harsh." I have no idea if Finn is seeing anyone at the moment, and his face is betraying nothing. I guess I could just *ask* him if he actually has a girlfriend, but first I'd have to care. Which I don't.

Finn snorts. "I'm sure your boyfriend is saved with about five emojis." He makes another swipe to grab the phone, catching a bit of side-boob in the process. "Did you go with the eggplant, or keep it classy and stick to the kissy face?"

"Hey, no redirects allowed." The phone keeps ringing. "Is this chick stalking you? Need me to intervene?"

"I think I can handle it," he says, holding out his hand.

"Oh, I know you are capable of juggling multiple ladies," I say. Finn winces slightly but doesn't look over at me. "Just tell me this." I'm still clutching the phone to my chest. "Does whoever's calling actually know she's not your girlfriend? Or are we still out here breaking hearts?"

"Trust me, I'm very open about the fact that I'm not in a relationship place right now." Finn's eyes are on the road, and I'm a little deflated that he's being so serious, even while admitting that he's basically a self-proclaimed player. I don't know why, but I'm in a teasing mood. Finn brings it out of me.

"You know, maybe I should take this for you. You are driving, after all." I pretend to press the answer button on the phone and hold it to my ear. "Sexual Emoji Department, Emma Townsend speaking."

"Hello?"

A tinny voice emits from Finn's phone, startling us both. I involuntarily toss the phone back to the floor then quickly grab it and pass it over to Finn. "Shit," I whisper. "I am so sorry."

He glances at the screen. "It's work," he says to me, and then into the phone he answers with a gruff "Hughes here."

I curl away from Finn, pressing my body into the passenger door, as if perhaps I'll be able to melt into the smooth leather interior.

Desperate for any distraction from my mortification, I pull out my own phone and scroll through my work inbox.

There's a meeting invitation from my boss for Monday morning with just two words in the subject line: *Performance Review.* I accept the meeting and close out my email. Great. Now I'll have that hanging over my head like a guillotine blade all weekend.

I take a deep breath in, hold it for seven seconds, then exhale for eight, just like the antianxiety app taught me.

Finn wraps up his call, placing his phone back in the cup holder, where I don't even dare to look at it.

"Sorry about that," I say sheepishly.

"That was one of my top investors." He stares straight ahead out the windshield, so it's hard to tell how pissed he is.

"Shit. Seriously, Finn, I am so sorry. Did I screw anything up for you?"

"Just a multimillion-dollar sale."

My jaw drops. I'm about to start groveling when I notice the corner of his mouth twitch. Finally, he looks over at me, and when he does, I can see that I haven't actually ruined his career with my stupid joke.

"Screw you," I say, relieved. I punch my window-down button defiantly. Despite Finn's counterargument, I *can* smell the salt air. I take a deep breath, not bothering to count my inhale this time. Traffic has cleared a bit, so we're moving with speed now. The wind whips my hair around my face, getting caught in my mouth, but I don't care. I'm suddenly transported back to bus rides to debate tournaments when Finn and I would pass the time by playing round after round of truth or dare. I glance over at him, trying to reconcile this version of Finn with the kid I met in middle school—shy, and sweet, but with a biting wit that could surprise you. The breeze ruffles the sleeve of his shirt, and for a moment, I can almost see *him*—and not this semi-stranger that Finn has become.

"I am selling my company though," he says, raising his voice over the sound of the air rushing by us. "Or really, I've sold my company. It's just paperwork at this point."

Things begin to click together. The investing, the Singer, the second-nicest cottage at an incredibly expensive hotel… suddenly I'm thinking the phrase *multimillion-dollar sale* might not have been part of the joke. I roll my window back up and look over at him.

"Oh, wow. Congrats." I almost wince at how sullen I sound. Sure, Finn may have stomped on my tender heart more than once, but why shouldn't he be a crazy-successful entrepreneur? It's not like I've spent the last five years praying for his demise. If it weren't for our respective friendships with Sybil keeping us tethered to the same gravitational force, my interactions with Finn would be negligible. I couldn't care less how many classic cars he owns or how many perfectly tailored T-shirts he can afford. It's just that my own current professional situation is a nightmare, all my friends are living somewhere else, and my love life's on ice. (Alas, no eggplant emoji to speak of. My most recent relationship ended last fall. He always put his wet coffee spoon back into the sugar bowl. Enough said.) Work is all I have right now. It's rough to see so many of my contemporaries thriving as full-blown, successful adults, while I'm barely managing to hang on to my job.

Until a few months ago, I had actually been doing really well. I was on my way to becoming one of the youngest senior designers in company history. But then the Hansons came along. They were a couple from Dallas who'd recently purchased a gorgeous, neoclassical mansion in Highland Park. Excited by the hometown connection, I lobbied my boss hard to let me take the lead on the project. She relented when the Hansons mentioned how much they liked the foyer I'd worked on here in NYC.

I put together my pitch and flew home to Dallas.

It was a shit show.

Turns out they weren't looking for the dramatic foyer that I'd done for Nikki's sister. They were talking about a hotel I'd worked on in Williamsburg, a sleek obsidian and malachite space for their lobby. I was proud of how I'd executed my boss's vision on that one, but it was never something I would have designed myself. The Hansons took one look at the bold, artistic design I'd drawn up for their home, and promptly fired our firm.

The only thing worse than seeing the dirt lot where they razed the historic mansion was the ominous references to "reassessing my role within the team" that my boss has been making ever since.

Finn flips on the radio, looking for a clear signal, eventually settling on some bland Top 40 station. I consider mocking him for the *Celtic Woman* CD, but the reminder of the disparity of our work situations has zapped the fun out of it. *Sure, you might be a tech wunderkind with career success and Mr. Darcy levels of financial stability, but* I *have cooler taste in music—so there!*

Instead, I take in the rest of the car. The back is filled with papers, a soft-sided Yeti cooler, a beat-up gym bag, and a ratty Duke sweatshirt. Pretty basic stuff, but it all feels strangely intimate and out of place here in the Singer. This is a car built for escaping your life. For driving along the Pacific Coast Highway with your windows rolled down, Tom Petty blasting. But Finn is treating the Porsche like a minivan. It's like he's dragging his whole life with him. I wonder when he was last home to his parents' house in Dallas. *Mother's*, I remind myself. Finn's dad passed away when we were freshmen in college.

A thought comes to me, quick as a reflex. It's one of those dark, selfish ones you don't say out loud: sometimes, I wish my dad were dead. It's terrible, I know. I don't mean it in a he's-so-awful-he-should-just-be-dead kind of way. Because he's not, most of the time. Most of the time he's just...nothing. A blurry vagueness whose absence has played a far bigger role in my life than anything he's actually done. I guess I just mean it like...maybe it would feel cleaner. Grief may be a heavier burden to carry, but I don't think it poisons you quite the same way that bitterness does.

The traffic stalls again, getting worse and worse as we head into San Diego. Finn looks something up on his phone, then puts on his blinker and pulls off I-5.

"What are you doing?" Finn turns down another street, and it's clear that we're no longer headed toward San Diego.

"I'm grabbing something to eat. There's a place up here that's supposed to have the best tacos in the state. Apparently, all the pro golfers hit it when they play Torrey Pines."

"No, we've got to keep going." Not only are we losing our window to find Sybil and bring her back in time for the welcome party, but Nikki will lose her shit if she learns we found ourselves within a nine iron's swing of Aaron.

"I didn't get anything to eat this morning, because a semi-feral woman dragged me out of the shower and didn't give me time to grab breakfast."

"You could've just given me your keys," I say sweetly. "Then you could've had all the pancakes you wanted."

Finn executes a flawless parallel park outside a buttercream-yellow building with a cheery green roof. "That was never an option."

We step out of the car, and directly across the two-lane road is a small inlet of water between us and a forested hill. If we had the time, it'd be a beautiful place to sit outside with the sea breeze and the still-gentle Southern California sun. I give myself one deep breath to enjoy the view then turn toward the taco shop. My breath catches when I see that Finn had been watching me. He breaks into a small smile as if laughing at his own private joke.

We head inside and wait in line behind a multicolored-tile counter. When it's our turn, Finn leans over the counter and grins at the cashier. "So, what's good here?"

The cashier, a sweet-faced Latina girl who can't be more than nineteen, smiles back at him. "Our loaded hash brown burrito is really good. I like to add avocado."

"That sounds perfect. I'll have one of those. Emma?" He turns to me for my order, and a loaded hash brown burrito honestly does sound delicious, but I don't let myself order the same thing. "Bacon, egg, and cheese burrito, please," I say primly.

Finn winks conspiratorially at the cashier. "Add avocado to hers too."

"Do you have to flirt with the cashier?" I ask once we move to the side to wait for our order.

Finn gives me a confused look. "I'm just being polite."

"Fine."

"Fine," he echoes. But then a smile breaks through his confusion. "Are you jealous, Emma?"

"Ugh. No." I wince slightly at how unconvincing I sound. Pulling out my phone to avoid any eye contact, I add, "I just don't think you should be pursuing children."

He leans toward me, and I can feel the warm brush of his breath against my cheek. "Emma, I promise you, I only ever pursue fully grown, enthusiastically consenting, adult women."

I don't dignify Finn's words with a response. Instead, I try to ignore the fact that my skin all of a sudden feels too tight for my body and pull up the Map app to see that we're only twenty-eight minutes from the Del. Less than half an hour, and I'll have this whole Sybil debacle wrapped up.

Through the window I see a black Range Rover Sport pull up. I'm weighing whether to add a side of jalapeños, when the hairs on the back of my neck stand up. Which can only mean one thing. Sure enough, I turn back to the window just in time to see Aaron Brinkley exit the Range Rover. His sandy hair is tucked under a baseball cap, and there's a smattering of freckles across his forearms. To be honest, I never really understood what Nikki saw in him. He's no better looking than every other douchey white guy that populates America's frat houses, and clearly his character leaves something to be desired. Aaron makes his way across the parking lot and I turn away from the window.

I nudge Finn. "Shouldn't he be playing?"

Finn, who still can't seem to keep a smile off his face, pulls up Twitter on his phone, then shakes his head. "Apparently he didn't sign his scorecard."

"English, please." I'm growing agitated. Finn is still gloating over my nonjealousy, and in just a few moments I'll be sharing breathing space with the man who destroyed my best friend.

"It's an automatic disqualification." Finn shrugs. "It's been a rule forever. It's to prove your integrity—you're signing that you're going to self-report your scores accurately. You have to be able to trust the other golfer's word, or there's no point in playing."

Integrity and *trustworthiness*. I can't think of two words less suited to describe Aaron Brinkley. He walked away from someone amazing who loved him despite the fact that he was an idiot who didn't deserve her. He lied to Nikki. Just like Finn lied to me, and my dad lied to my mom. Everything I've been feeling about Sybil running out on Jamie erupts to the surface, and before I know what I'm doing, I'm fully across the taco shop when Aaron walks through the door.

"Hey, asshole." My finger presses against the striped green of his polo.

Eyes wide, he puts his hands up reflexively as if this isn't the first time he's been accosted by an angry woman in a taco joint. "Do I know you?"

"No, you don't *know* me. I was just supposed to be a bridesmaid in your wedding, you cheating piece of shit."

He puts his hands down and looks somewhat relieved. "You're one of Nikki's friends."

"Thank god she didn't marry you, because if she had and *then* I found out you cheated on her, I would have torn into you like the bear from *The Revenant* and left you to die in the Canadian wilderness."

Confusion paints Aaron's face, along with a slight glimmer of fear in his eyes like he thinks I just might be unhinged enough to gnaw through his ribs.

"*LovedBy* was a reality TV show. She should've known what she was getting into." He heads to the counter dismissing me.

"She was trying to find true love, and you used her," I say to his back. Aaron just stands there. Meanwhile, Finn has collected our order and comes up beside me.

He nudges my shoulder with his. "Let's get out of here."

"No. I'm not getting out of here until this jerk admits what he did."

Aaron rolls his eyes, and something inside me snaps.

Before I can process what I'm doing, my hot and toasty burrito is out of the paper bag in Finn's hand and flying across the room.

Piping hot cheese covers Aaron's smug face. Egg and avocado drip down his green polo.

Two thoughts hit me simultaneously: one, Nikki is going to kill me; and two, it was worth it.

"What the fuck is wrong with you?" Aaron shouts, brushing off the piece of bacon that landed on his shoulder.

Adrenaline courses through my veins. I'm breathing heavy, in and out, in and out, exactly like the antianxiety app tells you *not* to do.

"Emma," Finn says, placing a firm hand on my shoulder.

"Don't touch me," I snap.

Finn pulls his hand away. "Emma, please," he says, softer this time.

Those words trigger a memory—the first time I made the mistake of trusting Finn Hughes with my heart. Suddenly I'm sixteen again, standing alone, waiting for the boy I liked to show up where he said he would. *Emma, please.*

I whirl on Finn, jabbing a finger in his chest.

"You know what? You're just as bad as him."

Finn's eyebrows shoot toward his hairline. "Excuse me?"

"You heard me." My blood is buzzing.

Finn's looking at me like I've lost it.

Behind the counter, the teenage cashier is recording the whole scene on her phone.

"Ma'am." A man with a name tag that reads "manager" approaches me warily. "I'm going to have to ask you to leave."

I let him lead me to the exit. But before I pass through the swinging glass door, I turn back to the cashier, looking straight into the phone camera.

"He broke her heart."

6

MISTAKE ONE: THE PROM

(Eleven years before the wedding)

IT WAS MAY OF junior year, and the air was sticky and thick with the scent of jasmine. We'd just won state, which, for debate kids, was the equivalent of winning the big game. I can't even remember what our topic was—stem cell research? The US adopting a monarchy? Something about the nuclear test ban treaty? What I *do* remember is the moment we won, Finn drew me into a bear hug and whispered, "We did it," in my ear. I remember his smell—woodsmoke and lavender—and his warm, surprisingly strong arms around me. I remember his whiskey-colored eyes sparkling as he looked into mine.

On the ride back from Austin, the team threw open the school bus windows and passed around a water bottle full of vodka, laughing and singing and celebrating our victory. As always, Finn and I were sitting together in the last row. I wasn't a big drinker in high school. I'd only snuck a hard lemonade or two from Sybil's garage fridge during sleepovers when Mr. and Mrs. Rain were out. But I was a certified pro compared to straitlaced seventeen-year-old Finn. After only a few sips from the water bottle, he was looser, bolder, gigglier, imitating our chaperone Mrs. DiTullio with such a pitch-perfect nasal drawl that I laughed until I cried.

We were just pulling back into the school parking lot when Finn turned to me and asked if I wanted to go to junior prom with him. I was floored. Up until that moment, I hadn't allowed myself to admit that I had a crush on Finn. Prom was only a week away, and I planned on just going stag with Willow and some of her theater friends. But now, I had a date. Not just hanging out at a friend's house at the same time—but my first-ever *real* date. I said yes with a smile, and Finn slipped his hand into mine.

A few days later, we all met at Willow's house before prom to take photos. I was giddy, wondering if Finn would shake my mom's hand when I introduced them, or if she'd bust out mortifying baby pictures saved to her phone. But twenty minutes passed, and there was no sign of Finn. I worried that maybe we got our signals crossed. Did he think we were meeting at the dance? I sent him a couple of texts but got no response. Meanwhile, everyone else was pairing off, both their mom and dad there to take photos of them. My mom, the only parent without a spouse, and me, the only kid without a date.

"Sweetie, let me get a photo of just you, okay?" I nodded

because I didn't trust myself to say anything. "We'll get a photo of you with Willow too." My mom waved Willow over.

"Em, are you okay?" Willow asked quietly as she put her arm around my waist.

"Why wouldn't I be?" Willow gave me a look like I was being ridiculous, but must've seen how I was barely holding it together, because she didn't say more. I mirrored her pose, throwing my arm around her waist, and putting on my most dazzling smile for the camera. Until it became clear that Finn wasn't going to show, I'd actually felt beautiful for once. But with each minute that ticked by with no sign of him, everything about my look began to feel wrong. My makeup was too harsh against my pale skin. My auburn hair clashed with the bubblegum pink of my taffeta dress. Willow has that photo framed on a gallery wall in her living room, but even now I can't stand to look at it. All I can see is a girl in an ill-fitting gown playing at a life she'll never have.

Sybil was going to prom with her boyfriend, Liam Russell, and their group was meeting up at his house. I felt grateful that at least I wasn't getting stood up there. Liam and his church friends treated me like I must be recovering from some massive trauma since my parents were divorced. It always grated that they thought my mom wouldn't be enough. She was more than enough, and I didn't need a date to have a good time. At least, that's what I repeated to myself over and over, standing there alone in Willow's backyard.

After everyone else finished up with photos, my mom pulled me aside before we got in the limo.

"Honey, take my credit card. For dinner." She pressed the thin slip of plastic into my hand, and I tucked it into my beaded purse. I realized that I was going to have to make it through dinner dateless before I could disappear into the crowd at prom.

The only one without a corsage or date in the limo, I kept flipping open my phone to see if I was missing texts from Finn, but there was just one from my mom: *You look so beautiful! Love you.* Finn's friend Seth leaned across Willow and said, "He's not answering my texts either."

After we'd finished our meal at the steakhouse, the waiter came by with the checks. "Just by couple?" He looked directly at me. "And you, you're alone?"

Seth said, "She's with us." It was the closest I came to crying that night.

"No, I've got it." I pushed my mom's credit card across the table with a soft scrape, relieved that she'd thought to give it to me. That I didn't need a guy to take care of me.

When we got to the Radisson, where the prom was being held, I went straight to Sybil to tell her what happened. But before I could start, she said, "Liam and I broke up."

"Oh, I'm sorry, Sybs." I was genuinely surprised. The two of them seemed so obsessed with each other. Actually, it always struck me as a little smothering. Maybe Sybil finally felt the same. But the look on Sybil's face was definitely upset—though she looked more lost and distracted than heartbroken. "But wasn't he your ride? How did you get here?"

"Finn let me borrow his car. I ran into him at the…" Sybil stopped as if catching herself. "At the mall." She tucked a strand of shiny blond hair behind her ear, looking past me toward the bathrooms. "I'm gonna go find Katie Dalton and those girls," she said—which I knew was code for going to bum a cigarette—and before I could say another word, she was walking away.

Frustration needled my temples. At Sybil—couldn't she see how upset *I* was? Why was I the one always comforting *her*, making sure *she* was okay? Of course, Sybil would always be okay. Her glossy hair looked perfect against her navy-blue gown. Her makeup looked effortless against her sun-kissed skin. But mostly, my frustration was directed at one Finn Hughes. "Cha-Cha Slide" blared from the speakers, but all I could hear were Sybil's words echoing in my head. Finn was at the *mall*? He'd let Sybil borrow his car? I'd felt sorry for myself before, and honestly a little worried about Finn, but now I was incandescent with rage. I looked down at my phone to see three missed calls and one text from him: *Call me, pls.* I remember being so livid that he couldn't be bothered to type out the entire word *please*.

The plan had been to drive out to Willow's family's lake house after the dance, but I asked Willow and Seth to drop me off at Finn's instead. I rang the doorbell, the sharp smell of fresh mulch mixed with the sweetness of Mrs. Hughes's jasmine. Finn opened the door and stepped out onto the porch with me. He looked visibly upset. Good. He should be upset.

"What the hell, Finn?" I'd rehearsed what I was going to say to him on the way over, but actually seeing him in person leached away some of my anger, and the space it left behind filled with a watery sadness.

"I'm..." He took a second to finish. "I'm sorry, I just totally forgot about prom." It was early May, but the heat of summer had already crept in and curled itself around us. Oppressive. Suffocating.

"You forgot? You didn't forget about Sybil," I said. "I'm sorry she wasn't available to take as a date and you only got her best friend as a consolation."

"What? No. That's not it at all. Emma, please. Do you want to come in? I can explain."

"No, I don't want to come in. You humiliated me in front of all our friends. You gave Sybil your car while you were shopping at the *mall*, and you couldn't be bothered to text me?"

"Is that what she said?" He let out a deep breath as if resigning himself to something. Finn Hughes, who never fumbled for words, just stood there silently. Until finally, he said, "I'm sorry, Em."

"Whatever. It's fine." I felt myself shutting down. Closing off. Severing the diseased limb before it could infect the rest of the body. "We were just going as friends anyway. Teammates, actually. We don't need to make this some big thing."

Finn's face fell a fraction, but he just nodded. "If that's what you want." It's not what I wanted. I wanted him to chase after me. To tell me that he was just as into me as I was into him. To explain how you forget your *prom date*, but not her manic pixie dream girl of a best friend. But in that moment, my pride won out. I stormed down his sidewalk, and when I was two blocks away, pulled off my heels and finally let the sadness totally overtake my anger. I cried the whole two-mile walk home, the hem of my dress ruined from being dragged along concrete.

Senior year, Finn dropped out of debate, and the junior I was paired up with in his absence was woefully inferior. We didn't even make it past regionals. And somewhere in that time frame, Sybil became best friends with Finn. To this day I have no idea how it happened. As the madness of senior year set in, I distanced myself even further from Sybil. If she was going to hang with Finn after what he did to me, then maybe she wasn't as good a friend as I thought she was.

We might never have reconnected if Sybil hadn't suggested we travel together one summer during college. On that trip the vestiges of our old friendship slowly began to regrow, eventually blossoming back into the fierce connection we have today.

All through college we never spoke about prom or the dark period where our friendship had waned or anything relating to Finn Hughes, outside of the occasional life updates that Sybil would toss my way and I'd pretend to only half listen to. But the truth was, I soaked up every word—half hoping to hear that he had suffered some humiliation on the level of the mortification he caused me…half hoping for signs that the sweet, nerdy guy I'd fallen so hard for was still there, deep down. And that, one day, we too might find our way back to each other. But I knew better than to hold my breath. Finn had revealed himself to be careless with people's hearts—with *my* heart. And when someone shows you who they are, you're supposed to believe them. So I did.

But over the ensuing years, there'd be moments where I'd forget. I'd let myself get swept up in dreams of what Finn and I *could be* instead of accepting the reality in front of me. When I eventually learned the true story of why Finn stood me up for prom—a story that proved more complex than it first appeared—I thought perhaps I'd misjudged Finn. That perhaps things *could* work out between us after all. But in the end, my hopeful musings turned out be nothing but another mistake.

7

THURSDAY AFTERNOON

(Two days before the wedding)

"I DO FEEL A little bad for Aaron," Finn says, tearing back the wrapper on his burrito. "It's no fun to be on the other end of your wrath."

We're back in the car, sitting in the parking lot. Finn hands me half of his burrito—mine having been a tragic casualty of my attack on Aaron Brinkley—but I decline the peace offering. I'm still savoring my righteous rage.

Finn just shrugs, as if to say *Your loss,* and goes on eating. After he takes a couple of bites, he says, "I remember the first time I saw you go beast mode like that. Some dick was making fun of your sister, and you totally lost it on him."

"I don't 'go beast mode,'" I insist. But I blush as the

memory comes to me. The dick in question had leaned over the bus seat and asked my redheaded nine-year-old sister "if the carpet matched the drapes." Liz had no idea what it meant but could sense that he was trying to make her uncomfortable, snickering with his buddy. As soon as I saw the tears start to well in her eyes, I launched from my seat, not bothering to wait for the bus to come to a complete stop before pouring an entire can of iced tea on his head while screaming at him to leave my sister alone.

Finn chuckles as if he's been replaying the scene in his mind too. "You really do, Em. But it's nice. You only go Hulk like that for the people you love." There's a softness in his voice, and when I meet his eye, I see something that almost looks like longing there. But then he breaks the moment, going in for another burrito bite. "Anyway, you must really love Nikki based on that display in there. You were impressively detailed in how you would kill Aaron. Like maybe you've thought about it. A lot."

"He deserves it. You can't claim to care about someone, and then abandon them. It's cruel."

Finn turns in his seat to face me, seriousness replacing the amused smirk that had graced his face moments before. "Is this about what happened between us?"

"No," I say, which is mostly true. Though I can see why Finn might think I'm making a slightly passive-aggressive reference to our shared past. I reflect on the handful of times I was led to believe Finn might care about me, only to have that misconception corrected in the most mortifying ways. Because in the end, Finn always showed me who he really was: thoughtless and untrustworthy. Just like Aaron, and just like my dad.

I think back to five years ago, when Sybil asked if Finn could crash at our place for a couple of nights when he was in town for work. I'd pretty readily given in and agreed, but later that night I began to regret my decision.

"Does he have to stay with us?" I asked, legs swinging off our fire escape. Struggling to find a good reason why he shouldn't, I landed on "He is such a flake."

"He is not a flake." Sybil rolled her eyes affectionately, and I shot her a skeptical look back. "Okay, so he sometimes has flake-ish tendencies," Sybil admitted as she handed me a Bluetooth speaker before climbing through my bedroom window to sit next to me. "But so do I, and you still love me."

"He stood me up at prom because he was at *the mall*." I connected my phone to the speaker, and Sybil's latest indie-pop playlist began to mingle with the sounds of the city.

Sybil opened her mouth to speak but then pursed her lips.

"Just spit it out, Sybs."

"Okay, yes. He did flake on prom, and standing you up was a shitty thing. He screwed up," Sybil conceded. "But does one mistake define a person?"

Yes, I thought, turning back to watch the world pass below on Second Avenue. Some mistakes do define you. Some mistakes leave you irrevocably changed.

Back in the Singer, Finn seems for a minute like he wants to press the issue, to actually get into what happened between us four and a half years ago at Katie Dalton's wedding, but he just puts the car in drive and pulls out of the lot. We drop down a gear as we turn back onto I-5. Finn keeps hold of his burrito as he lets go of the wheel and moves his left hand to the stick shift. It's an incredibly smooth maneuver, and I can't help but be a little impressed. Once, after I'd admitted to rewatching *The West Wing* for the eighth time, Willow told me I had a "competence kink" because I love people talking fast and skillfully solving for solutions. Her words inexplicably come back to me now as I watch Finn weave in and out of traffic. It's probably just that the Singer is such an exceptional machine, it can make anyone seem like a great driver.

My phone buzzes, and Nikki's name appears on my screen with an incoming call.

"What is the *one* thing I asked you before you left here?"

Shit.

I decide to go straight to denial and diversion. "To drive safe? Hey, by the way, any word from Sybil yet?"

"Aaron just texted me."

"He did?" Playing dumb never works. My pulse is causing my neck to throb.

"Yes, he very much did, Emma Mae."

Uh-oh. We're in full-name mode.

"In fact, to be specific, he texted, 'Tell your psycho friend with the red hair to leave me alone.'"

"That *is* specific."

Nikki is not amused. "He said you threatened to kill him like a bear."

I don't say anything.

"From *The Revenant*."

I might not be able to duck out of this one.

"I know how obsessed you are with Leonardo DiCaprio."

Damn. You have one cardboard cutout of a celebrity in your childhood bedroom, and everyone thinks you're obsessed. "I just really respect his climate advocacy," I say, folding my arms as Finn turns off I-5 and onto the Coronado Bridge.

"*You dressed up as that bear for Halloween senior year. I've seen the pictures, Emma.*"

I pull the phone away from my ear, but it's clear that Finn has heard every word. He sputters like he's trying to hold in a laugh. I did dress up as a semi-slutty bear and painted blood around my mouth. It was a real whiff of a Halloween costume because I had to spend the entire time we were on Sixth Street explaining it. People thought I was a satanic Winnie-the-Pooh or something.

"Look, I didn't mean to run into him. Finn was hungry, so we stopped to grab a burrito, and Aaron was just there being an idiot. Finn was the reason we stopped; you should be mad at him."

Finn flips me the bird as the crisp white wooden facade and the iconic red rooftops of the Hotel Del Coronado come into view.

"*Finn* isn't the one who threatened to disembowel him."

"Well, that only proves that Finn's not as good a friend as I am. Nikki, we're about to pull into the Del. Once I get Sybil back to Malibu, you can yell at me all you want."

"We're not done with this, Emma." Nikki hangs up, and I let my phone rest on my knee, trying to practice the app breathing again.

"I've really got to see a copy of those photos." Finn pulls the Singer onto the paved brick roundabout at the entrance of the Del.

"I will be dead and buried before you ever see those photos." And before he can press further, I'm out the door, leaving Finn to handle the valet. I've already asked the concierge to point me toward the spa before Finn makes it into the lobby.

It's impressive how they've managed to keep so much of the original wood and still leave the space feeling bright and spacious instead of dark and claustrophobic. The elegant, climate-controlled interior calms me, and I take a centering breath, reminded why we're here.

Finn catches up to me as I pass an ornate brass elevator—it looks like there's an actual bellhop inside. I call Sybil as we're crossing the courtyard to the spa, but it rings to voicemail. Unlike the opulence of the lobby, the spa is a bright, soothing white. Gentle Muzak plays in the background. Eucalyptus-scented diffusers sit on a lightly veined marble countertop. I try Sybil's number again on the off chance I can hear it ring nearby, but it goes to voicemail once again.

A severe-looking woman with slicked-back hair appears behind the receptionist's desk. "Hi," I say. "I'm meeting my friend here."

"Of course. What's her name?"

At least, I think that's what she says. She seems to be speaking in a decibel only dogs can hear.

"Sybil," I respond. But, suddenly, speaking in a normal volume feels like I'm shouting, so I repeat in a whisper, "Sybil Rain." The spa receptionist frowns a bit and taps at the computer in front of her.

"No one named Sybil Rain is scheduled for appointments today," she murmurs.

Finn steps up to the counter beside me. "Maybe it's under

her parents' card? Greg or Melissa?" I try not to think about how his raspy whisper is giving serious Morning Voice vibes.

"We're really not supposed to disclose the names of our guests," the receptionist says. "Perhaps you should wait for your friend in the lounge?" And with that she glides away.

"Now what?" Finn asks, his voice back to full volume.

"Now we go back there and find Sybil." I gesture to the double doors beside the reception desk that must lead back to the treatment rooms.

"Oh, sure." Finn nods like this is a wise plan. "I think I've seen this episode of *I Love Lucy*. So do you want to pretend to be the masseuse or should I?"

I roll my eyes but can't help the corners of my mouth curling up. I had forgotten that Finn loves old-timey TV shows. "We're not going to *Lucy* this—we're just going to go back there and see if we can spot Sybil. She's probably getting a wax or something and didn't want to put her own name down."

"You're going to walk in on your best friend getting *waxed*?" Finn raises an eyebrow.

"Wouldn't be the first time." I shrug. Obviously Finn has never had to come to the rescue after an at-home waxing kit goes wrong. When you're girls, best friends, *and* roommates, there are no secrets.

I'm about to walk through the doors, when my stomach lets out the most audible growl. Like a cross between a rumble of thunder and my East Village radiator in December. I flinch, half expecting slicked-back-hair lady to come out and shush me like a librarian.

"Let's grab you some lunch first." Finn reaches for my

elbow, and I let myself lean on him just for a moment as we follow the signs pointing toward the poolside bar.

On the Sun Deck, we find an unoccupied couch near a firepit and look over the menu. I want everything. I look up, hoping to flag a waiter, when my eye is caught by a petite blonde in a distinctive blue-and-white swim shirt.

"Sybil!" I shout.

"Where?" Finn asks, immediately standing.

"Over there. " I point several feet away, where the woman in the swim shirt is now stepping off the final stair that leads down to the beach, her back to us.

"Are you sure that's her?" Finn frowns, unconvinced.

"Don't you recognize her hair?" I ask.

"We're in Southern California, where ninety percent of the women are some shade of blond."

Men.

"Well *that* shade is hers. It has to be." Sybil bought that exact designer swim shirt last month. I remember her telling me encouragingly that rash guards were back in. She was seeing them all over her Instagram! My freckled shoulders should rejoice!

Finn dials Sybil's cell, but once again, it rings and rings, then goes to voicemail.

"Come on," I say. "Let's just go down there. Looks like she's heading toward that shed thing."

"That's the kayak rental hut," Finn says, pulling from his pocket a creased resort map he must have grabbed from the valet.

Why do I find his dorkiest qualities so frickin' cute?

We head down to the beach, and sure enough, I can see

the blond woman in the blue-and-white swim shirt paddling a bright green kayak.

"I still don't think that's her," Finn says, shielding his eyes with his hand and squinting into the sun.

"Well I *know* it is. Let's just paddle out there and find out. It won't take long."

Finn sighs and goes to pay the vendor.

"You're not really dressed for this," I say as we tip a two-person kayak off the rack at the rental shed and tuck two paddles into the seats. I'm still wearing the flip-flops, exercise shorts, and tank top that I had on for our spa day, but Finn is in tennis shoes and slacks.

"These are performance-wear pants," he says as he rolls up his cuffs to just below his knees. "They can handle anything." He says it like he's reading off a podcast ad.

"Oh, can they?" I grab the front end of the kayak. Finn takes up the back and then promptly drops it. Turning around to grumble at him, I see that he has two life jackets. He hands me the smaller one and says, "Safety first," as we maneuver the boat into the surf.

"You were an Eagle Scout, weren't you?" I say dryly.

"Two badges short," he says. "I'm a rebel like that."

The kayak sways precariously as we climb inside, and Finn makes a noise that is higher pitched than any sound I've ever heard him—or, you know, any full-grown adult—make.

"Did you just *squeak*?" I ask.

He clears his throat. "Absolutely not." He takes a moment to settle onto the kayak. "Just not a big water fan. If this boat tips over, you're walking back to Malibu."

"Don't worry. I promise to keep you safe."

8

THURSDAY AFTERNOON

(Two days before the wedding)

WE ROW A FEW strokes away from shore, quickly getting into a rhythm so our oars are moving in sync. The sun glistening off the water looks so inviting, I want to dive in, but I settle for dipping my hand into the waves and pouring some water on the back of my neck. I didn't realize how hot it was.

"That can't be her," Finn says to himself, but keeps rowing.

"Oh, sit right back and you'll hear a tale, a tale of a fateful trip..." I twist around to see his reaction to my off-key *Gilligan's Island* theme song, and he shoots me an annoyed look. "So I'm guessing one of the two badges you missed was the water-sports badge?" I try again to lighten the mood, but Finn just continues his withering stare. "Come on, she's just around that bend up where that kayak is going." I point with my oar to a neon-orange kayak a hundred yards ahead of us.

Finn has a point though; something doesn't feel right. Sybil has always loved being out on the water, but she's never been much for manual labor. Waterskiing across Lake Athens? Sure. Sunset cruise off Marina del Rey? Definitely. Riding in a little boat in Central Park taking selfies while her companion rows her around? Yes, and I have the blisters to prove it. But kayaking by herself through somewhat choppy waves? It doesn't really add up.

The kayak ahead of us disappears behind a rocky outcrop.

"Let's just catch up with that kayak up there and ask if they've seen her. If not, we can go back and keep looking around the hotel." At this point my empty stomach is churning and I am really regretting not ordering anything off that pool bar menu.

We lapse into silence, focusing our attention on paddling.

It's nearing one o'clock, and the sun is really beating down now. I feel a tightness settle in my chest. I pull at the neck of my life jacket to try to get some relief, but it doesn't help. Sweat trickles down my temples, leaving an itchy path in its wake. Shit—did I reapply my sunblock after my shower this morning? My nose tingles. It's probably already flaking.

We round the rocky outcrop, finally catching up to the blond girl in the blue-and-white sun shirt. I increase my paddling efforts, nearly capsizing us in my efforts to pull up alongside her.

"Emma!" Finn yelps, but we manage to right our boat before any damage is done.

I tap my oar onto the back of her bright green kayak. "Sybs, it's us." But the girl who turns around to face me is definitely not Sybil. My stomach drops as the stranger gives us a confused stare before paddling off.

Oops. I guess Sybil really *did* see that swim shirt all over Instagram.

Finn calls out an apology to the woman and begins to turn us back to shore. I can feel his unspoken *told you so* radiating off his body in judgmental waves. I don't know what it is about Finn that brings out this need in me to be right all the time. I have to consciously unclench my jaw and take in a deep breath. Except I can only seem to get air into the top half of my lungs. Between the mountain run this morning and the exertion of paddling this kayak under the baking sun, my body is spent.

"So I'm thinking the Del Double Cheeseburger with the works and one of those rumrunner drinks they were advertising by the pool before we get back on the road," Finn says.

Like a Pavlovian dog, I start salivating at the mere mention of a burger. But at the same time, the thought of it makes me nauseated—the heat and the motion of the kayak making my stomach churn harder now. I can't believe I'm out here, probably contracting melanoma, and definitely sweating off my mascara, when I could have been in a dark, soothing room with cool cucumbers over my eyes and the strong hands of some guy with a name like Jan gently easing twenty-eight years of tension from my trap muscles. The minute, and I mean, the *minute*, I locate Sybil, she starts paying for this. But wait…

"Get back on the road to where?" I ask Finn, turning around to make eye contact.

"Back to Malibu. Sybil's clearly not up for the welcome

party. We should just go back and explain everything to Jamie. Sybil will come back when she's ready."

"Clearly you don't know her as well as I do. She needs help. I promised to keep her grounded this weekend—to make sure everything goes smoothly."

"It's just a cocktail party, Emma." Finn rolls his eyes. "I'm pretty sure we'll all survive. Don't worry, you'll still have two days' worth of wedding-related events to micromanage."

I huff a sigh and turn back around to face front. Typical Finn. "Well it may be 'just a cocktail party,'" I say, mimicking his condescending tone, "but Sybil's the freaking host. She made a commitment. People are counting on her to be there. Not showing up would just be selfish and rude." I lean hard on those last two words.

I hear Finn's knuckles crack as they tighten on the oar, and he paddles us forward with more force than necessary.

"What are you saying?" he asks, clearly gleaning my double meaning.

But I'm not about to rehash old drama with Finn while we're trapped on a kayak together.

"Nothing. Forget it. I just think Sybil should be there. We don't need to make a thing of it."

Something in my words seems to trigger Finn, who slams down his oar to rest on the kayak between our bodies. "No, you know what? We need to actually talk about this."

"You shouldn't put down your paddle like that. It could slip into the water."

"Emma, you've been carrying this grudge against me for years. I know things between us have been"—*A nightmare? Infuriating? Soul-crushing?*—"complicated. But I don't think I deserve this passive-aggressive anger you've been throwing my way."

Of course he doesn't. They never do.

I start to turn around to explain to Finn *in detail*—with rebuttals, counterarguments, cited sources—why he does, in fact, deserve every second of the grudge I'm definitely not even holding. But as I do, I see what appears to be a jellyfish inching dangerously close to our boat.

I scream and poke my paddle at it, but it's just a grimy plastic bag. I sigh in relief, grabbing the sides of the kayak to steady myself, only to realize that my paddle is floating twenty feet away.

I watch it drift further and further, feeling like an idiot.

"You know," Finn says from behind me, leaning close so I can feel his breath on the back of my neck. "You really shouldn't put your paddle down like that—"

"Just give me your paddle." I yank it from Finn's hand before he can argue with me, and put all my energy into paddling us toward my runaway oar, but it keeps getting pulled further and further out to sea, and the kayak is getting pulled closer and closer to the rocks.

I should turn back. I should just let Finn row us back to shore. But it's like I'm possessed. The tunnel vision. The racing heart. The feeling like if you don't just do this *one thing*, then something terrible is going to happen. I had my first anxiety attack in the second grade, not long after Dad left. Not that I knew that's what it was at the time—we weren't really a therapy-going type of family. I had this favorite yellow cup that I always drank my water from at bedtime. But one night, Mom handed the nightly ritual to me in a new pink cup. Apparently the yellow one had a crack in the plastic, and she threw it out. I was devastated. Something inside me was unleashed. I ran to our garbage barrel, already out front ready for the next day's pickup, and started rifling through it like a madwoman, trash flying all over our lawn, tears streaming down my face. It was a complete overreaction to the situation, but I couldn't stop myself. I'd been holding my emotions together ever since Dad left, and it was like the dam finally burst. It felt like everything was changing, life as I knew it slipping through my fingers. If my favorite cup could disappear without warning, then so could Mom or Liz. I needed to get it back.

"The paddle's gone, Emma," Finn says—his voice now sounding much further away than it should. "You need to give up. Please give me my paddle so I can get us back." Through my own panic, I can hear the anxiety in Finn's voice, but my mind latches on to his words: *You need to give up.*

"I won't." *I won't give up.* I need to get us back to shore, and then I can ride out the rest of this anxiety attack and come up with a new plan.

"Emma, you don't need to prove anything," Finn yells over the waves. But I do. I need to prove that I can do *one thing* right even if that one thing is getting this kayak to shore.

"I'll get us to land," I say.

"You're being ridiculous right now."

"I'm following through, Finn. Something you don't know anything about."

"You're the one who has no idea what you're talking about, Emma." I've never heard Finn this angry before.

When we're almost back to shore, my panic has peaked and my mind is a dull throb of anxiety. My fingers are tingling and starting to go numb. As soon as the bottom of the kayak scrapes against sand, it's like my body gives itself permission to shut down. I wobble as I start to stand up out of the boat, and Finn's arm shoots out to steady me. "Do you need some help?" he asks, though there's definitely still an edge to his voice, or at least I think there is, but I'm finding it hard to concentrate because my ears are starting to ring.

"I'm fine," I snap. But I'm not. Blood rushes to my face, and my field of vision shrinks.

I can hear the waves slamming against the side of the kayak, and I vaguely register Finn's voice and a splash. The last thing I remember is my body sliding sideways off the kayak and being grateful that Finn made me put on that stupid life jacket.

"MA'AM, ARE YOU OKAY?" A suntanned man with blond curls and a perfect body hovers above me. Is this heaven? The possible angel hands me a water bottle with HOTEL DEL CORONADO emblazoned on the side. Right. Not heaven. San Diego. I'm lying on a lounge chair up on the Sun Deck poolside bar.

"Thanks," I breathe, taking a sip from the water bottle. I hear a huff from my left and look over to see Finn scowling.

The blond man smiles at me, and I can't help blushing when he winks. Finn makes a noise low in his throat, which from any other person I would call a growl. "I'm just glad to know you're okay. It looks like your boyfriend can take it from here."

I watch the Greek god—who I now realize was probably

the resort's on-site doctor—head back toward the hotel's main building.

"I think you must've gotten sunstroke," Finn says. "I had your head on a towel and your legs elevated"— My blush deepens. I know it's the appropriate treatment for a fainting victim, but my mind immediately goes to an *inappropriate* place. Finn laying me back, an urgency in his breathing, his hands pulling my legs up, up, and…— "and then I ordered you some fruit juice, for when you woke up," Finn continues, oblivious to my mind's dirty wandering, "but I thought I should probably get the doctor, just in case." Though he's looking like he's maybe regretting that decision, still staring daggers at the handsome doctor's retreating form.

"Sunstroke, yeah." It's true. I was overheated and underhydrated, and have barely eaten all day. But the anxiety attack I had out on the water definitely played a role too. It's been over a year since I've had one, but I guess I should have been expecting it. Between the stress at work, the stress of trying to find Sybil, and the stress of being thrown back together with Finn Hughes—it's probably been percolating for days. But there's no reason Finn needs to know that.

It's only now that I realize that I'm mostly dry, while Finn's clothes are soaked—his T-shirt clinging to his chest in a way that some people might find attractive.

Oh hell, I can admit it. I'm "some people." Finn's eyes are glued to my mouth, and I realize I'm biting my bottom lip.

I try to gain some self-control and clear my throat. "Did we fall off the kayak?"

There's a pause, and Finn pulls his gaze back to my eyes. "Sort of. We were basically back to shore, but you got woozy trying to step off the kayak. You kinda took me down as you slid off."

Oh right. It's coming back to me. Our fruitless search for Sybil. Losing the oar. The fight.

"But wait, how did we get all the way up here?" The Sun Deck is a long way from the shoreline.

"I, um, carried you," Finn says, like he's embarrassed.

Is he embarrassed? Should *I* be? Mostly I'm just pissed that I was unconscious for the whole thing.

"Oh, thank you," I say dumbly.

"It's no problem," he says. I think he's going to leave it at that, but he goes on. "You know being stubborn to the point of endangering yourself won't help you find Sybil, and…and I'd be very upset if something happened to you."

"You hate me." I take another swig of my water.

"I could never hate you, Emma."

"You just think I'm overly stubborn."

"I never said *overly* stubborn. But…" His eyes are twinkling like he's about to laugh.

"But what?"

"Well, I'll never forget the debate where you were so offended by the opposing team's tactics that you physically moved the podium so you wouldn't have to look them in the face."

I laugh, the memory coming back to me. "Are you making fun of me?"

He's laughing too, but he stops now, and the seriousness that suddenly fills his expression almost takes my breath away. "Never," he says. And I believe him. The way he looks at me, there's a new flutter in my stomach separate from the nausea.

It doesn't feel entirely bad, but it's even scarier. And for the first time in several years, I let myself imagine what it would be like to be with Finn. Like maybe our love story was supposed to start a decade ago. Like maybe I should have told Finn how much his actions over the years had wounded me. But instead, every time, I ran away before he could hurt me even more. He brushes away a lock of hair from my cheek, and he's looking at me right now like I'm something precious. He's leaning closer, and my chin tilts up. Somewhere from the dark recesses of my id, a phrase blazes across my mind: *Kiss me.*

Then my phone buzzes, and the moment collapses around us. There's a blush flaming across my cheeks, and my heart is slamming against my rib cage. Turning away to give myself a moment, I pull my phone out from the waterproof pouch the kayak rental had given us. It's Nikki. I answer ready to tell her we haven't seen any sign of Sybil, but before I can say hello, she says, "Open Find My Friends." I put Nikki on speaker and navigate to the app. It looks like Liz is still safely on the East Coast, my mom is in Dallas, Willow and Nikki are overlapping dots just north of my blue dot, and there's Sybil's photo floating up and to the right. It takes a second for it to hit me.

"She's in *Vegas*?" I can't keep the disbelief out of my voice. Finn comes to sit beside me on the edge of the lounge chair. His damp T-shirt presses against my shoulder, sending a shiver down my spine. A memory flashes across my mind. Me and Finn, water all around us, our mouths sliding against one another's. The very first time I kissed Finn Hughes...My eyes snap to his. Could Finn tell how much I wanted him to kiss me a moment ago? *God, I hope not.* I scooch over, putting an inch of separation between our two bodies, and turn my focus back to Nikki. It doesn't help. I can still feel the heat of his body radiating against my back. "S-so has Sybil been in Vegas this whole time?" I stutter out.

"I don't know," Nikki says. "It just occurred to me to look at the app a few minutes ago."

"Is Jamie meeting her there? Maybe they're eloping?" I ask.

"I don't *know*." Nikki's voice is reaching a slightly hysterical pitch.

"Shh, it's okay." A soft voice comes through over the background. Willow. "Jamie's still here in Malibu. But I think he's starting to suspect something's up."

"Guys—" Finn speaks into my phone, leaning even closer to me in the process. "Hey, it's Finn. I think we all need to calm down. Sybil will be fine. It's normal to want to blow off some steam before a big life event."

"First flaw there is assuming that Sybil is at all normal," I say. Sybil is so beautiful that most people can't see what an absolute weirdo she is. She snacks on raw pasta and is obsessed with romance novels and outer space. "Remember when she wore that 'Pluto Is a Planet' shirt for a solid month in eighth grade?"

"Good point," Finn concedes. "She was pissed about that Pluto thing for a long time. She wrote her senior thesis on it."

I guess Finn is one of those people who see the weirdness in Sybil and still love her. For once, the thought doesn't make me burn with competitiveness.

"Focus, people, please!" Nikki's shrill tone once again brings me back to the matter at hand.

And in that moment, I make a decision. "Finn and I are going to go to Vegas to get her."

"Are you sure?" Nikki asks. "Maybe we need to tag in Jamie, or her parents."

"Not yet. Finn and I should be the ones to track her down." I feel this deep in my bones. "Seeing Jamie or her parents might send Sybil spiraling even further, and Lord only knows where she'd flee to next."

"Okay, we'll try to hold down the fort here," Willow says, and we hang up.

Finn helps me up from the lounge chair. He forces a to-go turkey sandwich on me, and we head back to the valet. He hands them a ticket, and years of muscle memory has me reaching into my own pocket. I find my license, credit card, a few folded bills, and an old movie ticket all intact.

"Ooh, old license photo of Emma," Finn says with a devilish grin, reaching for the pile of cards.

"No!" I say a little too quickly, gathering all my items back up and slipping them carefully back into my wallet. "There's some important stuff in here."

"Oh, come on, like an old movie stub?"

"None of your business."

"Okay, okay," he says, hands up in surrender. As the valet brings the car around in front of us, Finn's tone changes.

"You know, it really seems like Sybil doesn't want to be found," he says softly.

"There are a lot of instances where what Sybil wants is not what Sybil really needs," I say, finishing up the sandwich and reaching into the to-go bag to pull out a piece of fruit. I'm already starting to feel more like myself.

"Emma, I think we should go back to Malibu. This is

Sybil's life. She has to make the call about whether or not she wants to marry Jamie."

"We can be in Las Vegas by dinnertime, grab Sybil, and then be back at the hotel by midnight." The valet pulls the Singer up right beside us.

"Doesn't that mean we miss the welcome party?" Finn says as he opens the passenger door for me.

"Who cares about the welcome party if there isn't a bride?" I ask.

"Answering a question with a question. A pretty weak rhetorical move there, Ms. Townsend." Finn rummages around in the back and comes up with a couple of towels that he spreads across our seats before I climb in.

"To be, or not to be..." I hold my uneaten orange in my outstretched palm like a Shakespearean skull. Finn lets out a laugh. It sends a jolt right to my heart, and suddenly it's like the past eleven years haven't happened. We're just Finn and Emma, playing truth or dare in the back of the bus on our way home from state, right on the edge of everything that we could be.

Finn goes around to the driver's seat and hesitates as he puts the key into the ignition. I can tell he's waffling. If I can just get him on my side, he'll see that we're the ones who have to bring Sybil home. We know Sybil better than anyone. The *two* of us. I'm grudgingly coming around to accepting the fact that Finn knows sides to Sybil that I don't. I need him with me on this mission. "What if I made a bet with you?"

"What kind of bet?" He looks over at me warily as he buckles his seat belt.

"We go to Vegas. You and me. If Sybil doesn't agree to come back with us—you win. But if she *does*, then I win."

"And?" Finn asks. "What are the terms of this bet? What do you get from me if you win?"

I hesitate. What do I want from Finn?

I want him to be someone he isn't, to be the guy I thought he was at seventeen. I want prom to have been memorable not because of the heartbreak I experienced, but because it was wonderful—even if we hadn't worked out and we'd gone our separate ways after graduation. I want Katie Dalton's wedding to have been the start of a new phase in our relationship, and not the last time I saw Finn in person until this weekend. I know it's irrational to hold these things against him. We can't go back and change the past. But my series of "almosts" with Finn Hughes still nags at my consciousness like a hangnail—it's not going to kill me, but I can't quite forget about it either. Maybe what I want from Finn is closure—to understand *why* things never worked out between us, even when there were times when it seemed like we were on the same page. When the spark between us was undeniable. But do I really want to know? No matter the missing details, it ultimately comes down to this: he just didn't care about me the same way I cared about him. And part of me still wants him to care about me that way, even now.

But those are wants. What I *need* is a ride to Las Vegas and to put any feelings I may have about Finn—good or bad—behind me.

"I haven't decided yet," I say eventually.

Finn takes a moment to respond, and I can see him calculating the risk of the unknown.

"How about this," Finn says. "You win, you get to drive the Singer." My eyes spark at that. "And if I win, you have to say one nice thing about me." I roll my eyes. "Do we have a deal?" He holds out his hand, and I grasp it.

"Deal." Our shake is a beat longer than it should be, neither one of us pulling away, the warmth of Finn's hand lingering on my palm.

"But if you start singing 'Viva Las Vegas' at any point, all bets are off." He squeezes my hand tighter, his dark brown eyes sparkling.

And in that moment, it's all I can do to keep those past "almosts" from flooding my mind all over again. It's going to be a long drive.

9

MISTAKE TWO: THE POOL

(Nine years before the wedding)

IT WAS THE SUMMER after freshman year of college, and Sybil and I were finally going to take the trip we'd always dreamed of—a four-week backpacking excursion around Europe. I was in the middle of trying to figure out how to fit twenty-eight days' worth of clothing into a knapsack, when I got a text from Sybil saying that a girl from our high school, Katie Dalton, was having a pool party and we *had* to go. I'd been getting nowhere with packing—too nervous about the upcoming flight—and the distraction was welcome.

Sybil picked me up, windows down, music blasting, just like she'd always done. It was somewhat strange to be back in her orbit after we'd drifted apart. We'd barely seen each other in a year—me at school in Austin, she in California—and I found myself uncertain about whether I wanted to get sucked into her gravitational pull again. I still hung out with Willow a fair amount, but I had tried to find friends at UT who weren't just the same kids I'd known since middle school. It was nice to be seen as my own person—not just Sybil's academically intense friend. And, truth be told, I was still a little stung by how things had fizzled out between us senior year. I was slightly nervous about the trip abroad together, and couldn't help but wonder if she'd only invited me because she knew she needed an anchor friend, someone to keep her out of trouble and help navigate all the logistics. But whatever the reason, I wasn't going to miss out on the experience of a lifetime, and I hoped that the time spent together would give us the chance to mend things between us and get back to the closeness we'd always had.

When we pulled up to the Daltons' house, Sybil hesitated for a moment before unbuckling her seat belt, leaving the car running. "Can you do me a favor?" she asked. "Can you do a quick check and let me know if Liam's in there?"

"Um, sure." I wasn't quite clear on why Sybil was sending me on this reconnaissance mission, but I took a lap of the party. I didn't see Liam Russell anywhere, and when I asked after him, one of his former football teammates confirmed he wasn't in town. I returned to the car and reported my findings to Sybil, who breathed a sigh of relief.

"Didn't you guys break up junior year?" I asked tentatively. "At prom?" I couldn't figure out why Sybil would suddenly be so awkward about seeing her ex from two years ago.

"Yeah, we did," Sybil nodded. "But then we were kind of on again, off again senior year."

"Oh." We sat for a moment in silence, and I could only assume that Sybil was thinking the same thing I was—how strange it felt that there was this gap in our knowledge of each other's lives.

Then, after a beat, Sybil broke the silence with "He proposed to me the day I got into USC."

"He *what*?" I turned to face Sybil so abruptly, I could feel the twinge in my neck. A thousand emotions competed for brain space, but shock took up the most real estate. Both shock that Liam, at only eighteen years old, would have asked Sybil to marry him, and, perhaps even more intensely, shock that she hadn't told me when it happened.

"I said no, obviously." Sybil avoided my eyes, instead rooting around in her bag for a ChapStick. "But I just didn't want to have to deal with...all that tonight." She smacked on a layer of lip balm, checked her reflection in the rearview mirror, and then turned to me. "Ready?"

I nodded, and followed her toward the Daltons' front door, but my mind was still reeling from what Sybil shared, more grateful than ever that we'd be spending the next month together. Clearly, I had missed out on a lot in the past two years.

We dropped our offering of Fireball onto Katie's parents' kitchen island, and after we forced everyone within shouting distance to do a shot, the Sybil Effect took hold. I watched as she took control of the makeshift dance floor in Katie's living room, pulling people off couches and into the center of the room. It was jarring to see the transformation right before my eyes, the quiet, uncertain Sybil I'd seen in the car shifting into this larger-than-life Sybil. Of course, I'd always known she was more than just a party girl. I guess I'd forgotten. But watching her twirl Katie Dalton around to the beat of whatever pop song was top of the charts that summer, I was reminded that even when Sybil was at her most effervescent, she could be masking something much heavier than anyone knew.

I danced a song or two with Sybil and the others, then went in search of fresh air, making my way toward the sliding doors that led to the patio. I'd no sooner stepped outside than I found myself face-to-face with Finn Hughes, who was sporting an ugly-looking black eye, standing beside an already sticky beer pong table.

"H-hi," I stammered.

"Hi."

Sybil spilled out of the glass doors behind me and spotted the two of us together, something gleaming in her eye. "Oh hey, there y'all are." Reaching into the cooler behind her, she handed us both cans of Keystone Light. "You two catch up while I obliterate Connor at beer pong." Finn already had a drink in hand, so he tucked the can into the back pocket of his shorts and took a long pull of his already-open beer.

Left without Sybil as a buffer, I struggled to come up with what to say. Sybil and I had an unspoken rule that we never talked about Finn. All I knew was that his dad had died recently, and that didn't seem like the topic to bring up at a party. I was tempted to ask him about his black eye, but didn't want to hear what I was sure would be an idiotic justification for an idiotic fight. So I asked the most innocuous question I could think of. "How was North Carolina?"

"I deferred to be home with my dad this past year." The bitterness in his voice surprised me. Finn had never been a big social media guy, so without any digital evidence to the contrary, I just assumed he'd gone to school in the fall like the rest of us. I didn't realize that while everyone else went on to live their brand-new lives, he'd stayed behind to watch his dad's end.

Two minutes into our conversation, Finn had already finished his first beer, and pulled Sybil's offering from his back pocket.

"How is UT?"

"Oh, you know, it's..." I trailed off. What was I supposed to say? If I said it was great, wouldn't that just make him feel bad about missing his own freshman year? And if I talked about the harder parts of my first year away from home, wouldn't that make me seem like an ungrateful jerk?

Finn ignored my floundering. "I visited Andrew in Austin when y'all played Tech," he said, referencing a mutual friend from AP Calc who also went to UT. "I think I saw you there."

"You did?" I was shocked, though I guess I probably shouldn't have been. After how Finn and I left things at the end of high school, it's not like he was going to text me to meet up on campus. But still, the idea that Finn was there, that he saw me without my knowing, was unnerving.

"Yeah, but you seemed pretty occupied with some guy."

"Ah, Scott." The weekend Texas played Tech, he'd punched through a dozen drop ceiling tiles in his dorm. Though whether it was in victory or disappointment, I couldn't remember—Scott was definitely a "win or lose, we still booze" kind of guy. Navigating the college boy scene while also juggling a full course load was one of the hard parts of freshman year. I was trying to figure out my own limits when it came to things like sex and alcohol. (Mom's were a lot more black and white: *Never. Ever. For any reason. Until you're thirty. Maybe older.*) I constantly felt like I had to choose between being the fun girl, who gets drunk and hooks up, or the serious girl, who didn't do either.

"He seemed like a fun time."

"He's definitely a fun time. Potentially too fun." I had tried to be the fun girl my first semester at Texas, but it hadn't felt right. I didn't just want to go home with whatever Sig Ep I found on Sixth Street.

"Is he your boyfriend?" Finn didn't look at me when he asked—his eyes were trained on the beer can in his hands—but even so, the question didn't feel casual. I paused for a moment, figuring out how to phrase my response.

"I'm not doing the boyfriend thing right now."

It was true, though perhaps not the whole story. Scott, who was the Houston version of all the guys I'd grown up with in Dallas, *had* technically been my boyfriend in the fall, but only because I'd forced him to define the relationship when he kept pressing for us to have sex. We broke up—or stopped hooking up—at the beginning of spring semester due to diverging ambitions (me: to close out the year with a solid GPA; him: to finally shotgun an entire six-pack of Keystone) and the fact that he didn't really want a girlfriend. He wanted the fun girl. He never missed a dollar-beer night at Abel's or a home game at DKR, but only ever managed to make it to a third of his classes. He got to UT knowing that when he graduated, he had a guaranteed job with one of his dad's golfing buddies in oil and gas. I didn't have a safety net. So I'd pivoted to being the serious girl for the rest of the school year: no alcohol and no boys. But being home now, and seeing Sybil, who never seemed to be tied down to anything but herself, I wondered how I could find my way to the girl I wanted to be.

"Fair enough," Finn replied. "I'm not really doing the girlfriend thing either." His eyes caught mine, and my gut did a weird dance, but then, out of nowhere, he started laughing. "So much for smoking Connor."

I looked over my shoulder just as Sybil was pounding one of the final cups of beer on her side of the beer pong table and groaned. "She's going to be so hungover on the plane tomorrow."

"Are y'all flying somewhere?"

"We're doing a backpacking trip. Starting in Paris then down to Willow's aunt in Provence, over to Italy, and through Eastern Europe. We end up in Istanbul."

"Oh, man. That sounds amazing." He seemed like he was about to say something else, but changed his mind and took a sip of his beer. "Where are you most excited to visit?"

"Istanbul for sure. This way I can knock out two continents on one round-trip flight."

"Does Istanbul *really* count as Asia? That's a bit of a Eurocentric historical construct," he says. "They've been trying to join the EU for decades."

"Does EU membership define what's European? Where does that leave Switzerland and Sweden?"

I missed sparring with Finn, and an argument about geopolitical borders put us right back on familiar ground. Again, he looked like he wanted to say something, but hesitated.

"What?" I worked the tab on my beer can back and forth until it came loose. It rattled into the empty can.

"Well..." He hesitated again. My beer can clinked as I motioned for him to continue. "Aren't you nervous about the flight? I remember how relieved you were sophomore year when that debate camp ended up being in Louisiana instead of Minnesota so we didn't have to fly."

"Ha, yeah." He wasn't wrong—one of the reasons that I had agreed to come to the party with Sybil was that every time I started to pack, all I could think about was being stuck in a metal tube that, as far as I was concerned, was hurtling through the air by magic.

"You should try the three-three-three rule."

"The what-what-what rule?"

"You name three things you can see, three things you can hear, and then you touch three things. Like, I see a hummingbird feeder, a striped orange-and-white towel, and a live oak. I hear cicadas, the jets from the hot tub, and Abbie asking Sarah if she wants another Modelo."

He moved toward a gardenia bush in an electric-blue planter and touched his finger to the rim. "Pot." Pulling a blossom from the shrub, he said, "Flower." His knuckles grazed my cheek as he tucked the gardenia behind my ear. "Pretty."

For a second we both stood still, staring at each other. Then, patting the flower to make sure it stayed in place, I pointed out, "Pretty is not a noun."

His face was still close to mine as he practically whispered, "Sometimes I make exceptions."

If I had leaned in a fraction sooner, something might have happened. But as I cleared my throat, trying to find a response, he leaned back on his heels and took the final sip of his beer, crunching the can. The moment was over.

"I'll give it a try on the plane tomorrow. Although, I feel like the only thing I'll be able to 'see' will be the inside of a barf bag," I said, trying to recapture the joking rhythm we'd been in just moments earlier. "Where did you learn that trick?"

He shrugged, gave a vague nonanswer. "Since my dad died, I've needed to be out of my brain more." He turned toward the cooler beside the grill, then looked back at me. "Can I get you another one?"

"No thanks." I could feel the dynamic shift between us, and before I could do anything about it, Sybil was at my other side, dragging me into the next round of the game.

THE NIGHT WORE ON, and the party moved into the pool, prompted by a chaotic game of chicken, but by now it was late. Most of the partygoers had trickled back inside to find towels and dry clothes. I had planned to head back inside, too, but took a quick lap to clear my head. When I came up for air at the deep end, there was Finn, hanging out underneath the diving board.

"Jesus, you scared me!" I blurted out as he moved out from under the shadow of the board, grinning. "What were you doing, hiding under there?"

"Waiting for the pool to empty so I can enjoy it alone," he said, still with that unreadable grin, his black eye giving him a slightly dangerous look.

"Oh, well let me get out of your way in that case," I said, but he swam in front of me, blocking my access to the wall. I floated there, treading water in front of him. "What are you doing?"

"Stay. I think there's room for one more in here."

I laughed as I turned back and saw that, in fact, it was true—we were the only two people left in the pool.

Earlier, Sybil had threatened to throw me in the deep end if I didn't join the fun, so I'd peeled off my jean shorts and olive-green crocheted halter until I was down to my black bikini. Sybil had also bullied Finn into swimming. When he took off the ratty *Calvin and Hobbes* T-shirt that he'd worn semi-ironically for all of high school, he revealed a chest and arms that made Sybil choke on her beer and start coughing.

"He's not *that* ripped," I had muttered as I patted her on the back.

She gave me a look like she was almost annoyed. "Emma, you need to see what's right in front of your face."

Now, floating beside Finn in the pool under the glow of the moonlight, I admitted to myself that he was beautiful. Oddly, the black eye made him even more gorgeous, like broken Japanese porcelain repaired with powdered gold.

"So how did you get that black eye?" I finally asked.

His smile faded a bit. "I haven't been making the best life choices."

The honesty surprised me. I had expected boasting or a joke. "What's stopping you from making good life choices?"

"My dad being six feet under, probably," he replied dryly.

My stomach dropped. I started to sputter an apology, but before I could, Finn raised his hand to stop me. "Don't freak out. Poor attempt at humor on my part. Though humor might be a better coping mechanism than what I've been doing of late."

The small ripples I made from treading water lapped softly against the side of the pool. After a few moments of quiet, I asked, "Do you want to talk about it?"

Finn took a deep breath, running his fingers across the water. "I—can't. Not yet." He cleared his throat and turned to look at a tuft of lavender growing beside the pool. "Definitely not without crying." He blinked quickly, but when he turned back to me, he was smiling. "And I make it a rule not to cry in front of beautiful girls."

I took my own deep breath, trying to convince myself that the lightness I felt was from the alcohol, not that Finn thought I was beautiful. At that moment, I needed not to be looking at Finn, so I leaned my neck against the sandstone edge behind me and let my legs drift up to the surface. Something between us had shifted, and I needed a moment to figure it out. Finn was never this openly flirtatious with me before. It was like we'd moved on from childhood, and come back slightly changed, a little more grown-up—but still with a little recklessness clinging to our final year as teenagers. It made me want to test the boundaries of this complicated relationship, simultaneously familiar and startlingly new. My skin, always pale, reflected the glow from the pool lights, and my bare stomach took on the teal-gray of a mermaid's ghost. Finn let his body come to the same position beside me, and we both looked up through light pollution to the few stars bright enough to outshine a metroplex's worth of electricity.

Finn's voice cut through the hum of cicadas. "I'm sorry how everything went down junior year."

It's the last thing I expected him to say—especially after we were talking about something as real and important as his dad. In comparison, it was hard to feel like prom mattered anymore. I was tempted to offer him some platitude to keep the moment going—it was so nice to feel like things were back to normal. But telling him it was okay would be a lie. He *had* hurt me. I took a beat too long to respond, and Finn kept talking. "We made a great team. We definitely would've won state again senior year."

I nodded, even though Finn couldn't see me, his eyes still skyward. It felt so good to be with him floating on our backs and looking up at the stars that I agreed with him because it was the truth. "We *were* a pretty good team." I pushed off from the wall. We had drifted to shallow enough waters that my feet brushed against the bottom of the pool as I turned toward him.

He gave me a half smile and turned toward me too. "The best," he whispered, his face leaning into mine. The fabric of his swim trunks brushed against the front of my thighs, and tornado sirens started blaring in my brain: *Finn is going to kiss me. Get to shelter.* But I didn't want to. I wanted to know what it felt like to kiss Finn Hughes. I wanted to get swept away, so I took half a step toward him.

His eyes didn't leave mine as his hand came up to my cheek, tucking a strand of wet hair behind my ear. He moved slowly as if he wasn't sure what I would do.

"Emma."

"Finn."

"Can I kiss you?" No one had ever asked me if they could kiss me before. I guess it had always been clear enough to other guys that I was *open* to being kissed, in moments like this, so they just went for it. But Finn's question forced me to acknowledge out loud that I wanted to kiss Finn as much as he seemed to want to kiss me. He'd very simply maneuvered me into a position where I was fully complicit in the kiss, and it thrilled me.

"You can kiss me." Saying the words out loud set my whole

body on fire, and I started worrying that if he *didn't* kiss me, I'd self-combust.

And then he did.

It started out like his question, his lips against mine for the first time, tentative and yet confident. I answered by putting my arms around his neck and pulling him to me. The weightlessness of the water made it easy to bring my legs around his waist and lock my ankles at his back. Finn's hands grabbed beneath my knees, and I pulled myself even closer to him, my flimsy bikini suddenly feeling outrageously, well, flimsy. My bare back pressed against the rough ledge of the pool, and the front of my body pressed against the slick warmth of Finn's chest. Finn's hands left my legs to tangle in my wet hair instead, tipping my head further back and deepening the kiss.

In that moment, I wasn't worried about being Fun Girl or Serious Girl. I was just Emma, and all I wanted was to get as close to Finn as I possibly could. Because no one had ever kissed me like this before. Like I was air and water, vital and precious. My entire body thrummed against Finn's, and when his tongue brushed against mine, I felt my grip on rational decision-making about to slip away. But as Finn's fingers twisted around the straps of my bathing suit top, starting to fiddle with the knot at my neck, a familiar spike of insecurity stabbed through my chest. I pulled back slightly, and Finn's hands instantly stilled.

"Is this okay?"

"Yes," I said breathlessly, and Finn leaned back in to kiss me again, his fingers resuming their mission of trying to undo my bikini top, and I flinched back once more. "It's just…what does this mean?"

Finn blinked twice. "I—Does it have to mean something?" His breathing was as ragged as my own, but something crystallized for me. It *did* need to mean something to me. Finn needed me to confirm I wanted to be kissed, and I needed Finn to confirm that this kiss wasn't just a drunken one-off. I had tried to bluff my way through it with Scott and pretend like I didn't care. But if I was going to have sex with someone, I knew now it needed to mean something to both of us. I needed to know I wasn't disposable. Finn just stared at me, his eyes dark and unreadable. A few excruciating seconds passed before it dawned on me that he was probably looking for a way to let me down easy.

My heart sank. "Forget it." I untangled myself from Finn and exhaled. "I shouldn't have expected this to mean anything to you." I splashed out of the pool before I could change my mind and wrapped myself in my towel.

"Hey. Emma. Sorry. I…I took it too far."

Now I had to struggle to hold back the flood of humiliation. "No, no, don't worry about it, it's all good! It meant nothing. Just a little stupid drunk moment." I forced myself to try to laugh. But the look in Finn's eyes was completely sober.

"I've been a wreck this past year. Like I said, I haven't been making the best decisions in the world…"

He was making it worse. Now, kissing me not only meant nothing, it was also a *bad* decision. A grief-induced mistake.

"Honestly, it's fine. I just need to get back because, you know, that flight tomorrow."

"At least let me get you home. My last beer was a few hours ago. I'm good to drive."

I looked around for any other possible option, but no one

was left. Sybil had fallen asleep on Katie's couch hours ago, and I knew she'd be crashing here for the night. I had already ruined one pair of shoes walking home after Finn disappointed me. I wasn't doing it again. I could handle a few minutes in a car with him. After all, it wasn't really his fault. There are lots of people who can be casual with sex. It just took kissing the guy I'd wanted to kiss for years for me to know I wasn't one of those people—at least not right then and not with Finn.

"Sure, yeah. I'll take a ride. Thanks."

My body was still vibrating from Finn's kiss. The drive home was awkward and silent, but when I stepped out of the car at my mom's place, Finn said, "Safe travels. Have some pommes frites and a croissant or fifty for me."

I nodded tightly and headed inside to finish packing. Through the window of the front door, I saw that Finn waited until I was inside to drive away. After I watched his brake lights flash at the stop sign on the corner and turn south toward his mom's house, I leaned against the foyer wall and slid down to the floor with a sigh.

Two days later, when I blinked up blearily at the Eiffel Tower, I couldn't help but think of Finn. Maybe I missed him, missed that moment between us. Or maybe I just wanted to show I was over it, that we could just be friends. That it was all fine. I snapped a photo of my croissant. It was five in the morning in Dallas, but Finn texted back immediately.

One down, forty-nine to go.

10

THURSDAY AFTERNOON

(Two days before the wedding)

THE MOVIE GAME IS all about strategy. You have to know your opponent's weaknesses, and you have to force them to play on your ground. For example, I know that Finn Hughes hates anything science fiction or fantasy. Whereas I have a blind spot for war movies, since I'm generally uninterested in watching people getting blown up.

"*Stardust*."

"Emma," Finn groans. It feels good to settle into an old routine knowing that some things never change. I sigh contentedly and settle back into the buttery leather of the Singer. "Is that the Matthew McConaughey space movie?"

"Is it?" I give him a wide-eyed look. "It could be." His eyes narrow, and I realize I've oversold it.

"It's not, is it?"

I shrug and take a sip of the black coffee we picked up a few miles back. Finn, who is not a doctor no matter how many medically adjacent apps he invents, spent five minutes explaining the effects of caffeine on the nervous system. That it would elevate my heart rate. That it was the last thing I needed after my fainting episode earlier. He even tried to force a chamomile tea on me, which made me laugh out loud. But his concern was sweet, so I compromised and only got a large drip instead of the red-eye I was desperately craving. Another moment where I exhibited an astounding amount of flexibility for which I will get zero credit.

"You can always challenge me," I say.

"I'm not going to challenge on an opening. You have to know at least one actor from the movie, or you wouldn't have said it." Finn takes a sip of his green juice, and I can't help making a face.

"Maybe I like to gamble," I counter.

"We're headed to the right place then."

Right. Vegas. To find Sybil. For a moment, I'd gotten so caught up in our familiar car-ride banter—honed over many a bus ride to debate tourneys—that I'd almost forgotten why we were on this road trip together in the first place. Locate Sybil, and return her to her happily ever after with Jamie. Despite the fact that Finn has been driving *way* over the speed limit, the GPS says we still have two and a half hours to go before we arrive in Sin City. As I watch the miles tick away, I can't help but feel the dull sense of a countdown. Like right now, Finn and I are suspended in a bubble where we can just be our old selves together, without any of the awkwardness and tension that have grown between us over the past eleven years. But as soon as time runs out, all of that will evaporate, and we'll be back to what we were before. Barely more than strangers.

I look at his strong hands, holding the steering wheel lightly. I take another swig of my coffee, trying to soothe the nagging sense of agitation I feel percolating in my veins, but the caffeine only makes my pulse quicken. Just like Finn said it would. Or maybe it's not the caffeine, but the fact that Finn has now moved one of his hands to the gearshift, dangerously close to my bare upper thigh…

"I don't know how you can drink that," I say, nodding to Finn's green drink.

Deflect. Banter. Jab.

It may not be as globally recognized as "lick, shoot, suck," but it's a routine I know well. One I always fall back on whenever things with Finn veer to close to…*something.*

The liquid of Finn's green juice has already started to separate into one level of water and one level of pulp. "Seriously, it looks like something our old cat puked up."

There you go. Nothing could be remotely romantic or sexy when the subject of cat vomit is introduced.

Finn gives his cup a swirl, and the juice partly rehomogenizes. "I want to live a long and healthy life, Emma."

"But at what cost, Finn? At what cost? Now come on, guess or challenge."

He takes a moment to consider. "Challenge."

"Claire Danes. And Robert DeNiro. And Michelle Pfeiffer."

Finn groans. "You're at m-o-v-i," I add, keeping score. Whoever gets to *movies* first loses.

"Okay, my turn. *The Revenant*."

"Ha ha." I roll my eyes. "You need to win this round to stay in the game. You're sure you don't want to try for an obscure World War II movie?"

"I'm sure."

"Fine. I could say, Leonardo DiCaprio." I linger over the vowels of his name with obvious pleasure, and Finn snorts. "But I'm going with Tom Hardy."

"*Layer Cake*." Finn looks over at me smugly. *Shit*. I vaguely remember Finn loving that movie in high school, but could not for the life of me remember who's in it or what it's about. "Edward Norton," I bluff.

"Wrong. That's m-o-v-i for you as well. The easiest answer would have been Daniel Craig. Pre-Bond, obviously."

"Obviously." And now we're tied. It's time to pull out the big guns: musicals. "*Les Misérables*."

But to my surprise, Finn responds immediately. "Anne Hathaway."

"*The Princess Diaries*," I say instinctively. As my brain processes what I've said, my hand automatically reaches for my wallet, trying to snuff out the flicker of regret that always flares to life when something reminds me of my dad. For an instant, I'm eight years old, sitting on our front steps, my eyes glued to the spot where his Jeep Wagoneer had turned off our cul-de-sac. I remember sitting on the stoop, running my finger back and forth over the edge of the ticket. We were going to have popcorn and Reese's Pieces for dinner. Mom begging me to come inside, and—

"Julie Andrews."

Finn brings me back to the current moment. I swallow down the memory.

"Wow, look at you, Finn Hughes!" I say, my mocking tone tempered by genuine warmth. Somehow, knowing that Finn has seen this classic movie of my childhood makes me feel slightly better than I did a moment before. I stare a beat too long into his dark eyes, until traffic moves and he's forced to look back at the road, and I'm forced to get back to the game at hand. "Um, okay, my turn? *The Princess Diaries...Two.*"

"Oh, come on. Challenge. Sequels don't count."

"Are you telling me *The Godfather Part Two* doesn't count?"

He presses his lips together. "*The Godfather Part Two* is a cinematic masterpiece." I clutch my coffee to my chest and fail at keeping the shit-eating grin off my face. It's a weak counter, and he knows it.

"Oh, I didn't realize we were playing the *cinematic masterpiece* game, Finn. That's a lot more letters. We'll be at this through the end of Sybil and Jamie's honeymoon. I'll obviously need you to define usage for the terms 'cinematic' and 'masterpiece.' Just so I'm clear, does that mean nothing ever released straight to streaming counts because it didn't run in a *cinema*? That knocks off *at least* one Scorsese movie—and I know how much you love him. Does the film have to be one of AMC's top one hundred? Does Criterion have to put it out on DVD? What makes something a flawless masterpiece? Truly—"

"A *masterpiece*"—Finn cuts off my questioning—"doesn't have to be flawless. It just has to make you feel something, even years later. Something you go back to over and over, and you're still surprised and delighted by it." He looks over at me as he says this, a playful gleam in his eyes, like maybe movies aren't the only things that still manage to surprise and delight him, even after all this time. I shiver, letting his words settle onto my skin like stardust.

Our brief moment of harmony is obliterated as Finn swerves, and a horn blares behind us. The seat belt jerks tight against my chest. One of my hands braces against the ceiling of the Singer while the other crushes the paper cup in my hand. The plastic top pops off, and the cup's entire contents fly out and splash down the front of my shirt. On instinct, I lift my hips and spread my body over as much of the seat as possible to keep any of the—still very hot—liquid from staining the leather. Finn pulls the car over to the side of the road, and I inspect the damage. The Singer remains unscathed, but *I* am soaked in coffee.

"Finn! What the hell?" I begin dabbing at my shirt, but the three tiny napkins I'd grabbed from the coffee shop are not up to the task of drying my shirt.

"Sorry! There was an animal. A kit fox, I think," he says apologetically, and peers into the rearview mirror. "He seems okay."

"Okay, well, I'm glad he's all right at least." The words come out more sarcastically than I mean them to. Obviously, I don't want to run over any animals. I twist to look through the back windshield, and sure enough, there's a four-legged, furry creature with oversized ears several yards back sauntering away, completely unbothered by his near brush with death. Unaware that he was saved only by the soft heart and fast reflexes of Finn Hughes.

Once he seems confident that the fox has made it completely

off the road, Finn turns the blinker on to merge back onto the highway. He looks over at the mess that is my shirt, and says, "I told you that you should have gotten the tea."

"How would that have changed the situation at all? I'd still be soaked in hot liquid."

"You wouldn't have been so edgy about slowing down."

"'*Slowing down*'?" I say incredulously. "Finn, we didn't 'slow down.' You swerved and slammed on the brakes."

"Well, at least it wouldn't have stained."

"Ugh, this is pointless." Pulling the shirt over my head, I use the driest parts to mop up the coffee that has pooled in my sports bra.

The car lurches again, and I cry, "Finn!"

"Sorry, thought I saw another fox," he says tightly. "What are you doing?"

"Trying to get dry."

"You took your shirt off."

"I did." But it's not like I'm wearing something scandalous and see-through beneath it. I've got on a very utilitarian Lululemon bra that has more coverage than some of the tops that Sybil wears to brunch. And besides, it's not anything Finn hasn't seen before. Memories flood my brain—our torsos pressed together in the glow of swimming pool light, Finn unbuttoning my shirt on a rooftop in New York...Suddenly I feel more exposed than I did a moment ago. "Um," I begin in a small voice, "do you have anything—"

"Oh...I...here." Finn keeps his eyes trained on the road as he reaches into the back seat and grabs the ratty Duke sweatshirt. I pull it over my head and try not to think about how it smells like Finn, hazy woodsmoke cut through with the sharp scent of lavender. The cuffs are a bit frayed, and the neckline has been stretched out so much that it falls off one of my shoulders.

Leaning forward in the seat, I reach behind me and unsnap my bra. Then I shimmy out of the damp undergarment and slide it off, all without removing Finn's sweatshirt. The Singer speeds up. Both Finn's hands are firmly on the wheel, and his vision is glued to the road.

"Do you need to do that?" Finn asks.

"Did you expect me to just marinate in my coffee-soaked sports bra?" The bra hangs limply from my fingers. I fold it up, careful not to let any off the coffee-stained parts touch the seat, and put it into the bag leftover from my to-go lunch.

"I'm sorry, but I don't have anything to offer you in place of a bra."

"You don't have a box of discarded bras and panties from all your conquests filling up your trunk?"

"No, I keep that in my Sprinter van."

"That is so murdery, Finn."

The car is back to a reasonable speed, and Finn seems to have relaxed. His hands unclench from the wheel, one of them returning to its spot, resting on the gearshift.

"To be honest, there's nothing interesting about women's underwear once it's no longer on a woman. When I'm with a woman, and she takes off her underwear, I'm very focused, and it's not on helping her sort laundry."

I swallow. My cheeks are burning. I'm reminded of how small the car actually is, and how easy it would be to reach over and touch Finn. Images—half memory, half fantasy—of Finn and me and underwear and lack thereof start bombarding my brain again, sending it whirring. I grasp for anything to bring me back to safer ground.

I pull the *Celtic Woman* CD from the car door. "Should we put this on? My mom used to record the PBS specials and play them on a loop, so I know all the harmonies."

Finn smiles. "Unfortunately, this car doesn't have a CD player."

"Then why do you have it?"

"My mom gave it to me when she was doing some house purging. I didn't have the heart to tell her that CDs are basically obsolete these days." He lapses into a short silence, as if he's sinking into reminiscence. "Whenever we traveled, my parents would go all out. Movies and books set in that country. We'd research all the local food and map out how to get to everything from our hotel. I thought it was annoying at the time, but now I really appreciate it. It was a sign of respect, and it felt like the vacation began months before we got on the plane. The last trip we ever took as a family—before my dad died—was to Ireland."

"Wow," I say softly. I remember Finn's dad from the odd school event—tall, his skin a few shades darker than his son's, but his eyes that same deep brown, streaked with amber. I feel an unexpected pang of regret that I didn't get to know him better before he died. I swallow the emotion. "Well, I guess I see where you get your affection for guide maps from." Finn rolls his eyes and grins over at me. "My family was never that organized," I say, grinning back at him. "When Mom took Liz and me on vacations, it was usually just a last-minute overnight trip to SeaWorld in San Antonio. One time we showed up, and the park was closed for renovations."

"Like in *National Lampoon's Vacation*?"

"A true cinematic masterpiece if ever there was one."

"Well." Finn's expression is soft, presumably from pleasant memories of his dad and family trips. "I guess I know where you got your freakish obsession with schedules from."

"What?" I ask, confused how he could possibly draw that conclusion from the story I shared. My childhood was anything but scheduled. More often than not, it was a chaotic, stressful whirlwind—Mom never having enough time to be in all the places a single working parent needs to be at once.

"It sounds like someone had to keep the family on track."

I'm struck by how much Finn's words echo the voice I've had running through my head for years. *Someone had to…* Someone had to make sure Liz got to every swim meet on time. Someone had to make sure we had cold cuts for lunches. Someone had to keep my mom's Subaru running…I never begrudged my mom. There were more things to be done than one person could handle, and if Mom was at work—which she was twelve hours a day—that person was me. My friends seem to think I just came out of the womb loving planners and sticky notes, but the truth is, if I didn't cling to those organization tools as tightly as I do, my life would have spun out of control a long time ago. And the look in Finn's eyes—perceptive, a little concerned, but still warm—tells me that he knows the truth.

My skin prickles along my spine. That exposed feeling is back. But it's even stronger than I felt when I was in just my sports bra.

"Let's play a song in honor of your dad and my mom," I say, trying to bring us back to safer ground. I open my music app and navigate to the *Celtic Woman* album. We sit in silence as the music plays. My eyes drift closed, and I imagine myself in a field of knee-high heather. Maybe a catnap is the reset I need. It feels so good to let my eyes close. I know the cardinal rule of being a good copilot is staying awake to entertain the driver, but maybe I'll just give myself a minute or two...

I'M IN A LIVING room that I don't recognize, but the beige built-ins and faux Tuscan wall treatment mean that it could be any of a dozen suburban houses my mom listed when I was a kid. Sybil is standing on the glass coffee table with a karaoke mic in her hand. I reach for her, but my mom walks in wearing a bright blue ball gown.

"There you are. I need you to help Liz finish her school project." My mom moves toward a table stacked with dozens and dozens of shoebox dioramas, each one a different room that I've designed. "I'm counting on you, Emma."

"I can't now, Mom. Sybil and I have to go."

"Sybil's isn't here, Emma."

"She is—" I turn back to the coffee table, but Sybil has disappeared.

"Emma, don't be difficult. Please just help for once."

I want to shout back, *All I do is help! I help you. I help Liz. I help Sybil. There's never anyone who helps me*, but my mouth feels like it's stuffed with cotton.

I charge through the kitchen and open the door to the backyard, only to find myself stepping into the spa at the Del, but there's still no Sybil. In the middle of the room is a massage table, and I realize Sybil and I had plans to get massages today, so I lie facedown on the table and let myself relax. A masseuse comes in, and the smell of lavender and woodsmoke fills the air as strong hands begin kneading up my back. All of the stress I've felt fades away, and I feel...safe. I exhale and let myself sink into the table.

Strong fingers press up and down my spine, then move to dig into the muscles beneath my shoulder blades. A low voice rumbles above me. "How's the pressure?" It's Finn. Excited anticipation coils in my chest, like a thousand hummingbirds fluttering in my stomach. "Turn over," Finn says. I obey, wondering when he'll realize it's me.

He begins by massaging the arches of my feet, but eventually his hands move from my feet to cup my calves and glide to behind my knees. Even lying down I can feel them weakening. As my heart races, I don't resist. I'm still covered by the sheet, but beneath it, my legs quiver as his thumbs begin to drift higher up my legs.

"Is there any other tension I can help relieve, Emma?"

His voice is some kind of permission for me to shift, allowing the sheet to drift further off one knee. Gradually, I reach down and begin to pull the sheet, inch by inch, up my body as his hands continue their journey...

A moan jerks me awake, and I realize to my eternal horror that it's my own.

My head is wedged between the seat and the car door. "Oh my god." I blink into the light, hoping that Finn attributes the red burning across my face and chest to sunburn—not complete mortification.

But seeing the look on his face does nothing to ease my

mind. He's smiling so wide, I'm positive I must have narrated the entire sex dream out loud in my sleep.

He trains his eyes back on the road, betraying nothing, but I can detect a hint of smug laughter in his voice as he asks, "Nice nap?"

And now, I'm officially dead forever.

11

THURSDAY EVENING

(Two days before the wedding)

My body is still vibrating from the dream, and I'm sure that Finn can read the lust pulsing from my face. Napping was the absolute worst decision I could have made.

"That position didn't look super comfortable," Finn goes on, and I can't tell if he's being sincere or hinting at more, "but I didn't want to wake you."

"Um, thanks."

"Maybe y'all can still get your massages tomorrow when we're back at the hotel."

The word *massage* just about murders the last shred of dignity I have. The only thing keeping me tethered to this life is that Finn must have thought I was moaning in pain.

I cross and uncross my legs and curl up against my side of the car as we continue past a field of windmills. The clear blue sky against the dusty brown of the mountains should soothe me, but it just reminds me of how I've lived like a cave dweller in New York, tucked away in either my office or my fourth-floor walk-up. I guess Sybil, even when she's on the run, is the only one who can get me outside trying something new.

For the past four hours, we've been mostly driving through a barren landscape, but now little signs of civilization have begun to crop up—a gas station, a pawnshop.

Which is good, because I'm definitely due for a pit stop. I need to stretch my legs, to shake off the lingering awkwardness from my dream. "Can we pull over for a bathroom break?" I ask Finn.

"Sure," he says. "Looks like there's a diner up ahead. We can stop there."

But when we pull into the parking lot, it's suddenly clear that this is no diner.

"Oh my god."

A large sign flashes INTERGALACTIC EMPORIUM in praying-mantis green.

An almost reverent look of awe comes over Finn's face—like he's never seen something so unabashedly tacky in his whole life. "What in the world..."

"No, no, Finn. I think what you mean is *out of this world*." A cheesy grin has overtaken my own face. "Come on. I'll be quick, I swear."

Finn pulls his eyes away from the neon monstrosity and meets my gaze, the corners up his mouth tipping up ever so slightly.

"Okay. Take me to your leader."

* * *

WE STEP INTO WHAT is clearly meant to be an air lock as a recording plays above our heads, “Prepare for a full-body decontamination.” I make eye contact with Finn, and he gives an overly pained grimace, like he already regrets agreeing to come inside with me—but then he grips my hand in mock solidarity and I can tell he’s secretly enjoying this ridiculous pit stop more than he wants to let on. The “decontamination” ends up being a blast of AC before the automatic doors open into the kitschiest roadside gift shop I’ve ever seen.

A life-sized display has a family of pearlescent gray aliens who seem to be meeting a family of cavemen. One of the adult-sized aliens is wearing a T-shirt—and nothing else—with a bowl of round green alien heads that reads WE COME IN PEAS. To the left there is a rack of the same shirt.

“How stoked do you think Sybil would be to find this place?” Finn asks, still holding my hand, but looser now, our fingers gently tangling together.

“This place definitely has Sybil vibes,” I agree. All I can think about though is our hands intertwined. Anyone walking by would assume we’re a couple.

Smoke from a fog machine cascades along the floor from one of the other rooms. We walk through an archway wallpapered in Bubble Wrap and iridescent cellophane into a room filled with alien costumes. I pluck a headband with two rhinestone-encrusted googly eyes bobbing above it, and place it on Finn’s head.

Finn turns around to take stock in the mirror. “More sparkles than I’m used to.”

"I think it suits you. You look like a beautiful alien princess."

"Do you think Sybil will let me wear it during the ceremony?"

"We wouldn't want you to outshine Sybil on her big day," I joke, but then my stomach clenches remembering Sybil's drunken worry that her gown didn't have enough sparkles. "Maybe we can get it for Sybil. She was worried she didn't have enough glitz in her wedding outfit."

"That's probably why she headed to Vegas. To pick up a pound or two of sequins."

"Let's hope so."

Finn takes off the headband. "I'll go settle up," he says. "Do you need anything else?"

"I need this hot sauce," I say, turning toward a floor-to-ceiling display of hot sauce bottles.

"How can you eat that stuff?"

"Asks the man who just drank twenty ounces of undiluted kale juice?"

"That doesn't physically hurt me."

"I can assure you that nothing on this wall"—I motion to the hundreds and hundreds of hot sauce bottles—"would hurt me as much as consuming that much kale in one sitting."

I'm trying to decide between a ghost pepper sauce with a pirate zombie on the label and a Carolina Reaper–based sauce, when my phone vibrates. It's Liz.

"Aren't you supposed to be heading to a networking event right now?" I wedge the phone against my cheek and shoulder to keep my hands free as I clink through more hot sauces.

"Aren't you supposed to be in LA right now?" my sister tosses back.

"How do you know I'm not in LA?"

"Have you been online recently?"

"Not really. I've been tied up with…wedding stuff."

"Oh, *have* you? I didn't realize Sybil was getting married to a breakfast taco."

I manage to hang on to both hot sauce bottles, but the phone tumbles to the ground. "Shit." Returning the phone to my ear, I say, "How could you know about that?"

"Um, because it's trending. You and #burritogate are all over *LovedBy* Universe right now. Aaron's expression when the burrito hits his face is what memes are made of."

I groan, realizing once again that I've underestimated the level of interest that anything related to the show garners from its fan base. I watched all of Nikki's *LovedBy* episodes for emotional support, but I tapered off after her season was over. Liz, on the other hand, has been a die-hard *LovedBy* fan since she was thirteen. Every time she runs into Nikki, she grills her over what it was actually like to be on the show.

I pull out my phone and cringe when I see the video. I guess Finn was right—I *did* go Emma-Hulk. "Shit. Shit. Shit." Nikki is going to be so pissed. For the first time since my run-in with Aaron, I regret acting impulsively. I'd wanted to protect Nikki, but all I've done is thrust her back into the spotlight and back to vulnerability, which I know is the last thing she wants. Then an even worse thought occurs to me. "Do you think Jamie would have seen it? Has it gone super wide?"

Liz considers for a moment. "Probably not. I'm a lot deeper in the *LovedBy* weeds than most people." I breathe a sigh of relief. I don't need Jamie getting wise to the fact that something is going on. As far as he knows, I'm having a pamper session alongside his fiancée, who is supposedly in the hotel spa and not halfway to Vegas. "Also," Liz continues, "I couldn't help but notice someone tall, dark, and handsome in the video with you. What's his deal? He looks so familiar. Is he from *LovedBy* too?"

"That's just Finn," I say. "Finn Hughes? He was in my year at school? He's helping me with some…wedding stuff," I say again, not wanting to verbalize even to my sister that the bride has gone AWOL. Our chances of finding Sybil and getting her back before Jamie realizes something is up are starting to feel slim. Finn and I need to get back on the road ASAP.

"Oh right," Liz says, as I make my way back toward the front of the store. "He was that kid from your debate team who always wore that *Calvin and Hobbes* T-shirt. Wow, someone outgrew his dorkiness."

No frickin' kidding, I think to myself as I spot Finn waiting in line to pay for his silly alien googly-eyed headband. My heart clenches, remembering his lankier teenage self wearing that old *Calvin and Hobbes* T-shirt, and I find I'm glad that even though Finn is now, yes, tall, dark, and handsome, he can still be a little bit goofy.

"Oh, wait!" Liz shouts in my ear. "I know where I know him from." She giggles. "My friend Callie from San Francisco totally hooked up with him a few months ago. She showed me his Bumble profile. She was obsessed. But he kind of ghosted her. Apparently he wasn't looking for anything serious. Are you on Bumble, by the way? You should be. Didn't you say it's been a while since you had a good—"

"Uh-huh," I interrupt before Liz can finish that sentence. I don't need reminding of how long it's been since I've had a good...*anything*. Irritation is suddenly prickling at my temples. Here I've been, basically waltzing around the store playing girlfriend and having erotic massage dreams about Finn, once again allowing myself to forget his true nature. How does this keep happening? "Liz, I really gotta go."

"Okay, wait. The real reason I called is I don't have anything to wear to the networking event," she says. "Nothing I have is businessy enough."

"What about those wide-leg black pants, and that blue top you wore to Mom's birthday?" I say, not bothering to mention that at this point, Liz is probably going to miss the event altogether if she's still stuck in a wardrobe crisis and not currently on the Q train uptown.

Liz was supposed to be interning in the city this summer in the hopes of lining up a full-time job for when she graduates next May. When I agreed to let her stay with me for two months, I assumed she actually had an internship lined up, but apparently she never turned in the requisite paperwork for her school program. I've been sending her posting after posting, helping her revise her résumé (okay, basically drafting the whole thing myself), and coaching her on interview prep. I didn't realize I was going to have to lay out her clothes and physically escort her to the interviews too.

I take a deep breath. There's no use getting frustrated with Liz. This is just who she is. A little scattered, but with a good heart. She just needs someone to keep her on track.

Someone had to keep the family on track.

Finn's voice echoes in my ears, but this time I sense a hint of judgment that I didn't notice before. Like he thinks I've been bending over backward to keep my family afloat, when that's not the case at all. I just lend a helping hand when I need to. The irritation prickling along my scalp intensifies. Who is Finn to tell me how to deal with my family? Not exactly my boyfriend. And despite all that's happened between us over the years, he never was.

"Liz, go to my closet and grab my black blazer and a pencil skirt. If you need to steam them, the steamer is on the top shelf of the closet."

"Okay," she says. Then there's a longer pause. "Also, my debit card is running low...do you think you could—"

"I'll put some money in your account. Now go—you're going to be late."

"Thanks, Em. You always save my ass."

Yes, yes I do.

Liz and I say our goodbyes, and I use the ladies' room before heading past a pile of alien pods to find Finn.

"Ready to head out?" I pull up my bank app, making sure that I angle it away from Finn. My account balance doesn't look especially healthy, either, but I send Liz a couple hundred dollars anyway.

"I haven't finished my alien poop."

I look up from my phone. "Your what?"

Finn holds up a cup filled with tiny balls of ice cream.

"That looks a lot like Dippin' Dots."

"It was labeled as Alien Poop, and I, for one, don't believe that the people who claim to have footage of Neil Armstrong playing badminton with an alien on the moon would lie to me. Do you want some?"

"Can you finish that in the car? I'll drive. Let's go."

"Good one," Finn says, like I've made a hilarious joke.

"You are not driving. Not unless you win our bet." But he must see how serious I am about leaving, because he just tosses what's left of his ice cream in a trash can, and we get back to the car.

"Everything okay?" he asks once we've pulled back onto Route 15.

"We should have just flown to Vegas from San Diego. We would've gotten there in two hours instead of nearly six." I press my hands down onto my knees in an effort to stop the nervous bouncing of my legs. "I guess it doesn't matter. We couldn't leave the car behind."

"I could have driven it back to LA while you went on to Vegas."

He's right, of course. That would have been a logical solution. But the thought never would have occurred to me. Somehow along the way this has become a two-man mission, and even now, with the irritation and the stress, I can't imagine it any other way.

"I mean, you did save my life on the beach this morning, so I figure it's useful to keep you around," I say. Maybe I'm just trying to justify it to myself. Why some clearly sadistic part of me didn't mind…okay maybe even *wanted*…to be stuck for a little longer in a car with Finn.

Finn gives me that perfect little grin that I've come to think of as his Emma Face—half-exasperated, half-affectionate. One hundred percent devastating.

"Plus you wouldn't have wanted to fly. You always hated it."

I feel the familiar swoop low in my belly that I get every time Finn makes a reference to our shared past—small things that he's managed to remember even after all this time.

"Things change, Finn."

He smiles. "I guess they do."

I check Sybil's location again. Still in the vicinity of Caesars Palace. I remind myself why I'm really here—to save a wedding. To find Sybil and get to the bottom of her disappearance. I think about what Liz said on the phone, about how I always save her ass. And Sybil basically saying the same thing last night—*You're my rock*. I think about Finn noticing how I keep the family on track, and how he seems to understand what a burden that can sometimes be. I know it's not my job to fix everything.

But it *is* my job to fix this. I owe it to Sybil. My oldest friend. The one who dragged me onto the dance floor to do an impromptu Macarena while all the other girls at the church social were dancing on their dads' feet. It didn't matter that the song was some sweet country ballad—Sybil shook her hips and flung her hands across her shoulders to the imaginary beat until I couldn't stop giggling. Until the pain of missing my own dad—the anger and confusion that he wasn't at the dance, would never be the father that these other men were for their daughters—became so distant, I almost couldn't feel it anymore.

Sybil makes me feel like there's nothing wrong with me, like I'm loved and included no matter what. She makes me feel safe enough to take leaps I never would have otherwise. And I keep Sybil grounded. That's been the unspoken rule of our friendship for nearly two decades, and I'm not about to break it now.

Also, I need to know why Sybil ran—and I need to make it right. Why doesn't she feel like she's good enough for Jamie?

It's something that's been bothering me all day, at the back of my mind. How small her voice sounded last night. What could make her feel that small? Certainly not Jamie himself. So what, then?

I need to find her, and find out.

Outside the Singer, the sky is streaked with pinks and purples. It's seven thirty, nearly sunset. Soon, everyone will be gathering back in Malibu for the welcome party—everyone, that is, except the maid of honor, the bride, and the bride's best guy friend. I fire off a quick text to Willow and Nikki.

Still on the road—cover for us at the party?

How??? Nikki responds almost instantly.

You'll think of something!

I'm about to ask Finn how much longer we have, when a sparkling sign comes into view: WELCOME TO FABULOUS LAS VEGAS.

12

THURSDAY EVENING

(Two days before the wedding)

FINN PULLS INTO THE circle drive at Caesars Palace and passes his keys to the valet. Polished columns stretch toward the ceiling and rings of golden marble ripple out from a huge fountain in the middle of the very ornate lobby. The fountain depicts three women, none of whom were carved fully clothed. It's not quite my personal design style, but I do always appreciate a theme. I pull up my phone again to check on Sybil's location.

"I think she must be staying here," I tell Finn, studying my app like I'm the investigator in some BBC detective series. "She's been up and down the Strip, but she always ends up back here. Let's start at the casino and then just work our way through the resort."

"Got it. And, Emma?"

"What?"

"Don't forget about our deal. If we can't get her back to LA, you have to say something nice about me."

He's laughing, but for me, it's game on. "Oh, we'll get her back, Finn. And I look forward to driving the two of you all the way back to Malibu, without ever having to tax my mind to think of a compliment."

The casino is to the right of the lobby, so we head straight there. We circle through wedding chapels and swimming pools—one of which I didn't realize allowed topless sunbathing until we were neck-deep in nipples. I look longingly at a passing server carrying a tray full of colorful cocktails with swizzle sticks and umbrellas. I could use something to calm my growing anxiety now that we're here. Deep down, there's this worry nagging at me. If Sybil actually wanted us to find her, she'd be broadcasting it via text, social media, and a very loud singing voice. So what does it mean that she's doing such a good job of *not* being found?

Finn and I wind through fake canals, and dozens and dozens of luxury shops, but there's no sign of Sybil. We stop in front of what appears to be a reproduction of the Trevi Fountain in Rome. "Maybe we should make a wish," Finn suggests.

"What—a wish for Sybil to finally appear?" I can feel a sense of hopelessness creeping into my voice.

Finn fishes into his pockets and hands me a quarter, keeping one for himself. "Is that really what you want to wish for?"

I'm startled by his question. "That's literally what we're here for, Finn."

"True. But look around, Emma. We're in *Vegas*. Surrounded

by people throwing caution to the wind. Look at that lady." He points behind me to a green-haired woman, who is laughing as she pretends to ride her friend's back like a cowboy, while swinging a pink penis-shaped sword above her head. "Everyone else is here for themselves. Isn't there something that you want just for you?"

For some reason his question is making my pulse pick up. "Why? Is there something *you* want?" I ask, a little defensively.

He shrugs. "Maybe. But the nice thing about wishes is they're also secrets." He kisses his coin as he turns his back to the fountain and, after a second, tosses it over his head and into the water.

I take a moment to think about my wish. My *real* wish. What is it I want, just for me? More success at work? For Liz to find a real job so I can stop sending her a third of my paycheck every month? To find someone who loves me for all my quirks, just like Sybil has found in Jamie? To not feel so secretly worn out all the time, like I'm chasing something invisible that I'll never catch? Why is this so hard?

"Come on, Emma. I didn't ask you to solve a calculus problem. It was just meant to be fun," Finn says.

And that's when the wish hits me. I just want someone to take care of me the way I take care of everyone else. With that, I kiss my coin and toss it toward the fountain, watching it sink swiftly to the bottom, where it quickly gets lost among the piles and piles of change on the slimy bottom. Then I turn to Finn. "Come on, I need a drink."

I check Sybil's location again while we wait for drinks at the least-crowded bar we can find, but the blue dot hasn't moved. It's still hovering in the general vicinity of Caesars Palace.

"She has to come out of her room sometime," I say, squeezing lime juice into my tequila soda. "She's an extrovert to the nth degree. There's no way she could resist being out with all these people." And suddenly, I know exactly where she'd go. "We should go to the roulette tables."

Finn raises an eyebrow at me. "Well, if we're going to the tables, we might as well play a round...right?"

"I suppose it couldn't hurt..."

So we lay down some cash for roulette chips. Holding the little striped disks in my palm gives me a surge of adrenaline, like I'm about to pull some fun feminist heist, *Ocean's 8*–style. Finn's right—while we're looking for Sybil, there's no reason we can't participate in some of the fun too. I've never been to Vegas, and it seems like it'd be a crime to come all the way here and not get the full experience. One table looks particularly rowdy, so we squeeze in beside a middle-aged Black couple speaking French. I let the heavy plastic click against my palm.

"I'm putting these on eighteen," I tell Finn. "Saturday's date. The day of the wedding." I slide one of my chips onto the table and tap it twice decisively, willing luck to be on my side.

"Wedding?" the woman beside me says with a French accent. "Congratulations! You have the glow of a couple in love!"

"Oh no," I start to correct this woman, who clearly misunderstood my reference to Sybil's wedding as a reference to my own. Well, mine and Finn's. "We're not—"

Finn places a hand on my shoulder. "Merci beaucoup. Elle est très belle, n'est-ce pas?"

"Oui, oui," the woman says with a knowing smile.

Then Finn bends down to whisper in my ear. "What if we

make our bet a little more interesting?" The crowd around the table is nearly three feet deep, so he's wedged in behind me. I can feel his breath against the back of my neck, and my mind flashes to the massage table from my dream.

"How so?" I turn to face Finn as the rest of the table places their bets, and I have to crane my neck up to look at him.

"If you win, you can drive the Singer *and* keep my sweatshirt."

"Who says I want your ratty old sweatshirt?" I say, but I blush as my forearm brushes against Finn's chest. He's leaning in even closer to me. "And if you win?" My words come out in a whisper.

"I haven't decided yet." He mimics my terms from earlier. "You'll just have to wait and see. But I might have an idea or two..."

My spine tingles. I'm shocked to find that not knowing is actually kind of a turn-on. I feel both tantalized by the thrill of the unknown, and safe enough to trust that Finn wouldn't actually demand anything too far outside my comfort zone. Maybe instead of trying to control everything, what I really need is to just let go. After all, what happens in Vegas stays in Vegas, right?

The croupier spins the wheel and drops the ball in. The clack, clack, clack of the ball pulls me back to the present, and I twist back toward the table.

"Sybil and I used to play roulette in our apartment all the time," I say over my shoulder. "It was our favorite pregame."

"I've been to that apartment. It was what, seven hundred–ish feet?" Finn asks incredulously. "How did you wedge a roulette table in?"

For a moment, I can't help the rush of memory—Finn visiting our tiny New York apartment. The way everything went down between us that night makes me flush with heat. But I recover quickly.

"It's an inlaid midcentury Italian games table only about thirty inches on each side. The top opens up to a roulette wheel inside the table." I pull up an old photo on Instagram of Sybil spinning the roulette wheel with one hand and balancing a martini glass in the other. The table is one of my favorite pieces of furniture with some of my best memories, but it's been covered in piles of fabric samples and unfolded laundry for nearly a year. I twist around to show it to Finn, and our bodies are pressed together in a way that makes me hyperaware of where our hips meet.

His hand curls around mine as he brings the phone closer to his face. It throws my balance off slightly, but just as quickly, Finn's hand is pressed to my back, steadying me. "If you were my interior designer, could you get me one of those?" Finn asks quietly. His eyes dip to my lips, and my tongue darts out nervously. His eyes darken, and the hand against my back presses me even more tightly against him.

"Yes." The word comes out more breathlessly than I intend. "Mine came from an estate sale on the Upper East Side, but I'm sure I could source one for you." I hesitate. "To be honest, you don't need me. Any designer could get one for you."

"But I don't want any designer. I want *you.*" The sincerity in Finn's tone sends a thrill down my spine, and I'm locked into the intensity of the way he's looking at me. A cheer goes up around us, but I can't pull my gaze away. My whole body is on fire, an asteroid burning through the atmosphere; all I want to do is crash into Finn Hughes, to get even closer to him than I am right now.

The dealer taps me on the shoulder. "Ma'am, you've won."

"Félicitations!" The French woman next to me motions Finn and me together. "Such a beautiful couple. You must kiss to celebrate your victory!"

The cry of "Kiss! Kiss! Kiss!" is taken up by the rest of the table, and Finn leans toward me. My mind goes brain-dead. Finn Hughes is going to kiss me. *I want you*, he said. And I want him too. My mind instantly jumps back to the summer after freshman year of college, the first time I felt Finn's lips on mine. It's like I'm right back in Katie Dalton's pool, only now, instead of our slick bodies pressing against the swimming pool's cement walls, my back is pressed against the roulette table—but just like before, my front is pressed against Finn. My entire body lights up like it's won the slot machine jackpot, pulsing at each point of connection between us.

"Not here." Finn's lips graze the edge of my ear, and his hand slips beneath the hem of the sweatshirt. His thumb drags along the bare skin of my back, and my heartbeat ratchets up another twenty beats per minute. *Not here, but soon.* I can hear his unspoken promise, and I haven't felt this out of control with lust since—well, since the last time Finn and I kissed.

The moment is broken by the roulette dealer. "Ma'am. The casino would like to comp you tickets either for the Ibarra-Kuzmin fight or Scarlett Westwood's World-Famous Burlesque Show."

I blink twice to clear my head, and spin toward the croupier, just as Finn starts to say, "We'll take the burlesque show."

I elbow him. "Excuse me, I won this game. We'll take the

boxing tickets." The dealer hands me two tickets, and I fan them out and wave them at Finn, who pouts at me like I've just spoiled his night.

"I hate boxing."

"It's not like we're going to go anyway," I remind him. "The match isn't until eleven thirty. We'll have Sybil and be on our way back to Malibu by then. Besides, why would you want to go to a burlesque show? I thought you didn't care about women in lingerie."

"Well, of course. I just appreciate the athleticism and the showmanship of these women. You wouldn't understand."

"Oh, I think I understand exactly." I swat his arm, laughing, and he grabs my wrist, lightly pulling me in closer to him.

"Emma," he begins. And suddenly I'm taken back to the many times we've ended up like this before—face-to-face, uncertainty hovering between us.

"Yeah?" I ask quietly.

"Is that your phone ringing?"

Shit. He's right. I reach for it, expecting it to be Liz telling me she missed the networking event, but anxiety and hope spike through me in equal measure when I see it's Nikki. It's either about #burritogate, or…

"Hey! Everything okay over there?" I ask, trying to keep my voice neutral despite the fact that I'm surrounded by an Elvis-themed mariachi band.

It's so loud in here I have to make her repeat herself after she says something scrambled into the phone. "What?" I scream back.

"Jamie *knows*," Nikki hisses into the phone. "And he's coming to Vegas."

13

THURSDAY NIGHT

(Two days before the wedding)

THE STRING OF CURSE words that fly out of my mouth would have my mother in conniptions.

"How did Jamie find out about Vegas?"

"Well..." Nikki hesitates. "I told him."

"You *what*?"

"Emma, stop shouting at me!" Nikki shouts right back. "He cornered me and asked where Sybil was, and I just panicked. I told him we wanted to do a real bachelorette for her in Vegas."

"Nikki," I groan, pulling Finn away from the roulette table to a quieter corner of the casino floor. "I thought we had a plan. You were just supposed to keep him in the dark long enough to give me and Finn time to find Sybil and bring her home."

"I know, I know. But he asked me straight out. You know

I'm not good under that kind of pressure!" It's true. Nikki's near inability to lie is something we have in common. Although in my case, the truth always seems to burst from me like a cannonball—too blunt, too critical, with the power to maim. Nikki's honesty is more like a bubbling champagne bottle, always delivered with a crinkle-eyed laugh or a sheepish smile—completely endearing. It's what made her such a fan favorite on *LovedBy*. "But you should be proud of me, Em," she continues on the phone. "I almost broke down and just told him the whole truth about Sybil running away—"

"Nikki!"

"But I didn't! I couldn't once I saw Jamie's face. You know him, he's such a sweet teddy bear of a man. I didn't want to be the one to break his heart." It makes sense. Nikki, more than anyone, knows what it's like to have the person you love leave you out to dry right before the big day, after you've promised to spend forever together. "Anyway, he said Vegas sounded like a blast, and one of his friends said they could borrow his PJ—"

"His pajamas?"

"His private jet, Emma." *Right*. Jamie really is such a sweet, unassuming guy, that I often forget that he and his circle of friends are loaded. "So now he and his entire half of the wedding party are on their way," Nikki continues. "He told his parents that he and Sybil have food poisoning, so they can't make the welcome party."

I pinch the bridge of my nose. "I'm going to need a spreadsheet to keep track of which lies we've told which people." Which reminds me… "Um, by the way, have you been online at all?" I ask as casually as possible, trying to ascertain if I'm still safe from her learning about the #burritogate video going viral.

"No. I've been playing nice with Jamie and his friends all day. Why?" Her voice turns suspicious.

"No reason," I say. Finn suppresses a chuckle, and I elbow him in the ribs.

"The plane is scheduled to leave at nine thirty p.m."

"What are we going to do, Nikki?" I hate the desperation in my voice.

"Find Sybil! Just follow that little blue dot and hog-tie her to a blackjack table when you find her. I've got to go change into something Vegas-y. I'll text you when we land."

I hang up with Nikki and start frantically looking up flight times and drive times, feeling like one of those headset-wearing tech-whiz characters in an action TV show, coaching the main character on how to defuse a bomb. "Okay, they leave at nine thirty p.m., an hour from now, it's a thirty-minute flight, and Google says it'll take less than twenty minutes for them to get to the casino from the airport. Which means we have less than two hours to locate Sybil before Jamie arrives and realizes anything is amiss. We need to find her. Now."

Finn gives me a nod and leads me back toward the lobby. If I wasn't so stressed about finding Sybil, I might be impressed with how smoothly Finn and I are able to transition from pressing against each other at the roulette table—seemingly moments away from crashing through the barrier of "just friends" yet again—to throwing ourselves headlong into problem-solving mode. How our chemistry extends beyond just the obvious physical attraction to the kind of mind-meld partnership that made us such a good debate team back in the day.

We make our way out of Caesars Palace, because Sybil's blue dot, which had been relatively stable for a few hours, has now started bouncing around, ping-ponging back and forth between the various casinos. She seems to have covered every square inch of the Strip.

"What is she even doing?" I ask, but Finn just shrugs his shoulders.

"Maybe she's trying to dodge us, or maybe she's trying to wrangle a troupe of lost circus monkeys. I can't pretend to understand what goes on in her mind."

"This is such a nightmare," I say. "We aren't any closer to finding Sybil now than when we got here an hour ago."

"Maybe we need to shift tactics. Why don't we throw out a little bait and let Sybil come to *us*?"

"What do you mean?"

"Like, post a photo of us having a good time. We'll see if Sybil checks it. Maybe she'll come out of the woodwork to join us." My face must show how unconvinced I am, so Finn continues. "Look, the last time you freaked out about finding Sybil, which was only"—he looks down at his watch—"seven hours ago, you literally fainted and fell into the ocean."

"I didn't fall. You caught me."

Finn smiles, and something flutters in my stomach. A pang of regret shoots through me that I was unconscious during Finn's rescue. As I look up into his deep brown eyes, my hand seems to move of its own volition, resting right over his heart. He curls his fingers around mine, and his eyes drop to my mouth. My body sways toward him, and he snaps to attention. "You're barely able to stay on your feet. The only thing you've had since lunch is coffee and tequila, so I'm making the executive decision that we're going to get dinner. We'll snap a selfie of us eating something amazing, and Sybil will join us before dessert. It just might work—and even if it doesn't, at least we get a meal." I'm not sure lack of food is what has me swaying toward him, but I don't correct Finn. He throws his arm around my shoulder and leads me toward the Bellagio. I try to ignore how perfectly I fit under his arm, how good he smells, and how safe I feel tucked up against him. I know this idea of luring Sybil to us via a fun selfie is ridiculous, but Finn's right—we need to eat. I won't be any good to Sybil—or Nikki and Jamie when they arrive—if I'm collapsed on the (questionably sticky) casino carpet. Plus, it's nice to let someone else take the lead for once. When we reach the Bellagio, Finn maneuvers us toward a swanky sushi restaurant.

Reluctantly, I pull myself away from Finn and say, "We can just go to the food court. We don't need to grab something fancy."

"You think we're going to lure Sybil out of hiding with Sbarro?" Finn asks with mock outrage. "No. This needs to be the meal of a lifetime."

I roll my eyes at his commitment to the bit—this excuse that we're concocting for ourselves about why taking a break for dinner is actually in service to our mission—but secretly I'm grateful. I'm not sure what it means that justifying things this way feels safer to me. Maybe it's because it saves me from having to be vulnerable and actually express my own wants and needs. But that's stupid. Why can't I just say that I'm hungry, damn it, and I want to eat sitting down…with Finn? I think back to earlier this evening, at the fountain. *Isn't there something that you want just for you?* Finn asked me. Yes, yes there is.

"And besides," Finn starts to say. Then he pauses, looking me straight in the eye. I suddenly feel light-headed, but that's probably just because, like Finn said, I've been running on caffeine and alcohol since lunchtime. Not because Finn is looking at me like it's *me* he wants to devour, and not some sashimi. "I've owed you a nice dinner since junior year."

And with that, Finn presses past me toward the host stand.

"A table for two, please," Finn says, beginning to look at the menu on the wall.

"Of course." The host smiles. "Unfortunately, we do have a dress code."

"Oh." I look down at my (Finn's) sweatshirt, shorts, and flip-flops. Not exactly fancy sushi restaurant attire.

To soften the blow, she adds, "We require that gentlemen wear jackets."

"Ah, right. I've got a sport coat in my car," Finn says, stepping away from the host's. "I'm sure it's wrinkled to hell, but it should do. Why don't you go grab an outfit from one of the ten million shops around. I'm going to grab a room so I can shower. I'll leave a key for you at the front desk so you can, too, and then we can meet under the Eiffel Tower in an hour? I'll find us a place to grab dinner."

I nod, realizing that my impromptu ocean dip during the kayaking fiasco has left my hair a crunchy, tangled disaster. A shower would be great. Though mostly I'm just fighting myself not to picture Finn taking his shower.

"See you soon," Finn says with an easy grin.

I wander into the first store that doesn't look like I'll need to spend a month's rent, and start flipping through racks. I haven't been shopping recently, partly because I haven't had the budget, but mostly I just haven't needed to. My life has been a predictable routine of work, home, work, home.

I'm about to go try on a simple black shift dress, when something else catches my eye. A jade silk dress with a high boatneck. It's definitely over the top, and I certainly don't *need* to be spending hundreds of dollars on a dress I can't also wear to the office. But I imagine what Sybil would say if she were beside me...*Em, you* have *to at least try it on. Look at that color. It's perfect for you.*

I pull the jade dress from the rack before I can talk myself out of it, and head straight to the dressing room. The bodice nips in at the waist, then fans out into an A-line skirt that's short enough not to look too demure. The fabric skims my upper thigh, and a shiver runs through me as I remember my dream from this afternoon. Finn's hands, grazing my legs...In the mirror, my cheeks flush pink as I wonder what Sybil would say about that. The answer is so obvious, it brings a smirk to my face: *Go get it, girl!* I leave the black dress swinging on its hanger in the dressing room and walk toward the register. I grab a pair of strappy gold sandals in my size and pay, wishing Sybil were actually here shopping with me.

I pop into Sephora to grab some makeup essentials, then hurry back to the hotel. There's a key for me at the front desk just like Finn said, and as I step into the room, my heart sticks in my throat, wondering if I might catch Finn like I did this morning, with his brown skin glistening, wet and warm and just a towel wrapped around his waist. The air is humid from a recent shower, but the room is empty. I try not to think too hard about the feeling of disappointment that settles in my stomach. I take a lightning-fast shower and blow out my hair using my fingers as a brush. The result is a softy, beachy look—a little more relaxed than the usual smooth treatment I give my long bob.

Taking a step back from the hotel mirror, I feel…beautiful. I know this outfit is just something we need to get a meal, but the butterflies in my stomach and the ritual of getting ready have started to trick my brain into feeling like this is a real date. A bemused snort escapes me as I realize that in all the years Finn and I have been circling each other, we've never actually gone on a real date. Never done the whole dinner-and-a-movie routine. It's kind of wild to think about, given everything we *have* done together. I grab my new brick-red lipstick and pull another swipe across my bottom lip as my mind turns over this realization. Is it possible I've been avoiding the typical courting rituals with Finn because I'm afraid of getting hurt by him again, like I did at prom or Katie Dalton's wedding? Have I been stopping myself from making a big mistake, or has the mistake been *not* letting myself really go there with Finn?

It feels like I'm about to find out.

Before I leave the hotel room, I gather up my discarded clothes into the empty shopping bag from the boutique. Looking in the mirror, I smack my lips once more and whisper a plea—my own reflection standing in for my absent friend.

"Wish me luck, Sybs."

14

MISTAKE THREE: THE ROOFTOP

(Five years before the wedding)

IN THE YEAR AND three months I'd been living in New York City, I had become an expert predictor of its rhythms, its complex choreographies. When to leap down a set of stairs to make it onto the L train before the doors sealed shut, how to tiptoe across a metal grating in stilettos so as not to get a heel stuck on the way to work, which corner of the street was best to hail a cab without having to get charged extra for looping around the block, whether sneaking up to our building's rooftop was worth the trouble from the landlord (always). But somehow, in the same exact amount of time, Sybil had remained inexplicably oblivious: always spending too much on fancy cocktails and then running out of money for rent; always falling for the guy who had the whitest teeth at the bar, even though he was guaranteed to be a player; always forgetting which of the burners on our junky little stove leaked gas, and then having to fling open all the windows of our shared apartment in a panic.

But even this—the clueless way Sybil conducted herself in this big, busy, cutthroat city—had become a pattern I could predict. And I loved it.

Usually.

It was a hot, sticky September, the beginning of our second autumn in New York, the kind of weather where all your cute fall sweaters end up flung to the floor, and the front door to our fourth-floor walk-up, swollen from heat, squeaked loudly every time we came and went.

Which was why I knew Sybil was home before I could see her. I had been sitting on the couch ever since I'd gotten home from the office, picking at my chipped nail polish while scrolling design blogs on my phone when, beneath the dying-cat yowl of the door, I heard Sybil call from the entryway, "Hey, babes! Can Finn stay with us while he's in town? I told him our couch isn't bad if he hangs his feet off the end."

I dropped my phone into said couch cushions as a bolt of adrenaline shot through me at the thought of Finn Hughes in our cramped apartment. Finn lying on this very spot, a mere three steps from the door to my bedroom. Sitting on one of our mismatched kitchen stools drinking coffee out of my Loch Ness monster mug. Finn in our shower, using my eucalyptus bodywash. I blinked away the thought of a naked, wet Finn just as Sybil appeared. A six-pack of Trader Joe's wine and three tote bags' worth of groceries hit the floor with a worrisome thump, and she looked down at me expectantly. That was another thing she still hadn't bothered to learn—how many heavy items you can feasibly carry up all four flights without inducing a heart attack.

"Doesn't he have his own friends to stay with?" I automatically moved off the couch and toward the grocery bags.

Sybil rolled her eyes and exhaled so hard her blond bangs fluttered off her forehead. "*I'm* his friend, Emma. So are you." Leaving the rest of the bottles on the ground, she grabbed a red and headed to the line of cabinets against a single wall that we referred to as "the kitchen," and began fishing around for a bottle opener. As the newest design associate for Maywell Interiors, I found it painful to coexist with the cheap yellowish oak and the peeling laminate counters, but it was worth it for the location—right in the heart of the East Village. We were two blocks from Tompkins Square Park, and there were fun bars and a diverse offering of cheap eats on every corner. It was the perfect place to ease into adulthood. And apparently, adulthood meant hosting your ex-friend/ex-maybe-something-more in your tiny New York City apartment. My stomach clenched at the thought, but I was determined to handle this unexpected reunion with grace and maturity.

"Yeah, it's fine." I started wedging celery and hummus into any open space in the fridge. "Finn can stay here. I'll just crash with Preston."

"Oh, perfect. He can stay in your room, then." My skin tightened at the thought of Finn Hughes in my bed, between my sheets.

I distracted myself by pulling out two containers of week-old Indian food, dropping them in the trash to make room for Sybil's soy milk. "When is he in town?"

The cork popped free of the bottle, and Sybil grabbed two wineglasses from the drying rack beside the sink. She started pouring, and as always, the wine came nearly to the rim of the glass—what she called a "country club pour."

Sybil handed me a glass, and I took it carefully so as not to spill. She turned and walked over to the spot I'd just vacated on the couch. Easing onto the cushion, she took a long slurp from the top of her glass. Then, as if just remembering the question I had left lingering, she tossed casually over her shoulder, "This Friday."

"Sybil! This Friday as in *tomorrow*? Isn't this kind of late notice?"

"Well...he may have told me about it a few weeks ago, but I must've forgotten to say something." There was another slurp, then silence.

I closed the fridge and narrowed my eyes at the back of Sybil's head. "You *forgot*?"

"Okay, fine, I did not forget." She twisted around on the sofa to look at me. "But in my defense, it was for your own good. I didn't want to stress you out about it. You had that big interview, and I didn't want you to go bananas and, like, try to reupholster the couch, or something." I looked down at the worn plaid of the couch, a Facebook Marketplace find. I would have liked to at least get a slipcover made for it—something a little punchier. There was a claret and eggplant stripe I'd been eyeing...but that was beside the point. The point was, Sybil was treating me like a child, withholding information in some misguided attempt to shield my once-bruised heart or something. Which was completely ridiculous. I was totally over Finn Hughes. Besides, I had a boyfriend. A real one, with a real job and tastefully sculpted biceps, and he paid for our meals.

Sybil gave me a look like she could tell exactly what I was thinking.

"I can take care of myself, Sybil," I said, slurping my own wine with as much dignity as I could muster.

"By the way, have you seen my new sweater?" she asked, clearly trying to change the subject. "I think I lost it."

"I returned it for you already." The sweater in question had been an impulse buy for Sybs, and while she could pull off just about anything, the rust-orange and neon-yellow combination on that cardigan was truly unholy. "It was on my way to work anyway."

"*Emmm*...Now I don't have an excuse to go to Midtown and casually run into Sebastian outside of his office!"

Ah.

So it wasn't so much a sweater as a ruse.

"Well, you could still pretend to do that."

"I could, but it's much more convincing with a prop. Having it helps me get into the role of Hot Twentysomething Who Doesn't Need a Man But Could Be Convinced If It Was Someone Very Special, Casually Returning Wool Sweater."

"That's a very specific role."

Sybil's current obsession was Sebastian Wallace-Conway, a photojournalist for the *Times* who always seemed to have just enough time in the city for Sybil to come to his place late at night, but never enough time to take her on a date. It was no secret that I wasn't his biggest fan. Mostly because he just drifted in and out of Sybil's life, always leaving a trail of running mascara and empty sauv blanc bottles in his wake. But on the rare occasions when he did stick around long enough for us all to hang out, I actually found his company enjoyable. He was a lot like Sybil—larger than life, emitting an energy that you just wanted to be a part of. And, of course, he was predictably gorgeous, in a rugged, artsy kind of way.

"Okay, well, I'm sorry I ruined Operation Return Heinous Sweater." I rolled my eyes into my wineglass. "But can we get back to the fact that you've been hiding critical information from me?"

"You mean about Finn coming? Sorry. I just assumed things might be weird with you two."

A jolt of worry ran through me that maybe Finn told Sybil about what happened, or rather, what *nearly happened*, in the pool four years ago. "Wh-why would you think that?"

"Oh, you know." Sybil waved her hand. "The prom of it all." I breathed an internal sigh of relief. The prom of it all had fallen to my second-most-emotionally-fraught interaction with Finn Hughes. Now, it was the thought of his hands tangled in my wet hair and his lips on my throat that left me taking another long pull from my glass. But that was four years ago—ancient history. Huge mistake. I was a totally different person now. I was finally with someone who checked off every box I could think of. Preston was smart, gorgeous, and ambitious. Honestly, I felt like he was out of my league. And sometimes, it felt like he knew it too. He had the same razor-sharp wit that Finn did, but it wasn't always tempered by the same sweetness. Preston could be quick with a zinger, but his sarcastic comments often had an edge to them that made me wonder if he was using humor to reveal his true feelings about me. *Babe, come on, you've never read Pynchon? Didn't they have an English department at that little state school?* Preston had gone to Cornell.

And then I remembered. "Ugh, Preston is going to a bachelor party in Montana this weekend." There was no way I was going to Preston's apartment if he wasn't there. He lived with four other former members of the Cornell crew team, and the floor only got cleaned if someone knocked over a beer can—sometimes not even then.

"Okay." Sybil shrugged. "Finn can just have the couch, then."

"So long as he doesn't bring a girl back. I don't need to stumble upon one of his Hinge hookups in the middle of the night." I clicked my teeth shut at the look on Sybil's face. "Don't tell him I said that," I muttered into my wineglass.

Sybil cocked an eyebrow at me. "That shouldn't be an issue. He's gotten serious with some girl out in SF."

"Oh." I ignored the wave of something—surprise, disappointment, indigestion?—that rippled through me. "That's great."

"Is it?" Sybil asked.

"Absolutely." I downed the rest of my country club pour in one go.

FINN HADN'T MADE IT to our apartment before I headed out for work the next day, but I knew he was there when I got home, thanks to the sad country boy music spilling into the hallway.

The twang of Tyler Childers's voice rose another decibel as I opened the door to our apartment.

"Hi." Finn leaned against the back of the couch, a Brooklyn Lager dangling from his fingers.

I cleared my throat and spoke over the music. "Hi."

The moment hung between us. He didn't make a move to get up, and I took the time to look at him. He seemed older. Which, of course he was. But all the lankiness of his teenage years had been filled in by muscle. He looked like a man. An incredibly attractive man. Sharp dark brown eyes against his brown skin, close-cut hair, and cheekbones that could slice through glass. Not that it mattered to me.

"I'm just going to..." I motioned toward the bags slung around my shoulder and tried to squeeze past him on the way to my room.

"Right, yeah. Sorry." He tried to give me more space, but we ended up blocking each other's path, like some strange partner dance. I went left, he went left. I went right, he went right. Once. Then twice. The third time, his hands came to my shoulders, and my neck craned up to look at him, and he smiled. "You stay, I'll move."

I stood completely still as he released his hands and slid around me. His body didn't touch mine, but my every hair follicle followed his path. I had to stop myself from turning toward him.

"Emma! You're here! Let's go get drinks!" Sybil's voice cut through the music, and the moment snuffed out as she appeared in the doorway of her room.

"One sec." I hurried into my own room, taking a quick look into the mirror above my desk. It could definitely have been worse. I swiped a tissue beneath my lash line and brushed on another layer of mascara.

"I'm starving. Can we do dinner first?" I called, dragging off the navy blouse I wore to work. The temperature had dropped several degrees today—apparently real autumn was finally ready to make an appearance—so I pulled on a pair of sheer tights beneath my short black skirt. On top I went for a filmy black sleeveless shirt with a beaded detail around the collar that I had found at a thrift store in Austin two years ago. I finished it off with a pair of slouchy black boots.

"I'll eat anything," I heard Finn say from the other room. It was a perfectly reasonable response, but for some reason my brain heard it as something filthy. *Get your act together, Emma*, I berated myself. *You have a boyfriend; you shouldn't be lusting over some guy from high school.* But of course, Finn could never be just "some guy."

I shrugged into my black leather jacket as I walked back into the main living area. Finn gave me an appraising look that made me shiver.

"You look so New York." He quirked a smile at me.

"I think that's a compliment?" I said, smiling back. Sybil looked back and forth between the two of us. "You look so SF. . . ." I motioned toward his standard-issue tech-bro fleece vest, then raised an eyebrow. "Well, maybe not the hat." Finn had on a familiar worn baseball cap with the Dallas Cowboys logo.

Outside, Sybil hailed us a cab to NoLita. She piled into the car first, which left me in the middle seat. For the entirety of the short ride, I tried to ignore Finn's thigh pressed against mine. With each stop and start of the taxi, the cotton of his pant leg slid against the whisper-thin nylon of my tights. I darted a quick look over at him, but he seemed totally unfazed, his eyes out the window. I decided that if Finn was going to be unaffected, then I would be too.

Now someone just had to tell my central nervous system.

We went to dinner at a Cuban-Mexican restaurant that Sybil loved, and between sips of frozen mojitos and bites of roasted corn slathered in mayonnaise and cotija cheese, everything started to feel a little more normal. Finn and I hadn't really been in touch throughout college, save for occasional run-ins back home in Dallas, so there was plenty to catch up on. And like Sybil had said, Finn was our friend. When the bill came and Finn's arm reached around me to grab it, it was a *friendly* warmth that suffused my entire body—nothing more.

After dinner, we headed a few blocks east to another bar, one that Sybil swore had the best music. Finn went to go grab us seats, while I leaned against the honey-brown wood of the bar and waited to catch the bartender's attention. After I placed our order, I looked over at Sybil, who had both hands, and her full attention, on her phone.

"Is there another puppy emergency at the Floyd household?" I asked. Sybil had been working as an assistant for B-list celebrity Amity Floyd for the last six months. Her previous gig, an internship at the clothing brand Zimmerman, had failed to turn into a full-time—and, more importantly, *paid*—position. So, when she had a chance meeting with Amity while waiting in line for Cronuts in Williamsburg, Sybil jumped at the opportunity to become her new PA. Amity sounded nice enough, but she seemed dogged (literally) by minor catastrophe after minor catastrophe. She never hesitated to send Sybil multiple texts in a row outside of work hours. She also had, in my opinion, a truly heinous habit where if Sybil didn't respond quickly enough, she'd tap back each text with a question mark.

Sybil smiled as she finished typing out her text. "No, Fitzwilliam has been sent to doggy Harvard for four months of obedience training." She looked at me, looked at her phone, looked back at me, and seemed to come to some decision. Tucking her phone back into her purse, she said, "Sebastian's back in town for the night. Then he's going to central Asia for who knows how long."

I didn't know if it was the mojito buzzing through my veins or the fact that things seemed to be going well with Finn, but I said, "You should go see him."

"No, I'm not going to abandon you to Finn," Sybil said firmly, but her hand drifted back to the clasp on her purse like she was itching to pull her phone out again.

"I can handle Finn, Sybs. You only get to see Sebastian like once a quarter." The bartender placed our drinks in front of me.

"Are you sure?" Sybil asked, but she was already pulling on her coat.

"I'm totally sure."

"Well, y'all do seem to be hitting it off," she said, looping her purse across her body. "Say goodbye to Finn for me. Just tell him he can crash in my bed. Or don't." Before I could argue, she pulled me into a bear hug, squeezing out a laugh from me. "You know, if you just talk to him about something boring like the mating habits of Australian marsupials, he'll be all over you."

"I don't want him to be all over me!" I said, wriggling out of her hug. "I'm with Preston."

"Preston is so bleh, and you are so…so." She didn't seem to be able to find the words, so she wiggled her fingers in front of my face like she was casting a spell.

"I'm so-so?" I asked.

She huffed out a laugh and dropped her hands. "No, you little weirdo. You're so *special*." Sybil's phone lit up again, and she glanced at it. "Okay, I'm going to go. Thanks, Em. I'll see you tomorrow. Don't do anything I wouldn't do!"

"That doesn't leave much," I called after her.

Sybil winked at me, then headed for the door.

I made my way to the high-top in the back where Finn was waiting, and slid all three drinks onto the table. "Sybil's gone."

"Where'd she go?" He didn't sound particularly concerned—or surprised. Which was fair; he knew Sybil almost as well as I did. It wasn't unlike her to bolt.

"Sebastian."

"Ah, the man, the myth, the legend," Finn said, and I got the distinct impression that he'd also been on the receiving end of endless texts about Sebastian all through summer and now into fall.

"He's not that impressive." I pulled the two tequila sodas toward me and pushed Finn's beer toward him. "She's been running after him for months. It's not like her. Usually her attention fades. But she really likes him, so I told her to go."

Finn raised his eyebrows and took a swig of his beer. "You told her to go?"

"I just want her to be happy, and right now Sebastian makes her over-the-moon happy." I didn't mention that the week after he leaves town we were usually knee-deep in Ben and Jerry's and nineties rom-coms. "Though I'm not totally sure why."

"Maybe she likes the thrill of the chase."

"Maybe." I squeezed the wedge of lime into my drink. Neither of us realized then that Sebastian would become one of the most important—and most turbulent—relationships in Sybil's life. But then again, there's a lot we hadn't yet realized.

There was a beat of silence, and I was aware that Finn and I were alone together for the first time since the Pool Incident. The memory of my lips on Finn's neck was the only thing I could think of. My glass paused halfway to my mouth, and I wondered what his skin tasted like without the hint of chlorine. My lips parted involuntarily. Finn's eyes darted to my mouth, but he took a drink of his beer and cleared his throat. "You should come out to SF sometime."

The offer took me by surprise enough that I was jolted out of the memory. I put my drink back down without taking a sip. "That would be fun."

Without Sybil, the easy flow we'd had at dinner dried up. Now there was a crackle in the air between us. Finn had rolled up the sleeves of his light blue button-up and begun peeling the label off his beer bottle. There was a slightly nervous energy to his movements. I watched the small muscles shift along the back of his hand as he ripped the green-and-black label into smaller and smaller pieces. It was indecent that men were allowed to walk around with their forearms just out in the open. I forced myself to think of Preston, who also had beautiful wrists and hands and arms.

"What's Pneuma?" I asked, motioning to the logo embroidered on his vest.

"It's my start-up. It means 'breath' in Greek. I'm actually out here taking some investor meetings." He looked slightly embarrassed.

"Oh, cool." I winced inwardly that I couldn't think of anything more interesting to say. Finn had his own company, and I was still assisting on projects. I felt that old surge of competitiveness I used to get around Finn during debate prep. The urge to prove myself his equal. But now, with the gimlet eyes of hindsight, I could admit that Finn had never actually made me feel like I was less than. In high school he was suitably intimidated by my arguing skills, and I knew if I told him about my new job now, he'd be excited for me. That he'd have nothing but respect for where I was in my career.

"Sybil said y'all have a rooftop."

Finn's voice startled me out of my thoughts.

"We do. Technically." As in, it was a roof. Not a roof *deck*. Not a roof *lounge*. Not a roof anything, just a tar-covered, puddle-filled, dangerously low-walled roof covered in pigeon poop...and perfect for parties. Our lease specifically forbade us from using it, but that had not stopped us in the past. Finn looked at me expectantly. "Do you want to see it?"

His eyes didn't leave my face. "I do."

"Let's walk," I said. I didn't think I could handle another cab ride.

"DON'T LET THAT GET knocked loose," I told Finn, motioning toward the old wooden cheese board I'd wedged into the doorjamb to keep it open, "or we'll have to spend the night up here.

There's no way I could get Sybil to leave Sebastian now that she's with him."

Finn headed straight to the waist-high wall at the edge of the roof, leaning against it and looking north at the rest of Manhattan. You could see both the Empire State Building and the Chrysler Building from our rooftop. Even after having lived in the city for a year, moments like this made me feel like I was inside someone else's life.

"How's the boyfriend?" Finn asked.

"I mean, you probably know as much as I do. He's a photojournalist who—"

"Not Sybil's," Finn interrupted. "Yours."

He angled his body toward me, one elbow propped up against the ledge of the rooftop. I hadn't spoken about Preston at all during dinner. Finn must have learned of his existence from Sybil.

"Preston's a, you know, crew guy," I said with a shrug, frustrated at myself that I couldn't come up with a more specific description.

"Ah, I know the type. They wake up at five a.m. to row," he said with a smirk.

"Exactly." Then, since Finn and I were just friends and this was the kind of thing you could say to a friend, I added, "And, you know, he's superhot, supersmart. All around...super."

"Oh, I bet." Finn smiled.

"So tell me about the girlfriend," I asked.

He squinted his eyes at me as if he was debating telling me something. Whatever he read on my face must have been enough encouragement, because he said, "Pilar asked me about an open relationship a few days ago."

I blinked twice, unsure how to respond. "Is that what you want?"

Finn's mouth was a grim line, communicating his unspoken *no.* "The deal with relationships," he said after a beat, folding his arms across his chest, "is that the person who wants the most freedom gets to set the terms."

"You could set the terms by no longer *being in* the relationship though," I offered. He shrugged and turned back to looking at the skyline. "What's she like?" I asked, mirroring his position and looking out at the sea of lights in front of us. I wondered what kind of woman could catch Finn's attention so thoroughly that he'd be willing to consider sharing her.

"Smart, ambitious." He turned to look at me. "Total smoke show. You know, my usual type."

"Of course." I nodded. Then, because I couldn't help picking at it, I asked, "Why even have a relationship if you want to have it open?"

"I think they work for some people. I'm not sure I'm one of them though."

"It'd be hard for me too."

"I bet. You're very territorial."

I reared back but was still smiling. "You make me sound like a she-wolf or something."

He flashed me a smile. "Just that you seem to go all in or all out on people."

My cheeks grew warm in spite of the cool evening air. I turned away from the skyline, away from Finn's gaze. As I rested my lower back against the ledge, I considered just how accurately Finn had described me—and tried not to analyze too hard what it meant that he was always able to see right to the core of me.

"So you think Sybil's got it that bad?" Finn asked.

We were close enough that I could feel the heat radiating from his body. I smelled woodsmoke and lavender, and I felt my own body leaning toward his. I tried to remember what Finn had just asked me. "I think it's that Sebastian's life is an adventure. He's always going to these far-off places, war zones, catastrophes, and Sybil's always looking for a new adventure."

"You have to admit that his job sounds pretty cool."

"Yeah, yeah, yeah." I waved away Finn's comment. "He'd be a lot cooler if he didn't string her along. He's always telling her he's going to meet up with her, then jumps on a flight to Venezuela. You have to be able to depend on people. You have to know that they'll be there for you. Anyone who stands you up is undeserving of your time."

I hadn't meant to imply anything about Finn, but the air around us thickened with a different kind of tension, and it was like the stupid night of prom had materialized before us both. *Oops.*

Finn was the one to break it. "So, I was at the hospital that night."

"What?" I looked over at him, but his gaze was trained north toward the Empire State Building lit up in blue and orange, probably for some sports team. I stared at Finn, waiting for him to continue, to clarify. What the hell did he mean he was *at the hospital*?

"The night of prom," he continued. "The night I stood you up."

"Oh, Finn, I wasn't even trying to bring that up."

But whether he believed me or not, he kept looking out at the skyline. "That was the day my dad got the news that his cancer was terminal." My heart sank as I watched his face in profile. "I had gone to meet my parents at the hospital. It wasn't until I got back home and saw my tux hanging on the closet door that I remembered it was prom." Finn tucked his hands into his pants pockets, his eyes darting down to his shoes. "I called you as soon as I realized."

I remembered my phone had been lit up with texts and missed calls that night, and how righteously hurt I'd felt at the time. A wave of regret crashed through me now.

"I'm so sorry, Finn. If I had known…" If I had known, I wouldn't have unloaded on him, but looking back, I realized I never even gave him the chance to explain. I was so confident I knew what had happened that I had just steamrolled over him. I could have just stayed with Finn—been there for him. Instead, I'd made an awful day for him into an even worse one. Now, I didn't know what else to say. Finn had pulled his hands out of his pockets, resting them on the ledge just inches from mine, so I reached over to give his right hand a squeeze. "God, I'm so sorry, Finn."

He nodded, then stroked his thumb along the outside of mine. "There's no way you could have known."

"Why didn't you tell me?"

Finn gave a one-shoulder shrug. "I almost did tell you. But then things fell apart between us anyway, and… Dad didn't want people to know about his diagnosis. And, honestly, I was in a lot of denial. It felt like my life was falling apart." Finn took a deep breath; he kept his eyes on the skyline, but his hand remained in mine. "I think maybe I hoped you knew me well enough to trust me—to trust that I would never hurt you without a good reason."

Regret sliced through me. Finn had stood me up, but I'd let him down too. He'd been nothing but a good friend to me for years, but at the first sign of trouble, I'd cut him out of my life. I'd been too dialed in on my own pain to see his.

"You're right," I said softly. "I should have trusted you. I'm sorry."

"I'm sorry too. I should have been honest with you instead of playing games."

I turned my hand upward, and he continued along the lines of my palm and down my wrist. I couldn't believe it. I had gone years thinking that Finn was just a flake who stood me up, when in reality, he had a completely valid reason for missing a stupid school dance. If only my pride hadn't been so bruised, sending me storming off his front porch that night, maybe I could have known the truth. Maybe we *would* have dated senior year. Maybe we—but wait. Through the haze of realization and regret, something occurred to me.

"But when did you see Sybil at the mall? You gave her your car to drive to prom, right?"

"There was no mall, Emma. Sybil was at the hospital too."

"She *what*?"

"You're going to have to talk to Sybil about that." I started to press further, but the look in Finn's eyes stopped me.

I suddenly had the feeling that I knew absolutely nothing—nothing about the world, about what had happened years ago, nothing about Finn, or myself, or this night, or what was possible. What had come before this moment was inexplicable; what would come after, wild and uncertain. So I just stood there, every part of me focused only on the small circles Finn made on the inside of my wrist.

My heartbeat grew faster and faster as his fingers moved softly against my skin, the blood in my veins growing fizzier and fizzier, and I knew the only thing that could bring me back to earth was Finn. I looked up at him. His eyes were on me, watching me watch him. His hand was now wrapped around my wrist. I drifted toward him, and he leaned into me, his mouth just a finger's width from mine, and I felt the warmth of his breath on my lips.

"Emma?"

"Yes?"

And then, just like he had in the pool that night, he asked, "Can I kiss you?"

It was as if the word drifted up from the noise and laughter in the streets below, and somehow ended up on my tongue. *Yes.*

As he closed the distance and our lips touched, I felt myself melt into his body, his hands drifting to my hips and pulling me against him. I'd convinced myself that I'd built up our last kiss in my head—but if anything, this was better than I'd remembered. It was natural. We fit together seamlessly. I could tell by the way his breath hitched, a slight moan escaping from somewhere deep within him, that he could feel it too. Finn kissed me again and again and again. Each kiss grew more and more desperate until he pulled me off the ground and carried me over to one of the two foldout lounge chairs that Sybil had found on the street weeks ago and dragged up there. He laid me down on the chair, then braced himself on his elbows above me, and kissed me again. This time, it was slow and deliberate. His knee pressed into the space between my legs. I heard a sharp inhale, and realized it was me.

He pulled away, and his hand ran up my thigh, skimming along my tights. “Can I take these off?”

I nodded mutely, too dazed by the thought of what was coming next to use words. Something fluttered in my chest at the thought that anyone in the surrounding buildings could look down from their window to see us, but despite all the city lights around us, the roof itself was a pool of darkness; we were exposed and alone at the same time.

Finn smiled and kissed me again. He pulled off both of my boots and let them fall on the rooftop beside us. Then, reaching beneath my skirt, he hooked his fingers into the waistband of my tights and used both hands to roll the thin material over my hips and down my legs. Every inch made me gasp with anticipation. My shirt was still on, but somehow most of its buttons had come undone, and the look in Finn’s eyes intensified, his knuckles grazing the edge of my bra as he leaned over me again, his chest warm and solid above mine. One hand cupped the back of my neck and pulled me toward him for a deeper kiss. The other dragged along the inside of my thigh. I gasped against Finn’s mouth, breaking the kiss as his fingers, cool from the night air, slipped beneath the soft cotton of my panties.

“Is this okay?”

“Yes, it’s okay.” It was more than okay. Finn’s fingers worked slowly and deliberately, as if he had all the time in the world. With each movement, he watched my reaction, moving slowly and then more quickly bringing me to the edge, but not letting me go over.

He slipped a second finger inside of me, and I lifted my hips so his fingers reached even deeper. It was nothing like sex with Preston, which was nice enough, but felt like paint by numbers. Simple strokes of soft pastels in pleasing shapes. With Finn it felt like I'd dipped the canvas in turpentine and lit it on fire. It was like oxygen, like water. Through the lace of my bra, Finn's mouth closed around my nipple, and I bucked against his hand as I came apart in a thousand pieces. Falling limply against the back of the lawn chair, I reached for the zipper on Finn's pants, but his hands stopped me.

His breathing was ragged. "Fuck."

"What?" I whispered. "What is it?"

"We shouldn't," he said, his words grazing my skin. He kissed me again.

"What do you mean?" I was in agony; stopping was the last thing I wanted.

"I mean Preston," he whispered. "Crew captain extraordinaire."

"I never said he was captain."

Finn laughed quietly, and so did I, reaching up to touch his jaw. But even as I did, reality was starting to come back to me in waves.

"You never said *you* were in an open relationship," he pointed out.

It took me a second to think through the lust fogging my brain, but of course, Finn was right.

"No. We aren't." Guilt sliced through me.

Shit.

I had *cheated.* Had I cheated? Of course I had. What the hell else could you call this? Hooking up with an ex, or an ex-whatever-we-were, wasn't a get-out-of-jail-free card. In fact, it was *worse*. Because I knew this was not just a hookup. I couldn't lie to myself and say it wasn't more than that. The want that was coursing through my body was not just because of the way Finn made me feel when he touched me, when he looked at me. It was all of that and something else too. I didn't want a hookup; I wanted *him*.

But he was already sitting up, straightening his shirt with shaking hands, and as I started to sit up and shift my skirt back down, I couldn't believe myself. This was a completely un-Emma thing to do. Preston might have been a self-important snob from time to time, but he didn't deserve to be cheated on. What kind of person does that? An image of my father popped into my mind unbidden, fully ruining the mood like a cold bucket of water. I began rebuttoning my shirt, feeling vaguely frantic. Was one of the buttons missing? Why couldn't I find my tights? How had it gotten so dark?

As if he could see me about to spiral, Finn whispered, "We'll figure it out." His lips brushed against my forehead. "Right?"

I found myself saying it for the second time that night: "Yes."

And despite the guilt, the self-recrimination, and the anxiety coursing through me, I believed him, believed *myself*. We would figure this out. Whatever *this* was. We would make it work, make it okay. We folded up the lawn chair, pulled the cheese board from the doorjamb, and took the steps back down to my apartment. Finn walked me to my bedroom door, pressing a featherlight kiss to my lips before saying good night.

Lying in bed, I replayed what happened on the roof in my

head, my body coursing with tingly heat all over again. The knowledge that Finn was just a few feet away in Sybil's room, and I was right on the other side of a thin door, in only a soft T-shirt and underwear, made it impossible to fall asleep. Then, my phone lit up the dark with an incoming text from Finn.

I've been thinking about what you said about "setting the terms." Maybe you're right. Maybe the best move is to just not be in a relationship with someone who doesn't want to be in one with me.

I took a deep breath, my fingers flying across my phone keyboard before I could second-guess myself.

Especially when there's someone else who does.

Finn hearted my response, and I rolled over, a giddy smile overtaking my face.

In that moment, it felt like we *would* figure it out. Like maybe now, with the air cleared, and all our miscommunications resolved, the time was finally right for Finn and me. He was clearly planning to break up with his girlfriend. And Preston? I knew in my heart that it was over. It should have been over sooner. I'd been playing along, playing a role, playing the girlfriend while some deeper yearning in me lay dormant.

Until now.

Of course, what I didn't know then, that night on the rooftop, was that trusting Finn would become just another horrible mistake.

15

THURSDAY NIGHT

(Two days before the wedding)

THE VEGAS EIFFEL TOWER straddles the Paris casino, and even in its cheesiness, it still manages to be romantic. It's helped by a glow that sparks off the windows of the hotels and settles into every crevice of the city. We're well past sunset now, but with all the manmade light around us, everything is infused with a luminosity. The Strip seems to wink back at the sky, providing its own glitter in a million twinkling lights and flashing neon signs. New York might be the official "city that never sleeps," but I think they got that one wrong—clearly that moniker should belong to Las Vegas, Nevada.

Finn is already there when I arrive. It looks like he was able to find somewhere to steam his jacket, and I'm grateful for the host's forcing him into it. For a moment, guilt spikes through me when I realize how happy and relieved I feel to take a break from chasing Sybil, but I try to push it down. Of course I still want to find her, and help her repair whatever went wrong, get her back on track, and make this wedding happen. It's my duty as a friend. But there's this quiet voice in my head, one that doesn't get a lot of airtime, that's saying, *What about me? When does it get to be my turn to be top priority?* Maybe it's the wish in the fountain, or just Finn's presence, but I feel myself wanting to pause time and stop running to fix things for other people. Just for this one evening. Not even the whole evening—just this one *dinner.* The world won't come falling down around me if I take this one little break to actually enjoy myself.

With Finn.

And besides, we may have missed the welcome party but we still have all day tomorrow to find Sybil and bring her back in time for the rehearsal dinner Friday night—and, of course, the wedding on Saturday.

We will just have to figure out a way to keep Jamie feeling positive and distracted. And what better place to do that than Vegas?

"You look really beautiful," Finn says, when I'm close enough to hear. We start walking, and his fingers barely graze my elbow, like he doesn't trust himself or he's worried I'll bolt.

"Wait!" I say, and Finn's hand pulls back like he's been stung. "Shouldn't we snap a picture for Sybil?"

Finn blinks as if he'd completely forgotten, which prompts a crooked smile from me. He's basically just admitted that the whole thing was a ruse, and that he's gotten swept up in the moment as much as I have. "Yes. Right. A picture for Sybil," he says, nodding. I stand beside him and try to angle our two bodies so that the Eiffel Tower sparkles behind us, but I can't get enough of the background in the photo. "Here, my arms are longer, I'll take the selfie." Finn slips the phone from my hand and pulls me to his side. I'm looking up at him as I hear the camera app click. Startled, I turn toward the camera and put on my happiest and most carefree smile. After a few more shots, Finn hands me back my phone, but leaves his arm around me. As we walk under the Eiffel Tower and into the Paris casino, Finn says, "I managed to get us a reservation at a place called Chez Nous. Is that okay?" He smiles down at me. "I know you love pommes frites."

"I'll eat anything." And I mean it. The boxed turkey sandwich from the Del hasn't been enough to make up for the fumes I've been running on for the last few days.

"Anything except pure unadulterated kale," he says.

"Anything but that," I agree.

The restaurant Finn chose is unequivocally French. The ceilings are high, and the mostly white floors are peppered with small black tiles. The mirrors that ring the restaurant double, triple, and quadruple the twinkling of the chandeliers. but the lights are dim enough that it still feels intimate as the host leads us to our table. Finn's hand settles on the small of my back, and I feel the warmth of it through the thin silk of my dress. We slide into either side of a small booth upholstered in a soft peach velvet.

"I have to say, I would have been okay with food court Panda Express, but this is nice too." *Nice?* More like the most frickin' romantic evening I've had in *far* too long. "Besides, I need to refuel so I can be at full strength to cheer on my guy,

Ibarra, later. Or maybe I'll root for Kuzmin. Who's the underdog? I'll root for whoever that is."

"I really do hate boxing," Finn says.

"Aww, your kind, otter-and-fox-loving heart just can't take a little pugilism, huh?"

"No, it's actually because I got into a pretty awful fight on Sixth Street the fall before my dad died. It was me and this white kid, and of course, I was the one that got dragged to the police station." Whatever quippy zinger I planned on tossing his way next dies on the tip of my tongue, anger rolls through me at the injustice, and I grip the napkin in my lap. "That was a really rough time for me," Finn continues. "I didn't know how to deal with everything I was feeling..." He trails off but I remember his black eye, from back at Katie Dalton's pool party all those years ago.

"That makes sense." I swallow, my mouth suddenly dry.

"After he passed, I was in a pretty bad place for a while. Got into a few more fights. None as bad as the one in Austin, but it's like..." He shakes his head and looks around, as if hoping the right words will appear on the tray of a passing waiter. "Strange as it sounds, it felt like the only way to make the pain stop." Finally, he looks straight at me, like he's desperate for me to understand. "I'm not like that anymore, Emma. Therapy helped a lot. And anyway, that's why I can't stand to watch violence now—even stupid boxing matches make my stomach churn."

I remember Finn's words from years ago: *I haven't been making the best life choices.* I think back to all the nights senior year when he and Sybil had holed up with plastic bottles of Azteca tequila and cheap weed. I thought they were just slacking off—feeding off each other's worst impulses. But maybe there was something more going on. At the time, I was too close to it and too in my own head to really see what Finn was going through. But when you're a teenager and your dad is dying, maybe reaching for another cold drink or another warm body—to punch or to kiss—makes the most sense. I look at him in his freshly pressed suit jacket, and for the first time, when he says he's changed a lot since those days, it sinks in. I actually believe him.

"I'm sorry. I was just teasing about the match." I release my death grip on the napkin, and reach across the table to grab his hand. "We'll be on our way back to LA with Sybil by the time the fight starts." At least I hope we will.

Finn squeezes my hand, and I expect him to let go after a beat. Instead, heat sparks up my arm and through my whole body as Finn's middle finger begins making small circles on the inside of my wrist. My mind races back to the roulette table. My body arched against Finn's, and his lips against my ear: *Not here…but soon.* I inhale sharply at the memory, and Finn's finger pauses. His eyes meet mine, and the small smile on his lips makes it clear he knows exactly how he's affecting me. His finger starts circling again. My lips part, and I press my thighs into the soft velvet of the booth. I wish he would grab my wrist and pull me across the table. It's taking every ounce of my self-control to stay on my side of the booth, and my mind flashes to the hotel room just a block away.

Just when I feel myself starting to break, the waiter comes by, and I pull back my hand and swallow, thankful for the opportunity to get control of myself. Finn looks down at his menu with a devilish grin.

We order drinks and mussels to start, and the tension between us fades to a physically survivable level. It's still crackling, but it's banked enough that my brain is once again able to access its use of the English language. "So, what are you going to do with yourself now that you've sold your company? Doesn't that basically make you unemployed?"

"I'm thinking of going home for a bit. I need to help Mom get her house ready to sell. She's been making noises about moving to Vail for most of the year and just getting a condo off Turtle Creek."

I straighten immediately. "She's selling the Dilbeck?"

The first time I ever saw a Charles Dilbeck–designed house was when I'd gone over to Finn's for a middle school science project, and it was an epiphany. I realized that houses didn't have to be boring square boxes with one central hallway. They could have a sense of humor. They could list to the side or pull you up a turret. They could be anything you wanted. Every Dilbeck looks different, but my favorites are straight out of a storybook with hand-carved mantels surrounding oversized fireplaces, detailed brickwork, leaded glass windows that glint like melted sugar, a maximalist's dream. It's not at all the normal Dallas look of bright, shiny, and new. Though, if you take a step back and realize that the city's vibe has always been "more is more," then Charles Dilbeck is a quintessential Dallas designer. His houses are whimsy piled on top of whimsy. Sometimes more whimsy than people know what to do with. They're getting torn down at an astonishing rate.

From what I remember, Finn's parents never really leaned into the fancifulness of their Dilbeck farmhouse. Their home was always beautiful, but they were minimalists. The interior was white and gray before white and gray was all the rage. No knickknacks or unnecessary pillows. It was so different from the house I grew up in, which had dozens and dozens of wine corks stashed in glass vases that my mother was going to "do something with someday." Liz's and my childhood art, framed as if it were as precious as a Picasso, hung all over the house. So many pillows on the couch that you needed to shove half of them onto the ground to have room to sit. My mother could never walk past a handmade quilt without taking it home. She couldn't stomach that something someone had put so much time and care into might end up homeless and unloved. She'd always meant to buy a chest for them, but never found one she really loved, so one corner of our living room became a landing zone. For most of Liz's elementary school career, she would come home, burrow into the nest of quilts, and do her homework on her lap while I pulled together dinner in the kitchen.

Finn's voice cuts through my thoughts. "A builder reached out to her about it, so she may just sell to him instead of going through the hassle of listing it."

A lead weight drops through my stomach. "You can't let her sell to a builder. That house is a treasure. A builder would just tear it down to build some lot-line-to-lot-line McMansion."

"I can't just tell her to hold on to it in this market. Not when she wants to be in Colorado most of the year."

The waiter comes by with our mussels, and Finn and I both order steak frites.

"Please, Finn," I say, once the waiter has gone. "Promise me you won't let her sell to someone who'll tear it down."

I imagine a world in which I have the funds to buy it myself and totally redo the interior as a proof of concept for my own design firm. But I'm barely able to save with my current gig—and with keeping Liz afloat. Mom certainly doesn't have the means to contribute to a down payment.

"I'll see what I can do," Finn says, which is really as much as I can expect from him. "How's your work going?" he asks, changing the subject. The lead weight in my stomach turns molten.

"It's fine," I say, hoping that Finn will just leave it at that. He opens his mouth, but takes a look at my face, and closes it. He's not going to push me, which I appreciate. But I find that I actually *want* to tell him.

"Honestly..." I take a long pull from my wine and decide to lay everything out on the table. "I think it may be time to jump ship. Though my boss may beat me to the punch on Monday."

"What makes you say that?" Finn asks.

I explain the situation with the Hanson property. When I finish, Finn's question isn't what I'm expecting.

"What's your end goal?"

"My end goal?"

"If you could be doing anything, what would it be?"

I don't have to think about the answer. "Running my own design firm."

"Okay. So does this job serve you toward that long-term plan?"

"I mean, I guess not so much at this point." I pluck a mussel from the pot and scoop the meat from its shell. "I've worked there for five years. I've made a good network of connections. And it doesn't seem like I'm going to be getting the chance to really grow my own creative aesthetic there."

"Exactly," Finn says as if it's just that simple.

"However, I do need this job to afford to eat and sleep with a roof over my head." I pop another mussel into my mouth. "Two things I've come to enjoy."

Tearing off a piece of bread and dragging it through the white wine broth, Finn counters with "I'm sure you could find someone to back you."

"Spoken like a true Silicon Valley–er."

"You could move back to Dallas. It'd lower your overhead costs. I've actually been thinking of doing the same."

"It just feels like failing," I say as the rest of our meal arrives.

"The firm you work for is the one failing if they fire you." Finn cuts into his steak matter-of-factly. "It's bad business to drive away good talent."

"I should have just done my job and kept my mouth shut."

I'm startled by Finn's knife and fork clattering onto his plate. He leans across the table and grabs my hand. "You absolutely should not have done that. I know you don't need my advice, but it sounds like you've just outgrown this job."

I can't help smiling. It's been a long time since someone—who's not my mom—has really believed in me. Or maybe it just feels that way because my other number one cheerleader now lives across the country.

I remember standing with Sybil on the street waiting for the Uber that would take her to JFK and then on to Los Angeles. When the app said her ride was one minute away, I could feel the tears begin to prick at the corners of my eyes.

"Don't work too hard, Em." She threw her arms around me. I let out a soft grunt as the momentum of her overstuffed backpack and tote bag landed her against me with a heavy thud. "I know Maywell is the dream, but you don't need them.

Come to LA with me and Nikki. Start your own shop. I'll do your website. Nikki can do your social media."

"Oh, sure, I'll just go throw some stuff in a bag before the driver gets here." I gave her a watery smile and squeezed her tight. "But really, I'll be fine. I've got a couple new projects lined up that I really think I can nail, and then I'll be up for promotion." I grabbed one of her roller bags as Sybil's car pulled up to the curb.

"I just worry about you, Em." It was strange hearing that Sybil was worried about *me*, and I wasn't sure how to respond. I was usually the one keeping everyone else on track, fretting about their missed doctor's appointments or questionable dating choices. What did Sybil have to be worried about me over? Maybe the same thing that had secretly kept me awake for the last several nights as Sybil's departure date drew near: *Am I going to be all alone forever?* I jammed her bag into the back of the Honda Accord that was going to take her out of Manhattan, and out of my life for the foreseeable future. I knew I'd see her in a few months, but I also knew that it would never be the same—that I wouldn't ever get to spend every day with my best friend again.

Blinking back tears, I pulled myself together before pasting a smile on my face and turning back to Sybil. "I'll be okay, Sybs. I promise." I gave her one last hug before she stepped into the car. As the sedan slipped into the flow of traffic on Second Avenue, I was struck by an unpleasantly familiar feeling. That gut-punching grief of watching a car drive away with someone I love inside of it, knowing they weren't coming back. It was just like when Dad left. It took everything in me not to run after the Honda, wave Sybil down, and tell her I was coming to California with her. Instead, I turned back toward our apartment door, and went back upstairs. Alone.

Finn's voice breaks me out of my memory. "Hey, are you all right? Where'd you go?"

"I'm just worried about Sybil," I say.

"So am I." His eyes are dark and serious, and I know he means it. Then he gives my hand another squeeze, his eyes growing warmer, so deep I want to fall into them, and says with a smile, "But don't forget to look out for yourself every once in a while too." I nod yes, the lump in my throat preventing me from forming words. "Good. And I guess if you *do* forget, I'll just have to do it for you."

FORTY-FIVE MINUTES LATER, FINN and I finish our meal, and I set my napkin on the table and scoot out of the booth, pulling the boutique shopping bag containing Finn's sweatshirt and my old clothes behind me.

My body is still buzzing from Finn's touch, which has been lingering all throughout dinner—squeezing my hand while he promised to look out for me, tucking a strand of hair behind my ear when it fell into my face, playfully nudging his knee against mine under the table, feeding me chocolate mousse so decadent it made me close my eyes with an indecent groan. I know we should start looking for Sybil again. But I don't want the feeling to stop, so as we leave the restaurant, I spit out the first half-formed idea that pops into my head. "There's an observation deck at the top of this casino. It might help us get the lay of the land, and we can get back on the hunt."

"Right. The hunt." The look on Finn's face makes it seem like *I'm* the one he wants to hunt down. He takes my hand as we move toward the elevator bank in the lobby, his thumb rubbing back and forth across the inside of my palm. A small shiver runs through me. But it's not enough. I want more. I don't know if it's the magic of Vegas, the wine from dinner, or just the haze of lust I've been fighting through since Finn bent me against the roulette table, but in that moment, I make a decision.

The elevator arrives with a ding, and the doors roll closed behind us. As it lurches upward, I step close enough to Finn that I have to tilt my head back to keep my eyes on his face. I barely recognize myself when I whisper, "Finn, kiss m—"

His lips are on mine before I can finish. It's nothing like the first time we kissed or even the last. This is explosive. There's no hesitation from Finn. He's kissing me like he may never have the chance again. My thoughts fracture as Finn takes a step toward me, pressing me against the doors of the elevator, and I'm surrounded by the scent of Finn, familiar and foreign. It's intoxicating. Both of his hands tangle in my hair, tipping my head further back to deepen the kiss. I reach out a hand to steady myself, and there are a dozen soft clicks as my hand swipes blindly, accidentally trailing down the button panel behind me. I give up trying to find purchase anywhere that isn't Finn, drop my bag to the floor, and wrap both arms around him. The feeling of Finn's tongue tangled with mine nearly pulls the air from my lungs, and I gasp against his lips.

He takes the opportunity to move his mouth down to my

throat, and his teeth scrape along my neck. "I've wanted to do this since I saw you walk out in this dress," Finn says, and I let out a soft mewling sound in response, suddenly wishing we were in a *different* elevator—the one back in the hotel that would lead to the room Finn booked. His hands tighten in my hair, and one drops to my lower back, crushing me even more tightly to him.

Through hazy eyes, I realize we're stopping on almost every floor—the doors opening and closing behind me. Finn must realize, too, because he spins me away from the front of the elevator and presses me against the back wall, shielding me from anyone who might see. The whole time, his mouth never leaves my skin. Our hips move together in a way that pulls another groan from Finn, and he wedges a foot between mine, pushing my legs apart, opening me up to him. My leg wraps around Finn's waist, deepening the angle. I wobble slightly on a single stiletto, and his hand is immediately behind my knee, holding me upright.

"I've got you." His lips brush against my ear before searing me with another kiss. From somewhere far away, I hear the ding of the elevator announcing it's reached its destination. I barely glimpse the rooftop observation deck and feel the breeze brushing against my skin before the doors close again, and we start to descend.

I'm about to float off the ground, and the only thing keeping me tethered to this earth is the feeling of Finn's body against mine, so I arch into him even more, trying to get as close to him as I possibly can. His hand skims up the outside of my thigh, and his fingers are so close to where I want him to be, where I want *all* of him to be.

There's another ding, and the doors open again. "I see this one's taken." A familiar Georgia accent has me dragging my mouth away from Finn's. I lean around his biceps to confirm what I already know.

I'm face-to-face with Nikki.

16

THURSDAY NIGHT

(Two days before the wedding)

LIKE ANY WOMAN, I believe all my friends are beautiful. Sybil in the way of a fairy princess. Willow has the tousled hair and je ne sais quoi of a French film star. But Nikki is beautiful like the Fourth of July: summery, sweet, and a little bit of a firecracker. Her smile invites everyone in and tells them to pull up a lawn chair and grab a lemonade. It's why they picked her from piles and piles of applicants to be on *LovedBy*. But she worked her way into the hearts of millions of viewers because she really *is* all those things.

At least she was until Aaron. Since their breakup, she's guarded in ways she never was before, and she's started arming herself with perfection. Even now, after what I'm sure was a hectic race to the airport with Jamie and his crew of groomsmen, her makeup is immaculate and her honey-blond hair is pulled back into a high ponytail, sleek and flawless.

"Don't let me interrupt," Nikki says calmly, but her eyebrows are nearly to her hairline.

Finn releases me slowly, as if he doesn't want to let go, but I can still feel the heat of his hands against my skin. My foot drops to the ground, and Finn positions himself in front of me while I try to put myself to rights.

I scoop up the bag that lies forgotten on the floor, and we step out of the elevator. The doors shut softly behind us as Finn's phone buzzes. "I've got to grab this," he explains, and steps out of earshot.

Nikki folds her arms across her chest. "I texted you, but when I didn't hear back, I decided to just come find you. Have a nice dinner, did we?" She raises an eyebrow. "Looks like you're still working on dessert."

"I'm sorry, Niks." Guilt has cut through my fog of lust. We wasted time when we should've been looking for Sybil. "We were just about to start trying to find Sybil again."

"Em, it's okay." Nikki's voice softens, and she loops her arm through mine and steers me through the lobby toward the ladies' room. Looking in the mirror, I catch a glimpse of what just a few minutes of kissing Finn has done to me. My lips are swollen, my cheeks are flushed, and the skirt of my brand-new dress is an accordion of wrinkles. Remembering how I got this way, I swallow past a wave of desire and try to press down the creases. "You're allowed to take a moment for yourself once in a while. I'm just..." She pauses for a moment, but then presses on. "I'm just really worried about

Sybil. When we left LA, the Rains still hadn't heard from her all day."

I pull Nikki into a hug. She smells like citrus blossoms and mint. "She does this, Nikki. You know that. She's okay." I will myself to believe the words as I say them.

Nodding, she sniffles and pulls away.

Steeling myself, I say, "I have to tell you about something that happened in San Diego."

"I know about the video, Em." She straightens one of the straps of my dress. "A dozen people have sent it to me today."

"Nikki, I'm so sorry."

"I know you were just trying to look out for me." Turning toward the mirror, she makes a quick appraisal of her own appearance. She nods, satisfied with what she sees, but then she deflates with a sigh. "And I know how infuriating Aaron can be. But you don't need to take care of me. I'm a big girl."

I nod, but something in me hurts. Because I *do*. It's my job to take care of the friend group—all of them. I really feel that, and I don't want to let them down.

"I like this dress." She brushes my hair from my shoulder, and then boops my stomach. "Let's get back to your BOAT man."

"Nikki!"

Nikki is the only person I've ever told about the hot-and-heavy pool make-out with Finn. Sybil and Willow were too close to the Prom Incident and knew too much about Finn, so I never felt like I could tell them. A week and half into the Europe trip, though, Nikki and I stayed up to finish a bottle of wine while everyone else went to bed. Overlooking the vineyard that Willow's aunt owned, the smell of lavender drifting up to us, I couldn't stop thinking about Finn. About that kiss. Drunk on rosé, new places, and making a new friend, I spilled everything. Nikki gasped at all the right moments, and when I finished she said, "So he's your BOAT."

"My what?"

"Best of all time," she said with the slow seriousness of someone very drunk.

"Don't you mean GOAT?"

"Who wants a goat when you could have a boat?" She emphasized her words with an overly enthusiastic wave of her hand, splashing most of her glass of wine on the gravel below. Devolving into fits of giggling, my angst over Finn eased as Nikki recast years of longing into very manageable boy drama.

"Maybe one day you'll get back on his boat and sail off into the sunset." She grabbed the bottle of wine to refill her glass. "Until then, lots of fish in the sea."

LITTLE DID EITHER OF us know how right she was then. Because it was just a few years later that the night in New York happened...I feel myself breaking into a sweat just thinking about it now.

Finn rejoins us at the foot of the (fake) Eiffel Tower, and it looks like he's taken the time to put himself to rights too—no evidence of my lipstick on his face, his sport coat only betraying a few new wrinkles. The three of us circle up to talk strategy, and I see that I have half a dozen missed texts from Nikki, and one from Liz from several hours ago.

The text from Liz is a selfie in my bathroom mirror of her in my clothes with the question *Professional enough?*

I'd hire you! I type back.

She sends back a blushing smiling face and an eye roll emoji. *Networking went well! I'll call you later!*

With the sun now completely down, the air has dropped a few degrees. I shiver as we walk back toward Caesars. Finn takes note and starts to hand me his sport coat, an action that once again has my brain flashing like the neon signs of Vegas: DATE DATE DATE. I wave Finn off. The cool air is bracing, a much-needed shock to the system to refocus me on the task at hand. Finn slides back into his jacket, then says, "Hey, where's my sweatshirt?"

"Don't worry, it's safe in here." I pat the shopping bag.

"You have his sweatshirt?" Nikki asks.

"She stole it," Finn supplies.

"I *won* it," I correct.

"She tried to get naked in front of me. I figured if I gave it to her, she'd stay clothed."

Nikki's eyes widen then her lips curl up into a grin. "Seems like you're *both* trying to get naked," Nikki says, but it's low enough that only I can hear it.

Clearing my throat loudly, I say, "Let's call Willow and tell her what's going on."

"There's not much to report, is there?" Finn asks.

"No, but maybe with our powers combined, we can come up with something."

While I dial, Nikki mouths "BOAT" at me silently behind Finn's back. Thankfully, Willow answers on the first ring.

"Tell me you've found her," she says.

"We have not found her." I switch the phone to my other hand, and Finn's jacket brushes against my arm. I try not to think about how close he is, or how close he was to me just a few minutes ago. I suppress a shudder as I remember the sensation of Finn's teeth scraping softly against my neck.

Willow sighs. "Shit." There's silence, then I hear a faint click and a puff of air. It's a familiar sound, but I can't quite place it. Until, wait—

"Willow, are you *smoking*?"

"I'm just lighting it! I'm not actually smoking it, Em. But I swear to god, if I can't at least hold a cigarette in my hand right now, I'm going to go insane."

"Okay, but open a window. Even breathing the secondhand smoke can impact the—"

"*Emma*," Willow cuts me off. "Trust me. I know. I'm not going to do anything to endanger my baby."

"Sorry," I say sheepishly. Once again, my stress instincts have me scrambling to fix whatever I can. "What's the latest there?" I ask Willow.

"Everyone's buying Jamie's lie about food poisoning, but the Rains are worried. They want to get the police involved." We all fall silent for a moment as the seriousness of the situation settles around us.

"Maybe we should." Nikki twists nervously at the end of her ponytail.

"Give us a chance to talk to Jamie," I break in.

Nikki turns to me. "What will we even tell him?"

"I don't know." And I really don't. At this point, lying to Jamie feels less like we're protecting Sybil and more like we're putting her at risk. "Maybe it's time to just tell him the truth."

We hang up and enter Caesars Palace. Jamie and his groomsmen are easy to spot across the lobby, all dark hair and expensive suits. They wave at us to join them, but before we can head in their direction, a bevy of boas and tiaras cuts us off.

"Nikki! Nikki Bennett!" A gaggle of white women—clearly a bachelorette party—beelines straight toward us, and Nikki's entire demeanor changes. She puts on a smile and cocks her head, but something shutters behind her eyes.

"Can we get a photo with you?" a woman with a light-up cowboy hat and a "Maid of Honor" sash asks.

"We loved your season!" another woman says as they congeal around Nikki.

"Aaron is the absolute worst," says one with a penis straw bobbing in her drink.

Nikki doesn't drop her smile, but the lines around her mouth tighten as she poses with each of the women. They all get together for a group shot with the lobby's fountain in the background and ask me to take the photo while yelling, "Best bachelorette party ever!" The maid of honor in the cowboy hat takes a second look at me as I hand her back her phone. "You're that girl in the video!"

I flinch at the reference to #burritogate, but suddenly I have a much bigger concern to contend with—Jamie has made his way over to us, his crew of groomsmen in tow. I note several members of this thirsty bachelorette party eyeing them up and down.

"Hey, Emma, Nikki." Jamie offers up a wide smile, but his eyes keep scanning behind us. "Where's—"

He's cut off by a loud voice from behind me, as one of the

bachelorettes—the one with a penis straw—crows out, "Ooh, you're yummy. You should go on *LovedBy* next." I turn to see her coral-pink nails clutched around Finn's biceps. He gives her an effortlessly devastating smile while gently extracting his arm from her grip.

"Ha, thanks. But not really my thing."

"Well, maybe you and I should just have our own little overnight date, then." She waggles her brows, and her eyes are glassy as she leans her body weight against Finn's torso.

"Um, no thanks." He looks over her blond curls at me, inclining his head toward the exit. "Emma, do you think we should…?"

I nod and start moving toward the door. "Jamie, let's step outside and we can—"

"Oh come *on*! Don't you like me?" Penis Straw's drunken voice rings through the lobby. "Just roll with it, cutie, it's a compliment!" I notice her hand drifting from Finn's arm to his chest now.

And I see red.

"Back off! He said no!" I whip around so fast that my elbow knocks into another bachelorette, sending her crashing to the floor with a yell. Her phone flies into the air, then plops into the fountain. The entire bachelorette party erupts into drunken shrieks.

Jamie looks from the fallen bachelorette to Finn, to Nikki, to me, the ghost of a smile still on his face, as if he thinks this whole fiasco might be part of some sort of flash mob and Sybil is going to pop out of the fountain any minute now.

"What the hell, you freak!" Penis Straw gives me a weak shove, hands on both of my shoulders.

"Hey!" Finn is behind me in an instant to catch my stutter step backward, his voice sharper and deeper than I've ever heard it, echoing off the marble lobby.

A security guard jogs over. "What's going on here?" he asks.

The woman I bumped into points up from the ground. "They attacked me!"

The officer immediately turns his eyes on Finn. "Did you put your hands on this woman?" His tone is sharp and accusatory.

"*I* pushed her." My voice echoes off the marble surrounding us as I shove my way between Finn and the security guard. "He didn't do anything."

"Ma'am, I need you to calm down."

"I'm calm!" I yell.

Penis Straw, the woman whose obscene groping of Finn started this whole commotion, looks aghast. "It was a compliment!"

"Emma," Finn says with what seems like practiced calmness. "Just let it go."

The bridesmaid in the cowboy hat pipes up, and turns to the security guard. "It's not the first time she's been violent. She attacked Aaron Brinkley just this morning."

This gets the security guard's attention. "She assaulted someone earlier today too?"

"There's a video." Cowboy Hat starts tapping on her phone.

The security guard turns to me. "I'm afraid we'll have to call the police if you don't vacate the property, ma'am." He crosses his arms and widens his stance.

"It's fine," I say. "We'll just leave."

As we file out of the casino, I lean over to Finn and murmur, "Sorry about that. I know you had it under control, I just couldn't get over the nerve of that girl."

"She was pretty drunk."

"Still," I say.

"Yeah, not a great situation." Finn shrugs. "But the upside is getting to watch you Hulk out on my behalf. I know righteous indignation is your love language. It's a privilege to have you defend my honor." He's making light of the situation for my sake, I know, but there's something else in his expression too. A kind of...vulnerability? Softening?

We step out onto the sidewalk, where the neon signs reflect twinkling light in Finn's whiskey eyes as he looks down at me. I can't stop staring up at him. He's got a full-blown Emma Face going. Half-exasperated, half-affectionate. Or maybe a little more than half. I'm sure my grin is radiating the same fondness I see on his. And I can't deny what he's just said. Because somehow, over the course of this crazy day, Finn has gravitated from "sworn enemy" to something else. Something I want to bask in, cling to, go slightly crazy defending. It's electrifying. And terrifying.

I feel an elbow nudge my ribs.

It's Nikki, standing in a clump with the bachelor party guys and Jamie, who still seems utterly lost. Right. Time to come clean about Sybil. I brace myself to break the news to him, but then he gives a little cough, as if to clear the air of whatever shit show just went down, and says, almost casually, "So...I heard from Sybil."

17

THURSDAY NIGHT

(Two days before the wedding)

At Jamie's words, a small gasp escapes from Nikki, which she covers up by coughing, and I realize that while I've been on the road trying to track down Sybil, Nikki hasn't had the distraction. Her anxiety is probably through the roof, like mine was earlier. Before I let myself get caught up with Finn, when I should have been focusing on my friends.

"Well, at least my voicemail heard from her." Jamie puts his phone on speaker, and we gather around to listen as Sybil's slightly tipsy voice spills out. "I love you so much, Jamie. Like, soooo much. You're too good for me. You're perfect. I'm so sorry I missed the welcome party. I'll—I'll talk to you soon." The line goes dead. I hadn't allowed myself to imagine the worst, but it must have been there in the back of my mind, because a wave of relief crashes through me. Sybil is alive and okay as of this evening.

"I've tried calling her back," Jamie says, "but it's gone through to voicemail each time." He tucks the phone back in his pocket.

Knowing that Sybil has called Jamie is a huge relief and sparks a renewed sense of optimism. If she's willing to reach out to Jamie, maybe she'll be willing to reach out to us soon. And we can get this whole debacle sorted in plenty of time for the rehearsal dinner tomorrow. I just need to eke out a few more hours… "We're supposed to meet up at a club to go dancing, but she might've already beat us there." The lie comes out almost too easily, and the guilt follows almost immediately.

Jamie runs his hands through his hair. "I'm glad she's getting a chance to blow off steam, but you know, usually when Sybil takes off to party like this, it's because she's upset about something." I'm struck by how on the nose his statement is. Nikki and I both nod in unison, and I wonder if the guilt at lying to Jamie is eating at her the way it's eating at me. Looking at Jamie's face, I understand why Nikki wasn't able to tell him the truth that likely Sybil has run off. There's an earnestness in his dark eyes, concern in the slope of his brows. He runs a hand through his wavy hair, mussing it up in a way that makes him look a bit like an absent-minded professor, or an exasperated hot young dad. Which is just so classic Jamie. He is in every way a great guy, and Sybil deserves someone great. The full weight of what's at stake bears down on me. Jamie truly loves Sybil, and I know Sybil loves him too. We have recorded proof in Jamie's voicemail inbox. Two lives could be ruined if we don't get this figured out.

"Let me tell Dan and Vittal that we're going to a club," Jamie says.

"Oh, you want to come?" Nikki's voice is an octave higher than normal.

"Sybil is always saying I need to go out dancing more."

"Um..." I look at Nikki, but twelve hours into our Sybil safari, we've finally run out of ways to divert Jamie.

"Why don't we let the girls catch up, while you and I go to the Kuzmin-Ibarra fight? Can I have my tickets, Emma?" Finn's hand is warm on my shoulder.

"Oh, yeah, of course." I rummage through my bag and hand Finn two rumpled tickets for the fight tonight.

"Man, are you sure? I mean, I'd much rather go to that fight than a club." Jamie turns to me. "You don't think Sybil will mind?"

"Not at all!" I say too cheerfully. "I'll let her know we're meeting up later."

Finn leans closer to me, his hand on the small of my back, and I shiver as his lips brush against my ear. "If there's no sign of Sybil by the time the fight's over, you've got to tell the guy the truth. Deal?"

I swallow and nod my head. "Deal."

Finn and Jamie head back inside, and I text Willow an update so Sybil's parents can relax.

"I'm so relieved Sybil's okay," I say.

"Okay-ish, I would say." Nikki reapplies her lip gloss using the mirror of a Rolls-Royce Wraith that the casino valet has left parked front and center.

"I wish she would just talk to us."

"Me too," Nikki says, popping the tube back into her bag and scanning me from head to toe. "So. I see you've taken the opportunity of Sybil's vanishing to go shopping?"

I laugh. "I had to. Finn made me spill coffee down my shirt."

"Oh, I see. He has an awfully bad history with your shirts, doesn't he?"

"Ha ha." I start marching away from the casino and from the memory that comes rushing back. Finn and I pressed into a ratty old lounge chair on the rooftop of my New York City apartment. My legs parted around him, my shirt hanging open, missing a button from where it came undone just a little too hastily... Another moment that I'd only told Nikki about. I can't seem to stop myself from trying to climb Finn like a tree.

She catches up with me and asks, "Seriously, how has today been? It seems like y'all were getting close to a happy ending." Nikki waggles her eyebrows at me, but before I can respond, we're briefly separated by a pack of tourists following a tour guide holding a polka-dot umbrella aloft as a beacon. When the stream of people has passed, Nikki links her arm with mine and continues her line of questioning. "I know this whole thing was your idea, but I *had* been worried about you—stuck in the car with Finn all day. Though from the look of things in the elevator, it seems like y'all have worked out your issues."

"That was..." I pause. "I don't know what that was," I admit. "I don't know what I'm doing. I feel..." *Out of control. Happy. Obsessed. Confused.* Like I always end up feeling when it comes to Finn.

A pang of longing for Sybil hits me. As much as I love

Nikki, she's an analyzer like me. She's great when I want someone to parse indecipherable dating app communications with, or someone to help me break down every pro and con of getting balayage at my next hair appointment. But sometimes, I just need to get out of my own head. And Sybil has always been there to help me with that. "Come on, let's go check at the MGM."

Nikki looks like she wants to say something more, but she lets the Finn thing drop and allows me to guide us through the throngs of people.

We zigzag down the Strip, crossing occasionally to the other side of the street, trying to mimic the ping-ponging of Sybil's earlier movements, but our journey is slow, the sidewalks packed with all manner of humanity—tourists, vendors hawking T-shirts, people dressed in character costumes, breakdancers performing right in the middle of the crowded pathway. We struggle to get a cell signal for Find My Friends, so instead we show Sybil's picture to people as we pass, but no one seems to recognize her—not that I can blame them. Every face I've seen tonight has blended together from the sheer sensory overload that is Vegas. When we get service, we try her phone a couple of times each, but it just rings and rings before going to voicemail. After forty-five minutes of this, it's becoming all too clear that trying to locate Sybil in this city is like trying to find a small blond needle in a Technicolor-neon haystack. Traffic is bumper to bumper, but the stream of taillights just adds to the cheerfulness of the lights flashing off buildings and billboards. One billboard announces a Miranda Lambert show, which reminds me—"Remember that year when Sybil disappeared at Stagecoach?"

"We finally tracked her down on a bus with half of the Turnpike Troubadours." Nikki smiles and leans over the rail of the pedestrian bridge where we've stopped.

"The fun half."

"Yeah," Nikki agrees. "Sybil always knows where to find the fun."

"Once, when we lived in New York together, she went out to pick up our falafel order and was gone for hours. I found her singing showtunes with the cast of *Wicked* at the piano bar next door.

"And she went AWOL in Tuscany for those two days."

"We found her in a literal castle."

"Yeah, but at least then, she kept having that guy's butler deliver those very official handwritten notes to our hostel."

We laugh, and I make a mental note to reference some of these classic Sybil moments in my maid-of-honor speech—the one I've still avoided spending any time thinking about, though I guess now I have a good reason to be putting it off. *Step one, locate bride. Step two, draft speech.* Besides, how could I possibly attempt to encapsulate my wonderful, weird, completely unique best friend in a two-minute toast? Yes, she's the life of the party, everyone knows that. But she's so much more than that. And her Technicolor-rainbow spirit has darker shades too.

The thought sobers me. "I know Sybs is always disappearing and falling into adventures. But then there are other times…like graduation night—"

"What happened on graduation night?" Nikki asks.

"She never showed up at the after-party. Willow and I assumed she was probably at some better, cooler party. Maybe already hanging with a crew of college kids. But we found her parked down by the creek, sobbing in her car." My heart sinks, remembering holding Sybil as she cried, her voice gasping out through her tears—*Everything's ending, Emma.*

Nikki nods. "There were a couple moments like that at USC too." We walk a bit in silence before Nikki turns the conversation away from Sybil. "So seriously, what's going on with you and BOAT Man? Y'all have clearly passed the 'I want to tear your head off' stage of your relationship, and are actively in the 'I want to tear your clothes off' stage." She chuckles, and even if it's at my expense, it's nice to hear Nikki laughing again.

"We've just had an okay day together, and we had a nice dinner. And then...we had a pretty fantastic elevator ride," I say, fighting to keep a silly grin from taking over my entire face. "He told me I should start my own design firm." I don't know why that detail has risen to the top, given everything that's happened tonight, but for some reason it feels important. I remember the absolute confidence in Finn's voice as he encouraged me to take the leap and strike out on my own.

"Well, obviously, Em."

"What do you mean 'obviously'?"

"Emma, you're so good at what you do. I don't know why you're still at that place that works you to the bone—for definitely not enough money—and doesn't appreciate you."

"Well, maybe it's something to think about," I reply, with no real intention of doing any such thing.

It's nice to dream big and all, but some of us need to live in reality and make pragmatic decisions. My little mental escape in Vegas has been fun, but it's not real life.

As if on cue, a woman in a neon-magenta feather headdress and not much else walks by.

"Sybil's probably in the penthouse of some high roller right now hand-feeding Wagyu beef to his pet tiger," Nikki says.

"Oh no, she'd never get with someone with a pet tiger."

"True. Maybe a capuchin monkey or something."

"I can see her being okay with that. As long as the monkey is well taken care of."

"Of course." We both laugh, but I do wonder—*would* Sybil cheat on Jamie on their wedding weekend? I'd like to think she would never go through with anything that extreme. Freak out with uncertainty? Sure. Flirt with some hot strangers? Probably. But I hope she wouldn't go so far as to ruin what she and Jamie have—or break his heart. I'd like to think that Sybil has moved on from her truly wild ways, because I'd like to think *I've* changed from the person I used to be, back when I was in my early twenties and still figuring out how to be a real adult. But then again, I know what it's like to get swept up in the heat of the moment. To let passion cloud your better judgment. To end up doing something you never thought you'd do—even cheat.

Finn texts me that they're finishing up at the fight, so we head over to the arena where the fight took place.

"Time to face the music with Jamie. I guess."

Nikki nods but doesn't say anything. She's not looking forward to disappointing Jamie any more than I am.

I can tell the exact moment Jamie realizes that Sybil's not with us. His face drops even as we approach from across the crowded concourse in front of the arena. Finn gives me a look, silently communicating our agreement from an hour earlier, and I know I have to tell Jamie—at least part of—the truth.

"Hey, how was the fight?" Nikki starts.

"It was good," Jamie says. Finn, meanwhile, is looking nauseated enough that I can tell he barely hung in there.

I almost want to laugh and tease him about it, but I clasp my hands together in front of me, all business. Time to rip off the Band-Aid. "Wait—before you tell us about it, we have to tell you something."

"Okay," Jamie says hesitatingly, as if he knows exactly what's coming. His shoulders sag in his perfectly tailored suit. His thick brows come together in a frown that's more concerned than angry. But his warm brown eyes project a steady sense of resolve. Like he's bracing himself for whatever's coming, but he intends to weather it.

Suddenly, I'm struck by a memory. It was a week after Sybil and Jamie got engaged, and she and I were both back in Dallas for the holidays. The day after Christmas, the two of us holed up in her childhood bedroom, working ourselves into a sugar coma from gingerbread cookies and spiked eggnog, giggling like teenagers. Then, finally, I lobbed the question I'd been wondering about since I got Sybil's elated FaceTime call telling me the news. "So, you really think he's the one?"

It was a reasonable question, I felt. Sybil had been proposed to twice before, and neither engagement had panned out.

Sybil took a bite of her cookie, chewing thoughtfully as she considered my question. "I used to think love was like a roller coaster, you know," she said. "The heart-pounding thrill of it all. The lows making the highs feel that much more exhilarating. But Jamie's not like that."

"What's he like?" I had only met him once at this point.

Sybil hugged a pillow to her chest. "He's like…he's like

the ocean. The feelings are just as powerful, but they're steadier—like the tide, rolling in and out. Sometimes it feels like he's the only one who can weather all my storms."

And then, the dreamy look of deep thought still on her face, she bit off the leg of her gingerbread man.

At the time, I hadn't been fully convinced, instead just brushing off her ocean metaphor as the semi-philosophical musings of an eggnog-tipsy Sybil. It took seeing her and Jamie interact several more times over the course of their engagement to understand for myself how true her assessment really was. And looking at Jamie's worried but resolved expression now, here on the Vegas strip, I'm reminded of Sybil's words. Jamie *can* weather her storms. I know he can. By this point, he has to know something is up. But knowing that deep down and having the reality thrust in your face are two different things. Jamie just needs us to shield him from the worst of it. At least, for as long as it takes for Sybil to complete her roller-coaster ride and realize that what she really needs is right here waiting for her.

So I send up a quick prayer to the gods of lying by omission, and say, "So...Sybil really wants some alone time right now." It's not a complete lie. In fact, it is absolutely very much the partial truth.

"Alone time...away from *me*?" Jamie's voice stretches thinly over the words.

"From everyone really," Nikki chimes in, which is also true. After all, no one has been able to get through to her.

For a moment, it seems like Jamie wants to push back, to demand more information, but mostly he just seems...tired. "Well, thanks for passing along the message. I know she's in good hands with you girls keeping an eye on her." I swallow down the lump in my throat. "But the moment"—he pinches the bridge of his nose—"and I mean the *moment* she doesn't want to be alone, you tell her to call me. Okay?"

"I will," I say, at the same time Nikki jumps in with "Absolutely."

"Okay, well. The rest of the guys are out…somewhere. But I think I'm just going to go to bed." His totally deflated look kills me. "Vittal scheduled the plane to go back tomorrow at nine a.m. I've texted Sybil the details, but I'll send them to you too."

I try to manifest into the universe a vision of Sybil sitting side by side with Jamie on his friend's jet tomorrow morning, but the odds of that happening feel incredibly slim. We still need to locate her *and* resolve whatever insecurities sent her running off in the first place, and I'm highly doubtful we'll be able to accomplish all that before 9:00 a.m., a mere eight hours from now.

We all give Jamie hugs and watch him slump back toward the hotel.

"Lord, that was rough," Nikki says with a sigh.

"You really think that was the best move?" Finn asks. "Keeping the charade up like that?"

"I didn't hear you stepping up to drop the bomb on him," I shoot back. Exhaustion and stress are settling into my bones, and that mind-altering kiss I'd shared with Finn in the elevator seems like a distant memory.

Finn holds his hands in front of his chest defensively. "Hey, I was genuinely asking. I have no idea what the right thing to do is here. I want to respect Sybil's wishes…" He trails off, rubbing a hand across his jaw. "But sometimes you just have to bite the bullet and tell the truth, even if it hurts."

I know he's right, but looking at Jamie's puppy dog face has stoked my protective instincts—the same ones that spun a story for three-year-old Liz about our dad being an astronaut who was on his way to the moon, and therefore couldn't take her to the daddy-daughter tea after church that Sunday. Eventually she learned the truth, but in that moment, the blow was cushioned.

"Let's give this one more try," I say as I navigate over to the tracking app for the first time in hours. "If we have no leads on her whereabouts by the time Jamie's heading to the airport, we'll fess up. Agreed?"

"Agreed," Nikki says.

Finn just nods.

As the tracking app loads, I pray that Sybil's little blue dot is headed toward Caesars Palace...and Jamie.

But I have to zoom out three times to find her. And when I do, my stomach does an unpleasant flip.

Sybil is no longer in Vegas.

And she hasn't just left the city. She's left the whole frickin' *state.*

"Oh shit," Finn says, peering over my shoulder at the map.

"Yeah, no kidding."

"It looks like she's headed to Albuquerque."

"Albuquerque?" Nikki repeats.

The anxiety that I've kept at bay through most of the evening curls around my chest. "How do you know?" I ask Finn.

"Call it a hunch," Finn says cryptically.

He leans back on his heels and stuffs his hands in his

pockets. "It's after midnight. I think we should just crash in the room I got, and try to catch up with her first thing tomorrow morning."

My entire body starts tingling, my mind already drifting to the feeling of Finn's hands around my waist in the elevator and his thigh pressed between my legs...

The sounds of a Rat Pack cover band spill out into the night each time the door to the casino opens, and the golden glow of the marquee lights shimmers around us. For a second, everything melts away—Nikki, Jamie, Sybil, pregnant Willow holding down the fort back at HQ...they all fade away, leaving nothing but Finn and me. His body pressed against mine at the roulette table. The hungry look in his eyes when he saw my new outfit. The way he opened up to me at dinner. The scorching kiss in the elevator. All the mistakes I've made with Finn have been in moments like this. Moments that feel too good to be true. Brimming with starlight or drunk on fresh victory. I'm not going to make the mistake of sharing a hotel room with him. The *actual* love story belongs to Sybil and Jamie. I can't let myself get distracted, imagining things will be different with Finn this time around.

"It'll be too late by then," I insist. "We should just go now."

"Are you sure?" Nikki asks. "I'm going to stay here for the night and catch the flight back with Jamie and the guys in the morning. You can crash with me, Em," she adds, like she knows I don't trust myself to share a hotel room with Finn.

"I'm sure. I'll pound some coffee and be good to go. Finn?"

Finn doesn't look especially excited about the prospect of getting on the road again, but he says, "We could make it to Albuquerque by morning if you're set on going."

"Then it's settled. We'll power through, and just get to Sybil." I start doing the math in my head. It's an eight-hour drive...then a two-hour flight to LA... "We could be back in Malibu by late lunch tomorrow—in plenty of time for the rehearsal dinner." It rings hollow in my ears though. I've kept moving the goalposts further and further back for Sybil, and now I'm not sure I can see the field anymore. But Finn is still here beside me, and for the life of me I don't understand why.

Nikki makes us promise to keep her updated regularly, then follows Jamie's path toward the hotel rooms.

"You grab the coffee, I'll go check us out of the hotel and call for the car," Finn says.

Luckily, there's no shortage of twenty-four-hour places from which to source caffeine. I return to the front entrance of the casino a few minutes later and hand an insulated paper cup to Finn, who takes a sip with a grimace.

"I hope Sybil appreciates the sacrifice you're making for her," I say. "You don't mind if I take a couple dozen photos of Finn Hughes drinking this death-beverage, do you? For posterity's sake."

"Ha ha," Finn says, pushing my phone camera out of his face.

The valet brings the Singer around, and Finn pulls open the door for me. It's a simple gesture, but despite all my protestations about staying focused on finding Sybil, the action of sliding into the passenger seat in my new outfit feels like heading home after a date, anticipating whether or not it'll end with a kiss—or something more.

After taking off his jacket and throwing it in the back seat to get crumpled anew, Finn joins me in the car, where we lapse into a comfortable silence—unusual for us. We are so used to debating and playfully—or genuinely—arguing, that there's something surprisingly intimate about the quiet. I rest my arm on the thin center console between us. Finn moves to shift gears, and the soft cotton of his shirt brushes against my forearm.

I expect him to pull his hand away, but it settles beside mine. I feel the slightest brush of his pinkie before it loops over mine. A thrill rockets through me. I don't understand how the slightest movements of Finn's fingers can have such a powerful effect on me. His eyes are still on the road, but he has a soft smile on his lips. Despite how late it is, and the weakness of the coffee I've only had a few sips of, I feel like I've drunk half a dozen Red Bulls, and the floating feeling from the elevator is back. But now it's ten times more intense because this is—or could be—real.

I leave my hand right where it is and stare out the window into the starlight.

18

VERY EARLY FRIDAY MORNING

(One day before the wedding)

IT'S AN HOUR OR SO into our drive toward Albuquerque—making good time but still not caught up to the little floaty blue tracker pin—when I force Finn to pull over at a rest stop so I can use the bathroom. I return to find him leaning against the side of the car, looking exhausted. He never did have more than two sips of the coffee I got him.

"Let me drive the rest of the way," I say. "I at least got a nap earlier." He smirks at me, and I instantly regret reminding him—not that he's aware of the lurid contents of my nap-time dream… I hope.

"Um, not a chance. The terms of the bet were that you only get to drive this thing if we were leaving Vegas with Sybil in tow. And that is very clearly far from the case. In fact, I'm pretty sure you owe me one official compliment. Don't worry, I'll give you a few minutes."

"That bet was made prior to the knowledge that Sybil would have crossed state lines again, and should thus be rendered moot. Besides, I'd like to avoid ending up in a ditch, and I can tell you need the shut-eye. Meanwhile, I'm buzzed," I say, holding up a Diet Coke I grabbed from the station on the way out.

A smile quirks at his lips. "Fine. You win, not because of the merits of your argument but because I forfeit with a plea of sleepless insanity." Pulling the keys from his pocket, he spins them once, and grabs my hand. "I can trust you, Emma, can't I?"

"Of course." The keys jingle quietly as he sets them in my palm. Both of his hands cup mine, and my body sways toward his as if drawn by an invisible force. He lets go and heads around to the other side of the car.

I grip the keys tightly enough to feel the teeth bite into the heel of my palm. "Just keep it between the lines," Finn says, sliding into the passenger seat, and I exhale. Finn can trust me. But can I trust myself? We haven't spoken about or even directly acknowledged our elevator make-out. The sudden twist of Sybil now heading east has captured our focus, putting a pause on the attraction that had begun bubbling over between us. But it's like a pot of water warming on the stove—I may have put a lid on it and turned the heat down to a simmer, but I know it's only a matter of time before we reach the boiling point again.

At least for now, though, there's a quiet calm between us.

Within five minutes back on the road, Finn slumps against the window and drifts off to sleep.

Moving from gear to gear, I remember how much I miss driving. There's no need for it in New York, and I've never driven anything as smooth as this Singer. The gear shifting is even more precise than a regular Porsche, the throttle is incredibly responsive, and the steering is almost intuitive. It's the kind of car my dad always lusted after but could never afford.

Instead, he spent his weekends restoring an old Jeep Wagoneer. He loved any excuse to drive it. When I was seven and the rivalry between Texas and A&M still meant something, we took it down to Austin for my first football game. There was never any doubt that I would go to Texas one day. Both of my parents went. It's where they met. I knew, even at seven, that one day I'd be a Longhorn.

My dad always said you were taking your life in your hands every time you got on I-35, so we took the long way down from Dallas to Austin on 281. In the spring, it's covered in wildflowers, but even in early fall, it's a beautiful drive. I remember when we went to that first football game, we left while it was still dark out so we could make the 11:00 a.m. kickoff. Wrapped in a burnt-orange fleece blanket with light limning the dashboard of the Wagoneer and dew shimmering along the fields, I watched the sunrise over the Texas Hill Country. Liz had just started walking that summer, and it felt like neither of my parents had any time for me—always chasing after my newly mobile little sister. Dad especially guarded his time alone, so it felt like a bit of a miracle that we would have so much of it together on this trip. I loved him for it.

My father's secondary motivation for taking the long way to the game—beyond his somewhat dubious claims of physical safety—was dessert. It gave us an excuse to drive through Marble Falls and stop at the Blue Bonnet Cafe for pie. We pulled into the diner at 8:30 a.m. and slid into a gray vinyl booth. My dad ordered a coffee, a hot chocolate with whipped cream, and two slices of coconut cream pie for us. While he doctored his coffee with cream and sugar, he said, "You're in for a treat. This is the best pie in the state, Emmie Girl. One day"—my dad licked the meringue off his spoon and pointed it at me—"I'll be driving you down to Austin for your first day of school."

"What if I went somewhere else for school though? Would you still love me if I went to A&M?"

"You should go to the school where you think you'll be the happiest." He wrinkled his nose. "But please, Emmie, don't go to A&M."

I nodded and went back to my pie, scraping the filling out so I could save the entire crust for last. In that moment, I would have promised him anything.

I don't remember much about the game beyond standing on the bleachers sucking down a Dr Pepper, basking in my father's attention, and knowing I could never be happy going to college anywhere else.

At the time, it was the best weekend of my life. By August of next year, he was gone.

The twice-a-year phone calls with my dad on my birthday and Christmas had mostly petered out by my senior year of college, but I called him as soon as I got accepted to Texas.

I could tell he was happy for me, but in the removed way

that he might be happy for anyone going to a school that meant so much to him.

"Maybe we could drive down together," I say.

"I've been meaning to get to Austin, Emmie Girl. Let me check my schedule." Months passed, and I never heard back from him, so near the end of summer, I sent him a text: *First day of school in a week!*

Two days later he texted back, *Proud of you! Hook 'em!* But nothing about driving me to school, like we'd once talked about. And I was too stubborn—and too hurt—to bring it up again.

Mom and I loaded up my Bronco with monogrammed towels, extra-long bedsheets, and my prized *Titanic* poster. Work was so busy that she couldn't drive me to school, and I knew the only reason I was able to afford college and all its peripheral costs was that my mom worked so hard. I couldn't ask her to take time off for me. And in the back of my mind, part of me still hoped my dad would be there. After my mom said a teary goodbye, she drove away to work, but I waited in our driveway for an hour. He never showed, so I took the straight shot to Austin down I-35 and didn't stop once.

FINN STIRS BESIDE ME and rubs at his eyes. "Where are we?"

"Closing in on Kingman."

Finn glances at the dashboard clock, which reads 2:42 a.m. "I can't let you just drive all night." He pulls up a map on his phone. "Take the next exit, and we'll make camp at Hualapai Mountain Park. Just for a few hours," he adds, to ward off any protestations from me. But at this point, none are coming. Thoughts of my dad have drained my energy, and now I feel one slow blink away from disaster. Following Finn's directions, we make it off the highway and onto a dirt road that leads to a small campground. After turning off the car, I recline the seat back as far as I can.

"Oh, we're not sleeping in the car." From the back seat of the Singer, he pulls out a Yeti blanket and a small nylon pouch, in which I assume must be a tiny pup tent or something. I step out from the driver's seat, but the green silk dress that had been the perfect thing for Vegas is deeply out of place in the woods.

Sensing my discomfort, Finn hands me a soft cotton shirt. "Here, you can wear this if it's more comfortable. I'll...um... turn around while you change."

I put on my shorts and slip Finn's oversized T-shirt over my head, but it's been worn so many times that the fabric is nearly translucent in some spots. I reach back into the car for the sweatshirt and put it on too. "I'm decent."

Finn turns back around and smiles. "You're all kitted out in Duke gear." He pauses. "It looks good." He clears his throat and shakes out the vinyl pouch into a large rectangle. He knots it between two pine trees, and in less than two minutes, we have a hammock. "It's not the cushiest, but it's better than the ground or trying to squeeze into the car."

"I'm incredibly impressed." I sit sideways on the hammock and give it an experimental swing. My feet leave the ground, and I'm looking up through a web of pine needles to the night sky. There's enough moonlight that I can see banks of clouds floating gently above us.

Finn produces a bottle of tequila from the car. "A night-cap?"

"Is that the tequila that sent Sybil into a tailspin last night?" I can't believe it was only twenty-four hours ago that Sybil went off the deep end. Only twenty-four hours since Finn Hughes came back into my life.

The hammock rocks as he takes a seat beside me. "It's one of many she tried." He passes me the bottle, and I focus on unscrewing the lid instead of the fact that the entire right side of his body is pressed against the entire left side of my body.

I take a small sip and let it linger on my tongue. There's a burst of flavor that almost tastes like my mom's gingerbread loaf with a hint of orange blossom. After I swallow, the faint taste of cloves lingers. It does taste remarkable. Score one point for snobby man-bun bartender. I guess some tequila *should* be sipped. I hand the bottle back to Finn.

"So why do you think Sybil is going to Albuquerque?" I ask.

Finn pauses with the tequila bottle halfway to his lips, as if he's not sure he wants to say.

"Come on, Finn. Just tell me."

He exhales. "I think she's going to see Liam."

"Liam *Russell*?" It's a name I haven't thought of in years—Sybil's high school boyfriend who broke up with her the night of prom and then proposed before graduation. "That was a million years ago. Why would she go see him?"

"It's just a hunch. I hope I'm wrong. He's bad news."

My mind races. I'd never liked Liam, but I hadn't realized that things between him and Sybil were that bad. The worry etched around Finn's eyes is real though.

"What happened with them?"

"That's Sybil's story to tell, Emma." His words sound familiar, but I can't place them. "I just have a hunch that she went to see him. He's a personal trainer in Albuquerque now."

"How do you know that?" I ask, pulling the tequila bottle back from Finn and taking another small sip. I know Finn still isn't on any social media, because every now and then I check—just to see what he's up to, just like I would with any old friend...

"He's an incredibly active LinkedIn user," Finn explains with a half smile. "A lot of multi-paragraph motivational posts." I grimace, and Finn nods. "Yeah, it's pretty cringey."

I pass the bottle back to Finn and pull the sleeves of his sweatshirt down over my hands, balling them into fists for warmth. "I can't believe she's chasing down an old boyfriend two days before her wedding," I say. "Honestly, I'd be a lot less surprised if she was trying to chase down Sebastian. That would at least make sense."

"Maybe she just needs some closure."

A breeze slips through the trees, and the susurration of pine needles slipping against each other fills the space between us. When I look up again, the cloud bank has moved with the wind, traveling westward. The vastness of the sky and forest settles on me, but it doesn't overwhelm me. Tucked beside Finn in this hammock cocoon, I feel rooted and safe.

"You know, my dad lives out this way. Around Flagstaff."

I don't know why I bring this up. Maybe Finn's talk of closure just now. That's something I never got with Dad.

"Do you get to visit a lot?" Finn takes a sip of tequila and leans back in the hammock, wedging the bottle between us.

I lean back, too, and the hammock sways softly. "No. This

is my first time in Arizona. It's been"—I do the math in my head—"almost eight years since I've seen him. He came to Austin for a football game junior year, and we got breakfast. It was super awkward because I hadn't really seen him for years before that—and I haven't seen him since. He's not a bad guy, he's just like a nonentity."

The silence from Finn is heavy.

"What?" I ask.

"I think leaving your family makes you an objectively bad guy."

"Yeah, definitely in some ways."

"I mean, I can understand a marriage not working out, but your kids are your kids. That's not something you can walk away from."

"And yet..." I let the sentence trail off, and reach for more tequila. "Do you want kids?"

"Not right now, but definitely someday. My dad and I had our differences, but there's never been a minute of my life that I doubted how much he loved me. Everyone deserves that. At least one person to love you completely unconditionally. I don't think you should have kids if you can't be sure you can do that."

"My mom is like that," I say and then tip the bottle back.

"Good."

His hand closes over mine, and he takes the tequila back for another pull. "I told you I got in a big fight in Austin when I was nineteen?"

"Mm-hmm." I don't know if it's the tequila, the rocking of the hammock, or being this close to Finn, but I feel totally at peace right now.

"They booked me and took me down to the station. Those

blue couches are burned into my brain. Even though my dad was dying, he drove down 35 and picked me up. It was a super-shitty drive home, but you can afford to make mistakes when you know you have a parent like that. I don't know that my mom has ever fully forgiven me. He took a pretty bad turn a couple of weeks later, and just never got better."

"Oh, Finn. I'm so sorry. It wasn't your fault."

He clears his throat. "Anyway. I think that if you can't love a kid unconditionally like that, then you shouldn't have one."

"I don't know if I love my dad unconditionally." It feels good to get the words out of my body. I've never been this candid with anyone before. Not Willow, or Sybil, or Nikki. Not even Liz. The anxiety that normally curls around my neck eases up, and I take a deep breath of mountain air.

"It's not a two-way street," Finn says. "Parents have to love their kids. Kids get to choose if they love their parents." He closes his eyes, and then, almost as if he's talking to himself, he says, "But I don't think romantic love always works like that. Sometimes, it's just...inevitable."

For some reason, this thought makes it hard for me to swallow. I reach for the tequila bottle just as Finn reaches out for it...and slips his hand around mine.

"But don't you think we *can* choose who we love and who we don't?"

I wait for him to let go of my hand, but he doesn't.

"I guess I just don't think we have as much control over our feelings as we'd like to believe."

"I disagree. You always have a say. No matter how tempting it may be, you can choose not to make the mistake of letting yourself love someone."

"I challenge your stance." He looks into my eyes. His face is serious, but his eyes are sparkling with something like laughter...or maybe it's something else.

I smile—I'm enjoying the references to our debate days. It feels right to accept the challenge. Natural. "Oh yeah?"

"Yeah."

"So what's your counterargument?"

Now he's grinning, definitely. "Sometimes, Emma, making the mistake is the best part about love."

19

EARLY FRIDAY MORNING

(One day before the wedding)

FINN'S WORDS SEEM TO linger in the cool mountain air. One word in particular…*love*.

I swallow, and he tucks a strand of hair behind my ear.

"Well, it's pretty late," he says, his voice barely more than a whisper. "I'm sure you want to get some sleep." As I swing my legs into the hammock so I'm settled the right way, Finn stands up, caps the bottle, and begins to tuck the Yeti blanket around me.

"Wait, where are you going to sleep?" It feels so nice, having him tuck me in so gently, like he really…*cares*.

"The car will do for me." The hammock gently sways as he stands and begins to walk away, and I feel the darkness of the night wrap around me, the piercing intensity of the stars, so far away—light-years. And even though he's only feet from me, Finn feels just as unreachable.

Maybe he's right about people not being fully in control of their feelings. Maybe the two of us are a ticking time bomb. What was the word Finn used? *Inevitable.* The memory of our kiss tonight in the elevator comes crashing back, and suddenly I don't feel a bit tired. Energized by this electric *something* that keeps pulling me to Finn, even though I should almost certainly know better by now. Maybe all I need to do is finish what we started in the elevator. What we started on the rooftop in New York. In Katie Dalton's pool. Really, what we started in the back of that debate team bus when Finn first slipped his hand into mine.

"Finn, wait," I call out.

"What, what is it?" he asks, backtracking until he's sitting perpendicular to me on the hammock. He pulls my legs across his lap, and the hammock sways slightly. "Are you warm enough?"

"Yeah, I'm just…I don't think I'll be able to sleep," I tell him truthfully. Despite the fact that I'm exhausted, my heart is racing, my mind numb with some feeling I can't name, some need I can't say out loud.

"Why not?" he whispers. His hand moves to my ankle. "Scared of the woods?" he asks, a slight, playful taunt in his voice.

"I just…" How do I say it? How do I make him understand? That I don't want him to stop touching my ankle, don't want him to walk away, to sleep in the car, to let this moment just slip away like all the other moments between us before. "I just—I don't want to make another mistake." My voice breaks, and I feel foolish for blurting that out. "I don't want to get hurt."

"I don't want that either," he says softly. In the darkness, I can't read his expression.

"I want to be able to trust you."

He sighs. "But you never seem able to."

The pain is in my throat, but I push past it. "And why do you think that is?"

He shifts. "Look, I know there were times when you felt like I wasn't there for you—"

"I '*felt*'?" I interrupt. I hate that kind of bullshit non-apology. He *wasn't* there for me. That wasn't just my perception of the situation, it was a fact.

"But I've changed. Only you can't see that because you—"

This time Finn cuts himself off.

"I what?" I demand.

"Forget it."

A wave of boldness holds me to the spot. "Come on. Tell me what you really think."

He shifts slightly so he's facing me, his hand on my knee now. "What I really think is that you don't *let* yourself trust me; you don't trust most people, in fact. You're afraid of anything—or anyone—that you can't control."

His words make me want to cry, but I refuse to let him see that. "Screw you, Finn." The words don't come out as venomous as I want them to—more just deflated.

"Am I wrong, then?"

I wish I could say he was. But what I'm feeling now? The mix of desire and confusion and...dread? He's right on the money. I'm terrified to let myself fall.

In the silence, he inches slightly closer to me, pulling my knees toward his lap. "I'm sorry, Emma, but you don't get to control me. That's not on offer."

There's something so sure, so powerful and confident in him, it takes my breath away. "I never said that's what I wanted," I protest, pushing the blanket off me, unsure whether to be angry or pleading.

My face is mere inches from his now as he asks, "So what *do* you want, then, Emma?"

The words are too hard to say, and so I don't say it, I show him instead. I lean forward, slowly, until our lips touch. There's no hesitation from Finn. He returns my kiss hungrily, opening my mouth with his tongue. Kissing him feels so good, I let the knot that had been forming inside me begin to unravel. He pulls me gently onto his lap. My legs are on either side of him. The hammock sways, driving my hips into his, and he lets out a soft groan. In this moment, the truth overpowers me, how much I want this, to be this close to him—out here in the middle of nowhere, where we could be the only two people on earth.

His hands reach for the hem of my sweatshirt; I help him lift it over my head, along with my T-shirt, both tossed to the ground in seconds.

I remember the last time I was bared to Finn like this. The mild crispness of a September night cut through with the heat of his breath against my skin, the lights of the city sparkling around us. Now it's cool mountain air and the sparkling of stars, but the heat is the same. And it's the same flicker of hope sparking in my chest that flares to life again. The intensity that I've spent the last two years trying to find with other guys, but never did.

Finn's words about Sybil and Liam echo through my mind. *Maybe she just needs some closure.*

Is that what I need too? But it doesn't feel like closure, it feels like another new beginning.

Through ragged breaths he says, "If you want to stop, just tell me. I'll stop. We'll stop."

"Do not stop." It comes out as more of an order than I mean it to.

He smiles against my mouth. "Yes, ma'am." And with that, he rolls me onto my back, switching our positions, and he's on top of me, kissing me, moving his mouth down the length of my body. He gets off the hammock and kneels on the ground, sliding me to the edge, slipping my shorts off. My breath hitches at the sight of Finn on his knees in front of me, and I lean back into the hammock. Slowly, he kisses one knee and then the other.

"Emma." I feel his lips now grazing along my inner thigh, and I nearly unravel in that moment. "Let me be the one in control this time," he whispers.

He drags his tongue along my skin, my thighs trembling, as he's kissing and licking, up, up, until I can hardly breathe, feeling like I'm coming undone at the seams.

"Can you let me take charge?"

"Yes."

My underwear is gone in seconds, strewn somewhere I may never find it.

Just as I feel like I can no longer hold on, he pulls away, and I can't help reaching for him. I tug at the neck of his shirt until he pulls it off. Bare chested, he grabs my hand and presses a soft kiss against my wrist. His tongue flicks briefly along my skin. When he releases me, a breeze blows across the damp spot where he'd pressed his lips, and a shudder racks my body.

"Emma." He stands, looking down at me. Exposed beneath the full moon, I feel luminous and otherworldly. And the way Finn is looking at me, it's like he thinks I am those things too. I don't feel any closer to closure. I just want more of him. All of him.

"Are you sure?" Finn rasps, reaching smoothly for a condom.

I nod, and then gasp as he pulls me back in, against him. A small sound escapes from him too.

"Emma," he whispers, moving deeper, holding my hips. Totally in control. Even though I'm completely naked, Finn's body is a furnace against mine, keeping me warm. He cups one of my breasts, and I gasp as his mouth closes around my nipple. His tongue swirls around it, and there's a soft scrape of teeth. I buck, and the hammock rocks me further into him, forcing him even deeper inside me. He lets out a soft curse, and the puff of air against my damp skin sends a shiver through me.

"You are so beautiful," Finn breathes into my neck, and then he begins moving against me with more urgency, and I begin to let go of everything, of all control, until my whole body breaks apart in shivers, and I'm free.

After, we lie together for a long time, my legs wrapped around his body and my cheek pressed to his chest, where I can hear the beating of his heart.

* * *

A FEW HOURS LATER, I wake up to birds chirping and the warm glow of morning brushing over the tops of the trees. I don't know exactly what time it is, but it's clearly well past dawn. I smile to myself. I guess there are ways to turn off my body's internal alarm clock after all. I'm tucked against Finn's chest, and his breathing is still deep with sleep.

For once, my mind is soft, languid. I want to hold on to this sense of calm, to be fully present in this moment. I start running through the 3-3-3 rule like Finn taught me. *See: Slate-colored mountains. The Singer. My discarded shorts... Hear: Birdsong. A car starting in the distance. The wind rustling through the trees... Feel: Warm skin. Soft skin—*

Finn moves beside me, and I look up to see his eyes on me.

"Good morning," he says. His eyes search mine while his fingers find a lock of my hair. He begins twirling it, and something flutters in my chest.

"Good morning," I say back, smiling. He returns the smile, and something like relief flashes briefly across his face. For a few more minutes we lie suspended in the hammock, listening as the forest around us begins to wake up too.

My stomach growls, and Finn lets out a laugh. "Let's get you something to eat." He presses a kiss onto my forehead before swinging both legs out of the hammock. "Maybe one day we'll make it to a bed."

My heart leaps at the thought of more nights with Finn, a future with Finn, but it's quickly followed by a tightness in my chest. Just yesterday (is it possible it was only yesterday? The whirlwind that started Wednesday night and carried through to our wild-goose chase on Thursday has completely messed with my sense of time), he said he was "not in a relationship place right now." When has Finn ever been in a "relationship place" in all the time I've known him? He's never wanted that. At least, not with me. Finn and I had one mind-blowing night together, but that doesn't erase an entire track record of non-commitment. Last night was just fun, I remind myself. Two people with a decade's worth of sexual tension finally relieving the pressure. *What happens 120 miles outside of Vegas, stays 120 miles outside of Vegas.*

After we've dressed (me slipping into my clothes sans underwear because I truly cannot find them anywhere) and shoved all of our gear into the Singer, Finn presses me against the car door, the aluminum still cool from the night before, and kisses me. It's slow and easy.

Until it isn't. After a few kisses, I'm back to the same level of desperate for Finn that I was last night.

One more time, I think. Just to make sure he's *really* out of my system…

I reach for the zipper of his pants, and he helps me. He scoops me against him, places me on the hood of the car, then focuses on pulling down my shorts. In the daylight, it feels even more erotic than last night. Just watching him get the condom is a turn-on. My legs are splayed open on the hood of the Singer as Finn pulls me forward onto him. He begins moving against me, and I can't believe how quickly I find release. His hand reaches between us, and I nearly slide off the car as an orgasm courses through me. But Finn's hands are firm, holding me. He groans into my neck a moment later, spent.

We're still holding each other, leaning against the hood of the car, when my stomach lets out an audible growl again. I feel Finn's chuckle against my neck.

I want to laugh too. I feel giddy, almost unhinged with happiness.

We re-dress hastily, like naughty teenagers, giggling. He whistles as he makes his way over to the driver's side and shoots me a grin over the roof that makes my knees buckle.

I put a hand on the car to steady myself. The sun beats down over the campground. I feel sticky with sweat—from the growing heat, sure, but more from the exertion of what we just did on the hood of the car. The languid feeling from earlier this morning has faded away. I can't focus on the things I can see, hear, and feel. Because my head is suddenly full of questions. Doubts. Anxiety begins to creep into my nerves. *What did I just do?* What does it mean for Finn and me and the friendship we were just finally starting to rebuild?

I linger with a hand braced on the hood of the car as Finn fires up the ignition. But before I get into the Singer, reality begins to sink in, serious as daylight. I take a deep breath, closing my eyes for a second, trying to hold myself together. *As soon as we're back home, this—whatever it is—is over*, I decide. I don't want it to be, but I have to give myself some boundaries. I have to make this promise to myself. I can't let this become just another mistake on our list. And I know—even though I hate to admit it to myself—I know I can't trust myself to stay casual with Finn, and that he doesn't want anything serious. He said so himself. I can't let my heart run away with me again. The last time I did, things ended in disaster—a mortifying scene at a wedding that still haunts me nearly five years later.

There's a pressure in my chest, but I ignore it. I can't let Sybil's wedding be ruined like Katie Dalton's was. I need to be mature this time. I need to be the one in control.

I square my shoulders and slide into the car. I can do this.

We look up the nearest diner—taking a moment to check Sybil's progress. She's still chugging along, headed east on I-40 toward Albuquerque. I watch the small blue dot that is Sybil creep across my screen, and avoid looking at Finn. Tapping the steering wheel along to the Stevie Wonder song spilling from the radio, he doesn't seem to notice.

I roll down my window to clear my head. It's all I can do not to beg him to pull over again, and again, wanting not just the feeling of him inside me, but the closeness, the intensity. But however good Finn makes me feel, it's no match for how much he could hurt me. How easy it was to forget that last night—and again this morning—and I know I could keep on forgetting it and keep on getting heartbroken. He's done it before, and it'd be foolish of me to think it won't happen again. People are who they are. It's not Finn's fault. He's been nothing but up-front with me. I'm the one who's been a liar—I've been lying to myself, about how much I care.

The wind whips across my face, making my eyes water, but I blink away the tears.

Once we're seated at the diner and the jet-fuel-level coffee the waiter pours us starts to take effect, I'm more in control of my feelings. I know what I need to do. I need to strike first, just like in debate. Sitting across the table, Finn reaches for my hand and drags his thumb along the top of my knuckles while he reads through the menu, and the casual intimacy of the touch makes me feel more vulnerable than the sex we've had. I pull away and reach for the sugar. My hand isn't steady, and I end up dumping more than I mean to into my cup.

We place our orders, and I imagine what it would be like

for this to be my morning every day: waking up next to Finn, knowing how he takes his eggs (over easy) and his coffee (actually Earl Grey tea). Those thoughts are too dangerous. Time to make sure Finn and I are on the same page.

I clear my throat. "About last night," I begin. Finn's face breaks into a grin, which slices through me like a knife, but I force myself to continue. "I think we can both agree it was a onetime thing."

A stillness settles over Finn. "If that's what you want." He carefully sets his mug of tea on the table. "I thought we had a pretty good time last night."

"I had a great time," I say with forced brightness. "This isn't an indictment of your..." Waving my hand in a circle, I search for the right word and land on "prowess."

There's a beat of silence. Finn's eyes take on a dangerous intensity that sends a rush of heat through my body. "I'm not concerned about my 'prowess,' Emma."

"Oh, that's good. You shouldn't be."

"Thank you," Finn says tightly. I hope he'll leave it at that, but he presses, "Why was last night a onetime thing?"

Taking a long pull from my too-sweet coffee, I say, "It's not a big deal. Just two people getting something out of their system, right?"

His eyes don't leave my face. "And am I out of your system now?" His voice thrums through me, and I have to look away. I make the mistake of looking out the window at the hood of the Singer, and the memory of this morning comes flooding back to me. I can still smell Finn on my skin. I feel myself blushing. *No.* I don't know that I'll ever get Finn out of my system.

"Yes," I lie.

Something vanishes from his eyes. Something like hope. "All right then."

THE CAR CRUNCHES OUT of the gravel parking lot, and Finn maneuvers us back to the highway. He doesn't tap along to the beat of any oldies now. Instead, he switches the station to Bloomberg Radio, and I learn more about the bauxite commodity market than I ever wanted to. I take the time to reply to a few work emails and text an update to Nikki. We're almost past Flagstaff before I think to look up flights from Albuquerque for Sybil.

"If we can get her on one of these five p.m. flights back to LA, I think she can make it to most of the rehearsal dinner." Our window to catch up to Sybil is tightening, but we might still have a shot at getting her back in time for tonight's event.

Something flickers across Finn's face, but he just nods. "Let me top off our tank before we get too far past Flagstaff." Those are the most words he's said to me in a row since we left the diner.

Finn handles gas while I run inside to get snacks. We're getting to the end of our time together, and I don't want to end it on such a sour note. I grab all the snacks I remember Finn packing for debate trips. One time, sitting on the bus, he turned to me very seriously, and said, "The secret to a perfect snack is the combination of salty and sweet. You need your sweet snacks." He held up a half-eaten package of chocolate cupcakes. "And you need your salty." He pulled a Slim Jim from his backpack and twisted it in half, handing me. "It's all about balance, Emma."

As I drop a handful of Slim Jims into my basket, I wonder it's even worth the effort. It's really not fair that Finn is so pissy right now. Isn't this what he wanted? No strings. After paying, I head back toward the Singer. Unwrapping a Snickers bar, I take a few bites as I cross the parking lot. Finn is still parked beside the gas pump, but he seems to have finished filling the tank. He's on the phone, his back to me, but I can still hear him, and my ears perk up when I realize who he's talking to.

"Sybil, I know you. I know you sometimes just need to take things to the end of the road. To see how far they'll go. But remember what I told you that night—you deserve someone who will love all of you. Okay?"

Relief floods through me that Finn has been able to nail down Sybil. He ends the phone call and turns around. I smile at him. "What did she say? Can she meet us at the airport?"

But as soon as he sees me, Finn freezes.

20

FRIDAY AFTERNOON

(One day before the wedding)

"I DIDN'T MEAN FOR you to overhear that." Finn's tone is clipped.

"Okay..." I look at him quizzically.

"It's just, I didn't want to get your hopes up. She didn't pick up. I was leaving her a voicemail."

"Oh. Too bad." I stand there like a moron, holding the plastic bag of gas station treats. The sun is high in the sky now, and the heat beats down between us. Finn squints at me, but he doesn't say anything. At a loss for what else to say, I venture, "So...should we get back on the road?"

"We should." Finn lets out a deep breath and returns to the driver's side. I slip into the passenger seat, feeling like a character in a horror film who doesn't know there's a psycho with a knife behind her. Like there's some big obvious reason why Finn is so edgy about my overhearing his call with Sybil, but I'm just too blind to see it. He fires up the Singer and pulls out of the parking lot, leaning a little heavier on the gas than he usually does. I reach out to steady myself on the center console.

"That voicemail sounded pretty intense," I toss out, hoping Finn will elaborate.

"I'm just worried about her," Finn replies, his eyes trained on the road. "I don't like the idea of her getting back with Liam."

I wait for him to say more, but he slips back into silence. "What did you mean?" I ask. "On your voicemail to Sybil when you said, 'Remember what I told you that night'?"

"It was nothing." Finn reaches out to turn on the radio, the international signal for *I don't want to talk about this anymore*, but I'm not letting go that easy. I'm getting the distinct impression that Finn knows more than he's telling me about where Sybil is, about why she might have run in the first place.

"If it's nothing, why not just tell me? Was it something that you guys talked about on Wednesday night at the tequila bar? Because if you said something that set her off, then I think I deserve to—"

"I was talking about prom night," Finn says through gritted teeth.

Prom night? Why would Finn bring up prom night? I rack my brain trying to come up with a reason for why, nearly a decade on, they'd still be talking about prom—especially since Finn wasn't even at the dance. I think back to that night. I remember standing on the dance floor, Sybil evasively telling me that she borrowed Finn's car to come to the dance.

I remember storming to Finn's house, telling him I wasn't a consolation prize… Then I remember another night, years later, on our rooftop when Finn revealed he'd been at the hospital the day of prom—not at the mall like Sybil had said. He told me Sybil had been there too. When I asked her about it, she brushed me off—*I was just picking up a prescription for my grandpa*. I had accepted this explanation at the time, too wrapped up in Finn and everything that had happened on the rooftop to give it much thought. But now, there's a squirming in my gut. I can't shake the feeling that something major happened between Sybil and Finn that night that they're not telling me about. Something that Sybil has been carrying around with her for eleven years. Something that might explain why she bolted from her happily ever after.

I take a deep breath, trying to stave off a wave of anxiety and agitation. I'm operating on barely three hours of sleep, and I can feel myself growing snappish. "Finn, please. You have to tell me what happened with Sybil at the hospital."

Finn looks over at me, starts to open his mouth, then closes it. Finally, he sighs and says, "It's not my story to—"

"For the love of god, Finn!"

"Let it go, Emma!" Finn matches my volume. "You don't get know every single detail of everyone else's life, okay?"

"Seriously? You think this is just me being nosy?" I bark out a scoff. "This is about me protecting the people I love. I have to know what's going on in their lives in order to fix things when they go wrong."

"Well, since I'm clearly not one of those people, why don't you just drop it?" The bitterness in his voice fills the Singer. "You can't control everything."

"So fucking what if I want to control things?" I'm nearly shouting now. "How does not wanting to let my friends get hurt make me such a shitty person?"

Finn doesn't say anything to that.

I'm not an idiot. I know I have a bossy streak a mile wide. That I badger, and nag, and relish being the big sister—not just to Liz, but to all my friends. It's more than that though. My need to fix everything isn't just about being responsible or looking out for my friends. It's about trying to protect my own heart. To hold the shattered pieces of myself together by whatever means necessary. Because when there's one massive thing in your life that you have *zero* control over—like when a parent abandons you—then you look for stability where you can get it. So Finn can say I'm controlling all he wants. Frankly, I think I'm justified. Especially when it comes to him.

I turn my body as far as it will go within the confines of the seat belt, hunching my shoulders and leaning my head against the window.

We drive another forty minutes in silence.

I try to regulate my breathing, but I'm still fuming. Angry at Finn for not telling me the full story about what happened with him and Sybil that night, and angry at myself that I let myself get sucked back in. I've been here before—fresh off the high of Finn Hughes touching me with more passion and reverence than any other man has, only to have the cold shock of reality set in soon after. But I'd made contingencies this time to protect myself. I'd told Finn this was a onetime thing *specifically* to avoid succumbing to this same feeling, but I can't help the memories that start to bubble up. I'm suddenly bombarded by scenes of Katie Dalton's wedding…just a few months after the night Finn and I shared on my rooftop. Me, thinking things were finally going to happen between us; Finn, ripping my heart out of my chest, yet again…That was supposed to be the last time. But I let a stupid hammock and a starry sky and the magic of Vegas cloud my vision. I let my guard down once again and got burned. What was I thinking, pretending I was someone who could just make fun mistakes and not suffer the consequences? Whatever proclamations of casualness I made at the diner were just wishful thinking. I'm not Sybil. I can't just ride the roller coaster, experiencing the highs and lows with equal exhilaration. What I need is stability. Honesty. Trust. And Finn Hughes is not someone I can trust. I need to remember that.

Just then, Finn's phone rings, and we both reach for it, but he's faster than me. He takes a look at the screen, answers, and tucks the phone between his shoulder and ear.

"Hi, Christine," he says, his voice a little rough from disuse. I try my best to listen in, but I can't hear the words of the caller. "I've been hoping you'd call." He smiles into the phone, and his mood seems to lift a bit. I hate the jealousy spiking through me. "I'm a little tied up right now—I'm at a friend's wedding this weekend." There's a pause while Christine replies, then Finn gives another grin—but this time, it's his too-cool-for-school smirk, the one that doesn't quite reach his eyes. "Nah, no plus-one. You know that's not how I roll. But hey, let me text you when I'm back. We'll get something on the calendar…Looking forward to it."

I'm burning to ask who it was, but I won't give Finn the satisfaction of calling me nosy again. So I offer up my own explanation instead.

"One of your dating app matches, then? Make sure Christine knows you're an open relationship kinda guy."

Finn flinches as the barb lands, and I almost regret saying it. "Why would you even care? I'm out of your system, remember?" His tone is angry, but there's a thread of hurt running through it.

I can't believe the hypocrisy. "I *don't* care." Much. "I just don't understand why you're so mad at me, when you're literally setting up a date while I'm sitting next to you in the car." Images of Finn with a leggy blonde—which is what I've decided Christine looks like—flood my brain.

Then, without warning, he swerves to the side of the road. "You've got me all figured out, don't you?" He slams the car into park.

"What are you doing?"

"I think there might be an issue with one of the tires." Finn's answer is completely out of left field. "Haven't you heard the clunking for the past five miles?" No, I hadn't. For half a second, I'd thought Finn was pulling over so we could have this argument out, once and for all. Is it possible that part of me is disappointed it's just Singer maintenance? Not that I would even really know what I'd say. I wish the lines were more clearly drawn. I wish I knew what side I was supposed to argue for. Am I team pro or con?

Finn gets out of the car and circles around back, bending down to take a look at the rear tires. Seconds later, I'm out of the car too. I may have a million conflicting feelings about Finn swirling around inside me, but I have nothing but love for his vehicle. I walk around to the back of the car and hover over his left shoulder.

"Do you need any h—"

"I've got this," Finn says coldly.

And that sends my blood boiling. Sybil might need me to be her anchor, but spending all this time with Finn has left me drowning. The best thing I can do for Sybil is get back to LA and get my head on straight. "You know what? I think we should just call it. We should go back to LA and help the Rains with whatever damage control they need to do, and I can figure out how to help Sybil from the resort." And then I can handle my *own* damage control. I thought I could handle sleeping with Finn and staying friends, but I clearly can't. I need to put an end to this road trip from hell and get back to my real life.

"We can't stop now," Finn says. "We're so close."

I almost bark out a bitter laugh. It's a complete role reversal of the positions we've held for the past two days. Just when I'm fed up with the chase, Finn hooks his claws in.

"We're no closer now than we were when we left Malibu," I say. "At this point, Sybil's going to make it all the way to the Atlantic before we're able to pin her down. Give me these." I yank the keys from his hand, and before he can stop me, I'm in the driver's seat with the door locked. I crack the window down an inch. "I will let you in the car if you agree to head back to LA."

Finn crouches down, and a muscle in his jaw twitches. I'm upset that even angry, Finn manages to look gorgeous. My skin is flushed a mottled red from my hairline down to my chest, but he just looks like a knight heading into battle.

He exhales once, and his nostrils flare. "Fine." He makes his way over to the passenger side and tugs at the door handle.

It's still locked. I roll the passenger window down one inch, too, and say, "And you promise not to take the keys from me."

Very deliberately, he unclenches his fists. I can't see his face, but through the passenger side window I watch his chest fill with air and this time when he exhales, it's laced with a growl. "Yes, Emma. I promise not to take the keys—to *my* car—from you." The low rumble of his voice sends a shiver through me. My eyes dart to the hood of the car, remembering the feel of Finn's hands holding me steady, keeping me from slipping to the ground. I shake it off and unlock the car. He slides into the passenger seat, buckles his seat belt, and looks straight ahead. I plug the resort's address into my map app, point the car west, and we're off. In eight hours we'll be back in Malibu, and we'll both go our separate ways.

The mood in the car is heavier than it's been the entire trip. This stretch of Arizona highway is a flat expanse of nothingness—scrubby little brown plants stretch out in every direction. The occasional semitruck is the only sign of life. Finn hasn't said a word for twenty miles, so I nearly run off the road when he yells, "Stop!"

I slam on the breaks. "What?"

"There's a raccoon."

"Are you serious right now, Finn?" This should be sweet, Finn's eagerness to save another little furry animal's life, but for some reason all I can think of is all the times Finn was sweet to me, and in the end, it didn't mean anything. *Sorry, Miss Raccoon, you might think he loves you now, but tomorrow you'll be roadkill.*

"You have to try to save everyone, don't you?" I say, pulling back onto the road. "No creature is safe from Finn Hughes,

Boy Scout extraordinaire: stray animals, Sybil, your dad." I regret the words as soon as they're out of my mouth.

The silence in the car hangs heavily until Finn breaks it. His voice is soft as he says, "Maybe you're right, Emma. But at least I don't avoid my own problems by trying to run the lives of everyone else around me."

"*Excuse* me?" I demand.

"You're bending over backward to keep your sister afloat instead of just letting her learn by failure. You forced Nikki to go on *LovedBy*, and she got her heart broken. You're constantly badgering Willow to stop smoking. You drag us across three states trying to force Sybil to get married."

"I don't force my friends to do anything. I just know what's best for everyone."

"And what about what's best for *you*?" Finn challenges. Then he sighs and rubs a hand across his face. "God, Emma. Sometimes I swear you don't even know yourself. You push everything down but expect people to read your mind."

I flinch, knowing that the words wouldn't sting so much if they weren't true. But I can't deal with being lectured by Finn right now. "This whole trip has been a mistake," I mutter to myself, thinking back on everything that's gone wrong over the past thirty-six hours. The kayak fiasco at the Hotel Del Coronado, all the Vegas mishaps…

"Well, maybe your life would be a little better if you were a little more willing to make mistakes," Finn says, "and forgive other people for theirs," he adds pointedly.

"The only mistake I've made this trip is feeling like I could trust you. Especially after what happened the last time we saw each other."

Again, images of the Dalton wedding spring into my mind. The dripping of an ice sculpture and the loud banging of a commercial kitchen. The hot wash of shame slicing through the sting of winter cold.

I turn to look at Finn, daring him to tell me I'm wrong, and in that moment, I lose control of the wheel.

21

MISTAKE FOUR: THE OTHER WEDDING

(Four and a half years before the wedding)

IT WAS DECEMBER 31; a new year was just on the horizon, and in a few months, I'd be turning twenty-four. I was full of glittery, naive optimism. Sunlight burst against white-topped mountains, and the gently drifting snowfall made it seem like crystals were dancing everywhere in the air. That amazing feeling of being on vacation after months of the hard grind in New York settled into my bones as Nikki and I traipsed in our heavy ski gear onto the shuttle heading to the lodge.

Katie Dalton's wedding was tonight, and a bunch of us had made plans to arrive early and spend the day skiing. Wasn't that the point of a wedding in Vail?

To be honest, though Katie Dalton and I ran in the same friend circles in high school, we were never super close, so I was a little surprised to have rated an invite to her wedding—surprised and thrilled. And not just because it gave me an excuse to travel to Vail for the first time. But because Finn was invited also.

"He's totally in love with you," Nikki said. I had brought her along as my plus-one, since Willow and Sybil had been invited as well, and we never missed a chance for the Core Four to reunite. Currently, Nikki was wedged between me and the window of the ski shuttle, scrolling through the last three months of my text chain with Finn—everything since that night on the rooftop back in September. Though I couldn't see the screen, I could probably recite most of the messages verbatim, I'd reread them so many times:

Things are complicated with Pilar

I want to make it work.

You're one of the most important people in my life. I can't lose that.

After those initial texts from Finn, it was like a dam broke open. We'd text all day and into the night like teenagers—sending funny memes, having heated debates about our favorite TV shows (Mine: anything Shonda Rhimes. His: a 1970s show called *M*A*S*H* that he swears still holds up). But it was more than just that. Finn confided in me his insecurities about the next round of funding for his company. I told him how worried I was that Liz wasn't taking her SAT prep seriously. Maybe it was the buffer of sending messages through a screen instead of talking on the phone or speaking face-to-face, but it felt like we were finally able to open up to each other. Like we were connecting on a deeper level and growing the intimacy that had sparked to life on my rooftop three months ago.

I'd broken up with Preston the day after he returned to the city from his trip. He'd been slightly taken aback. I don't think anyone had ever broken up with him before. But it wasn't fair for him to be with someone who wasn't all in. And there was no denying that I had *fully* moved on.

Beside me on the ski shuttle, Nikki squealed as she read, and I forced her to show me which texts had elicited that response.

Sybil and I went up to the roof tonight…

Oh yeah?

Thought about you.

Emma, please don't do this to me.

Finn clammed up whenever I tried to steer the texts to a flirtier place, which I understood. Sexting wasn't really my thing either. And like he had said, things *were* complicated. The logistics alone were tricky—we were living on opposite sides of the country, for starters. But even so, it felt like we could work through all those issues together. Like maybe this would be the weekend where we'd finally talk about making *us* official.

After all, there were only so many times you could hook up with a friend before they stopped being a friend and started being something more. Right?

* * *

After a couple of runs (blues only, since I did not want to risk injury before getting to enjoy the dance floor with Finn tonight), Nikki and I stowed our gear in a locker and broke for lunch at a cozy German restaurant at the foot of the mountain.

"What am I going to do if I can't text you for eight weeks?" I asked, blowing on the steaming cup of cider our waiter had just set in front of me. Nikki had just been cast on *LovedBy* and would have her phone confiscated once filming began. After months and months of listening to Nikki complain that none of the guys in LA wanted something serious, I decided to sign her up, and just as I predicted, she'd sailed through auditions with flying colors. But now that it was really happening, I found myself almost regretting having sent in her application…and giving yet another friend a reason to move away without me.

Sybil had been grumbling about suffering through another New York City winter, and I could sense that she was itching to move back to the West Coast, where she'd had four years of seventy-five degrees and sunny during college. And then there was Willow, who had been spending more and more time abroad, dealing with family stuff over there, and now Nikki was going to be sequestered in a TV mansion for the next two months. Instinctively my hand reached for my cell phone, itching to text Finn. I wanted to tell him how I felt like adulthood was pulling my friends in all different directions, and how I hoped that he'd be the one exception to that rule.

"Don't worry. I won't forget you while I'm gone," Nikki said, taking a sip of her cider. "And I won't replace you either. After all, *I'm not here to make friends*," she said with exaggerated bitchiness, holding up her manicured claws. I snorted, and she released her cat pose and slouched back in her seat. "What?

You don't think I'd make a good villain? I could totally flip a table or something."

"I think you would be the worst villain of all time. You'd flip a table and then be back two minutes later with a mop and broom," I said. "I think you should just be yourself, and then whoever the guy contestant is, they're guaranteed to fall in love with you." Our waiter was back, placing our orders in front of us. I dove in immediately, smearing a forkful of spaetzle and schnitzel with lingonberry sauce before dipping it in gravy.

Nikki picked up her knife and fork, but didn't make a move to eat. "What if *I* don't fall in love with *him*?" she asked softly. "Everyone on these shows acts like it's a foregone conclusion that all the girls will fall for the guy, but what's the likelihood that the one guy they pick is my soulmate?"

I set my fork down and reached across the table for her hand. "I guess you just have to be honest—with yourself, and with him. But either way, it's going to be a once-in-a-lifetime experience."

We decided to try to squeeze one more run in before we had to start getting ready for the wedding. The packed snow squeaked beneath my ski boots as I walked over to the rack where we'd left our skis. I had just clicked my boots into my bindings and was pushing over toward the gondola when I spotted him.

Finn was just a few yards ahead of us, standing in dark ski pants and a hunter-green jacket, his helmet tucked under his arm.

My heart rate ratcheted up as I called out his name. He seemed startled at the sound of my voice, then smiled and gave me a small wave. The sight of him, live in person and not just a series of gray bubbles on my phone screen, made me suddenly nervous. I tried to skate over to him, and promptly crossed my ski tips and fell flat on my face, even though I was basically standing on a flat patch of ground. I could see Finn chuckling behind his neck warmer. Nikki pulled me up and unclipped my boots from my skis, thrusting them into my hands and not so gently pushing me toward him and the gondola that went to the summit.

"Oh, man. Y'all, I realized I forgot my...ski...goggles," she said.

"They're right on your—" Finn motioned to the goggles on her head, but Nikki was already moving away from us, blocked by the next scrum of skiers jockeying for a gondola.

"She'll figure it out." I shrugged, quietly grateful that I'd get this time alone with Finn before the onslaught of wedding activities. Nikki might have been worried about being villainized on *LovedBy*, but she'd clearly be adored by the other women because she had the wing-woman role down pat—including when to bow out not so subtly.

"Allow me." Finn pulled my skis and poles from my hands and put them in the ski rack of the slow-moving gondola. The group in front of us had filled up the previous gondola, and there was a gap behind us, so Finn and I ended up in a little cable car by ourselves. The liquid caramel sensation of finding myself alone with him for the first time in months seeped through my veins, warming my frozen toes. We sat on the bench seats opposite each other, our knees almost touching, our breath mingling in little puffs of cold air. Even though I was wearing about a dozen layers, including a very unsexy set of thermal long underwear, I suddenly felt naked in front of

Finn. Probably because the last time we were together, I *was* naked in front of Finn. Well, half-naked, at least.

As the gondola started up the mountain, I turned my gaze out the window, trying to slow my racing heart. Below us, little kids in ski school were pizza-wedging their way down an easy green trail, led by their instructor. I watched their wide slalom path down the hill for a minute, trying to regulate my breathing in time with their turns.

"So, how have you been?" I asked as casually as possible.

But Finn was glancing at his phone. A gust of wind hit the gondola. As it swung slightly on its cable, I felt the lump of spaetzle from lunch shift in my stomach. Finally, Finn finished with whatever he was reading and tucked his phone into the sleeve pocket of his ski jacket. "Sorry. Just wanted to make sure my group up ahead was okay." There seemed to be tension radiating off Finn as he turned back toward me. "Um, I'm good. Great."

"Great." The sound-deadening snow that blanketed the mountain amplified the silence filling our small space. I looked around for something to say.

"That's a nice coat."

"Have you been down any black diamonds?"

We spoke at the same time, then smiled sheepishly. Finn's face relaxed, and I could feel the awkwardness starting to evaporate, and in its place, I felt that that familiar Finn feeling: safe, but with a crackle of excitement, like walking a tightrope, but knowing there's a net to catch you. I realized that I was so keyed up about seeing him that I must have been projecting that sense of tension I thought I had seen on Finn's face. He was probably just as nervous as I was. Like with Nikki and

LovedBy, it was one thing to fantasize about something, playing out all kinds of scenarios in your head—but when you're actually in the moment and the reality hits you, it can be kind of nerve-racking. And besides, the short ride up the mountain was probably not the time to do a deep dive into our future plans. Or even our plans for later that night…though I'd had more than a few fantasies already about the dance floor, and the after-party, and maybe having our own little *after*-after-party. Still, it was better to just let things unfold naturally, I decided. Like I'd been doing with our texts over the last few months, it was better to take things slow and let him lead.

"We didn't really grow up skiing," I said, trying to keep the lustful thoughts off my face by answering his question about the black diamonds, "so I'm more of a blue square kind of girl. Have you been skiing a lot?"

"Not really as a kid. Pilar's family had a place in Deer Valley that we used to go to a couple times a year, but they sold it."

"One less reason to date her," I joked weakly.

A slight frown formed across Finn's brow. "About Pilar, Emma—"

But just then the gondola jerked and slowed as we reached the summit. Finn and I stood up, stepping out of the car and onto the landing, grabbing our skis and carrying them over to the trailhead.

"What were you going to sa—"

But the words froze on my tongue, and I felt my imaginary high wire snap along with the stomach-dropping realization that there was nothing to keep me from slamming into the ground.

Because there, at the top of the lift, wearing skintight black ski pants and a silver puffy coat, skiing over to plant a kiss on Finn's lips—was Pilar. Beautiful, effortless, and very clearly *not* his ex.

"DO YOU WANT TO talk about it?" Nikki asked me carefully from the bathroom as she swiped mascara onto her lashes.

"No."

On the mountain earlier that day, I had sent Finn a look of utter shock and disgust, then strapped on my skis and flown down the first trail I could find—which happened to be a black diamond. Somehow, I'd managed to make it down safely. Too upset by what I'd just seen to worry about dying, I was fueled down the steep hill by a surge of hurt, anger, and adrenaline. Feelings that were still coursing through my system now, hours later.

I jerked my dress off its hanger and yanked it over my head. Last spring at an estate sale in the West Village, I'd found a bolt of the fabric tucked into the back of a closet. It was a ruby-red brocade that made my skin look soft and milky instead of translucent and ghostly. In exchange for helping my friend Kendall, an FIT grad, redesign her studio apartment, she'd offered to make me something bespoke, and I knew I wanted to do something with that fabric. I waffled between a jumpsuit and a dress, and finally decided on a gown. At the time, it'd been a totally frivolous request, pure luxury, but so much of my life seemed to involve barely scraping by, I couldn't resist the indulgence. The dress with its deep V-neck and voluminous flounced skirt had hung in my closet for months. As soon as I found out Finn was going to be at Katie's wedding, I knew this was the occasion to wear it. Unlike my dress for prom, this one was literally made for me. Pulling out my pair of pumps, I stomped my feet into them and then shrugged on a white fox fur coat that I'd inherited from my grandmother.

Nikki walked into the room, giving me a once-over while she finished putting on her earrings. "You look gorgeous, Em."

"Thanks. You do, too, babe." And she did, in an elegant ice-blue dress with a plunging neckline. I inhaled deeply and blew out a gust of air. "Let's get this over with."

Walking into the hotel lobby, I spotted Finn among the crowd, and for half a second, my rage gave way to longing. I suddenly realized I'd never seen him in a suit before. For a moment I was glad he didn't take me to prom all those years ago, because grown-up Finn filled out his formal wear far better than teenage Finn ever could. But then my brain processed the full image—this suit-clad Finn had a beautiful brunette on his arm. *Pilar.*

"She's here," I said, pulling Nikki away from the warmth of the lobby toward the patio where the outdoor ceremony would take place. We grabbed fleece blankets from the baskets set up on either side of the aisle and took our seats, huddling beneath the blankets.

"Are you sure it's her?" Nikki asked for the third time since I'd told her what happened.

I nodded once, not trusting myself to speak. Pressure built behind my eyes, but I forced it down. After that night on the rooftop, I had managed to get the girl's full name out of Sybil and did some serious cyberstalking. Pilar Riva: twenty-four, from LA. Worked in tech, like Finn. She was building her own start-up focused on bringing fresh drinking water to high-need areas around the world. "She's like a Californian Amal Clooney," I had groaned to Nikki over the phone back in September when I first unearthed Pilar's Instagram. Of course, back then, her perfection had only been *slightly* jealousy inducing. Because Finn had made it clear that he and Pilar weren't going to last as a couple. They wanted different things. Isn't that what he had said?

Now, I looked over my shoulder through the hotel ballroom's floor-to-ceiling windows, toward the crowd of guests still inside who weren't desperate enough to hide out in the cold. Nikki craned her neck to get a better view. "Don't look," I managed softly. Nikki heard the croak in my voice and looped her arm through mine.

"You have to explain this to me again. I thought they broke up." Nikki had been Team Finn for years and couldn't believe that he had strung me along.

"I did too." I took a deep breath and blinked rapidly. I was not going to cry over Finn Hughes. Nikki reached over and rubbed small circles on the back of my neck.

I mentally ran through our texts, trying to remember if Finn had actually typed the words "I broke up with Pilar," but I couldn't picture them. I had texted him immediately after breaking up with Preston. His response had been quick: *I'd say I'm sorry, but my mom taught me never to lie* 😉. But even though it had seemed implied throughout our many text exchanges, I was suddenly realizing that Finn had never explicitly said that things were over between him and Pilar. Even still, his showing up here with her felt like a betrayal.

And deep down, it hit me that he must have *known* I'd be

upset—otherwise he could have just told me the truth. Maybe that's what stung the most; not that I'd been foolish and wrong about what was going on between us, but that I *hadn't* been. He may not have made a single promise, but the flirting, and the implications, and the closeness we'd developed over these past months…that was all *real.* And he obviously knew it, too, knew I had real feelings for him, or he wouldn't have felt the need to avoid ever saying her name to me.

More and more guests began to filter out to the ceremony site, but luckily, Finn wasn't yet among them. I took in the scenery. When the invitation came, I had been dubious about a winter wedding in such a cold climate, but it really was beautiful. Mountains scraped against a lavender sky that was giving way to a soft tangerine as the sun set. The air was crisp, but I was warm cuddled up next to Nikki in my fur coat and with the fleece blanket draped across my lap. Then, I felt Nikki's frame tense beside me.

"They're outside now," she whispered. My spine stiffened, but I refused to turn around. "They're sitting on the other side." Nikki continued to give me the play-by-play while I kept my eyes trained on the silvery-white floral arrangements that lined the aisle. "Her dress has cutouts." Nikki looked at me meaningfully, "Who wears cutouts to a wedding? In December. On a *mountain*. She's obviously a monster."

But Pilar was *not* a monster. I snuck a look out of the corner of my eye. She was gorgeous. Tall and willowy. Glowing warm brown skin, long black hair swooped down her back. Even in the bulky winter coat she wore over her gown, she managed to look chic. She was nearly as tall as Finn. With six-inch heels, I'd still be half a foot shorter than he was. Maybe he wanted to be with someone who he wouldn't have to develop a hunchback to kiss, I thought bitterly. My mind flashed to the rooftop when Finn had scooped me up and kissed me, and how, at the time, our height discrepancy had made me feel delicate, easily protected by Finn's strong arms. I squashed down the memory.

Nikki's phone lit up. "Willow and Sybil said they're here."

I turned to look for them, but it was Finn who caught my gaze. He gave me a half-hearted wave. I crossed my arms over my chest and pulled my jacket more tightly around me.

The service was short and sweet. Katie looked beautiful in a scoop neck A-line dress in ivory moiré silk and a white fur stole, her chestnut hair twisted into a bun at the nape of her neck. As she stood beside the man she loved, her veil fluttered behind her. I teared up during the vows just like I always did at weddings, but this time the familiar reciting of 1 Corinthians 13:4 hit extra hard. *Love is patient. Love is kind.* I wanted to believe it was true, but my entire life experience seemed to negate the sentiment. I had been patient for the past three months, not pressuring Finn to define our relationship, even after everything that had happened between us. And all along, he was in love with someone else.

KATIE'S RECEPTION WAS HELD in one of the hotel's ballrooms, which had been transformed into a winter wonderland, complete with birch branch centerpieces, white roses, and a giant snowflake-shaped ice sculpture. A quick glance at the seating cards revealed that FINN HUGHES +1 had been assigned table twelve, while I was with the girls over at table four—thankfully, at the opposite end of the hall. I just needed to avoid Finn for the next few hours, and then I could return to New York City and put this whole embarrassing ordeal behind me. During dinner, I tried to enjoy my friends' company, but Sybil and Sebastian were all over each other, and Willow spent most of the night texting her long-distance boyfriend. Even Nikki was flirting shamelessly with some buddy of the groom's who had ended up at our table. I felt like a poster child for pathetic singledom. I listlessly chewed my preselected beef tenderloin and zoned out during the speeches. Then, at the first few notes of Tim McGraw's "My Little Girl," I bolted from the table. One thing was for sure: I was in no emotional state to sit and watch a father-daughter dance.

I wandered over to the bar on the edge of the ballroom and asked for a glass of white wine. While I waited for my drink, Katie and Mr. Dalton's dance wrapped up, and the bandleader invited everyone else to take the floor. Suddenly, there was a piercing screech of feedback. I pressed my fingers to my ears while the band members traded glances, looking for the source of the sound.

"Timothy!" A woman's voice cut through the noise to my left, and I turned to see a mother grab the extra microphone that had been used for speeches out of her five-year-old son's hands. I hadn't even noticed him, sitting on the floor, half under the banquet tablecloth covering the bar.

"Mooooom, I wanna go home. Weddings are stupid."

I'm with you, kid.

The mother hoisted the little boy onto her hip, trying to shush his whining. Then, she turned to me, pressing the microphone into my hand. "Sorry, he's way past his bedtime. Can you figure out what to do with this?"

I stood there, glass of wine in one hand, microphone in the other, like I was about to perform some boozy cabaret number, when all of a sudden, I spotted Finn heading toward me. I looked to my right and left, but the only escape was the swinging doors behind the bar leading to the kitchen. I darted through them, the first few notes of "Proud Mary" spilling in after me, and heaved a sigh of relief.

But my relief was short-lived as Finn squeezed in just as the doors banged shut.

"Leave." I pointed back toward the ballroom with the mic.

"No. Why are you so pissed?"

"Are you serious, Finn?" I decided to go on the offensive. "How's the open relationship?"

"It's closed again," Finn said. "I told her what happened in New York—"

"You *what*?" I pressed the microphone into the crisp white cotton of Finn's dress shirt. He took a step back, tripping over his feet and clanging into a stainless steel rack filled with dirty dishes. I advanced a step further. "I mean, how do you even have that conversation? 'Hi, honey, how was your weekend? Mine was fine; fingered an old friend on her rooftop.'"

Finn winced. "Emma, come on. She and I had an open relationship."

"Yeah, one you didn't even want to be in in the first place," I scoffed. Then realization hit me. "Oh my god. You used me to make her jealous." Shame sliced through me at the thought that I hadn't just been rejected, I'd been used. That night on the rooftop hadn't meant anything to him. He'd just been testing the limits of his "open" relationship, trying to get the girl he *actually* wanted to commit.

"What? No, Emma. I—"

But I didn't need to hear his pathetic excuses. "Does she know you text me every day?"

Guilt flashed across his face. "Emma, you've always been one of my best friends—I was glad that we were reconnecting. But I told you I wanted to try to make it work with Pilar. I thought you understood."

"You are so full of shit," I hissed. "What happened to 'I would never hurt you without a good reason'? Or 'I'm sorry for playing games'?" It felt good to throw Finn's words from that night on the roof back in his face. But right then an avalanche of reality crashed over me. The texts I'd spent months poring over hadn't been *I want to work it out with* you. It had been *I want to work it out with* Pilar. What if Finn hadn't been stringing me along? What if I had just been reading into things, building a fairy tale in my head that didn't exist? That stupid flirty text I sent about the rooftop flashed in my brain like a neon sign. Finn had replied, *Emma, please don't do this to me.* I took it to mean "don't make me hard when there's a whole country between us and I can't do anything about it." But maybe all he meant was "don't make things awkward."

Here in the hotel kitchen, with caterers pushing past us unbothered, Finn continued, "I know I've been unfair to you in the past, that there were times when you weren't able to count on me. But I'm trying to change. I'm trying to be a better person here, not just someone who bails the second things get hard. That's why I wanted to give things a real chance with Pilar."

Around us, the kitchen staff bustled about, preparing

the dessert course. A chef was touching up sugar roses on a silvery-white three-tiered cake. Finn continued to look at me, a crease between his brows. But it was the tinge of pity I saw in his dark eyes that sent me over the edge. Here he was, claiming that he was trying to change, when all he'd done was prove to me yet again that he was the same Finn Hughes who stood me up at prom all those years ago. Someone who dangled happiness in front of me, only to snatch it away again. I grasped for a way to turn this back on him, for any proof that Finn had lied to me. "I told you that I broke up with Preston after that night, and you said it was the right decision."

"Yeah, because he sucked. I didn't think you were breaking up with him for me."

"I didn't do it for *you*." I hadn't—at least not totally. Preston and I weren't a good fit. But it took being with Finn for me to realize that. And I *had* assumed that Finn was going to break up with Pilar too. That we were both on the same page. That we were both making the same decision. Instead, Finn had apparently weighed the pros and cons and decided that Pilar was the better option.

"Good." Finn's tone was heavy with a bitterness that he didn't have any right to. "I mean, how was it going to work between us, Emma? I can't leave California right now. You just got a new job in New York."

"You're right. It would never work out." The words came out of me, dull and lifeless. I was so stupid for thinking it would. I felt like an idiot for googling design firms in the Bay Area even after I'd gotten my dream job in New York.

Finn paced across the kitchen, then wheeled on me. "You were never explicit about wanting to be together."

"I *don't* want to be together," I shot back. "Not now. Not ever." And I didn't. I wanted to be as far away from Finn Hughes as I could possibly get.

"Okay, then."

"Fine!"

We stood there, Finn's arms folded across his chest, my hands still helplessly gripping a wineglass and a microphone, both of us breathing heavily. Then, there was a screech of feedback that we could hear even in the kitchen, and the door edged open. The wedding planner, eyes wide, pointed toward me and mouthed, "It's on."

The microphone.

I looked down at it in my hand, its green light shining up at me. My breath started coming in short bursts. "Did...did anyone..."

At the look of pity in the wedding planner's eyes, I knew. Everyone in the other room had heard me get rejected by Finn Hughes. Everyone on the other side of that door knew that I'd been pining for him while he was "becoming a better person" for his perfect girlfriend.

Even worse, I had gone into explicit detail about exactly what Finn did to me on that lawn chair.

Oh my god.

Mortification unlike I'd ever known washed over me in waves.

The wedding planner pulled the microphone from my slack fingers—along with the wineglass I clearly did not need to be drinking from—and I turned away from the doors to the ballroom in a trance. I couldn't bear to see any more pitying looks or barely concealed smirks. I made my way through the kitchen and into the hotel lobby, and kept walking.

Wrapping my arms around myself to keep warm, I'd gotten half a block from the hotel before I heard a shout. Sybil waved both of our coats in her hand as she caught up with me.

She draped my coat around my shoulders and pulled back. There was a heavy pause, as if she was waiting for me to fill in the blank. I couldn't bring myself to explain all that had happened with Finn, because then I would have to explain what I *thought* was going to happen this weekend. Instead, I looked down at the hem of my dress sagging with melted snow and swallowed down a sob. Another dress with another shitty memory attached to it. How could I be in the same situation all over again? Besides, she and all of our friends from high school had had a front seat to the shit show. What else was there to say?

"We don't have to talk about it if you don't want to."

My shoulders dropped in relief, and I let out a small hiccup. "It's nothing," I said, shaking my head and wiping at my eyes. "I'm just an idiot."

"You are one million things, and not a single one of them is an idiot." Sybil's arm came around my shoulder, and she pulled me away from the wedding and all its disappointments.

"Where's Sebastian?" I asked.

Sybil waved back toward the hotel. "He's fine. He loves being around a new group of strangers." She took a deep breath and looked up. "It's nice to be able to see the stars. Do you want to get a hot dog?" I blinked at her, not sure if I'd heard her correctly. She continued, "There's a place that's open late that serves fancy hot dogs. I think you need to eat something."

I let her lead me through Vail Village to a hole-in-the-wall restaurant. I slumped into a booth, and Sybil ordered for us.

She handed me a hot dog slathered in ketchup, and a large water.

"I can't believe you'd rather have ketchup than mustard on your hot dog," she said, taking a seat across from me.

"Mustard is disgusting, Sybil."

"And ketchup is a condiment for children." I wrinkled my nose at her and took an enormous bite of ketchup-covered hot dog.

"Well, it's perfect for me, then," I said after swallowing. I hated the tears that prickled behind my eyes.

Sybil reached across the table and took my hand. "You are the most grown up, put-together woman I know. It's not child-like to want to find your person." She smiled. "Besides, it's nice to have an excuse to take care of you for once. It's always the other way around." A warm feeling settled around me. It was nice to be taken care of every now and then.

"Do you think Katie will forgive me for ruining her wedding with my meltdown?" I took a much more manageable bite of hot dog this time.

Sybil shrugged. "I'm sure she will. If her grandfather recovers from the heart attack he had when you said 'fingering,' that is. Kidding!" she added at my look of horror. "It'll make a good story. Something always goes a little wrong at a wedding. No one will remember in a few months."

"You'll have to tell me what it's like when you get married."

"You'll find out yourself."

"I don't think that marriage is in the cards for me. I will just be godmother to all y'all's kids, get an Upper West Side apartment, and fill it with trinkets from my travels. Maybe I'll get really into birding."

Sybil looked at me solemnly. "I would love you, even if you got really into birding."

I snorted. "Gee, thanks." The picture I painted actually did sound like a lovely life, but it wasn't the life I wanted. I'd spent the last few months imagining what a life with Finn might look like, and now I wasn't sure I could ever trust myself to imagine a happily ever after again.

22

FRIDAY AFTERNOON

(One day before the wedding)

FINN'S HANDS CRADLE MY cheek. "Emma, are you okay?" His voice is thick with fear.

I blink twice to reorient myself as everything comes racing back. Our fight. The crash. The driver's side door is open, and Finn squats on the road beside me. "I'm okay."

"Are you sure? Your head…"

I reach up to my temple—it's sore, but I don't feel any blood. I've had a concussion before, from a nasty field hockey check in high school—luckily, I don't feel any of those symptoms now. I'm grateful we were going under the speed limit when I lost control of the Singer. "My head is fine," I say to Finn.

"Thank god." His hands drop to my shoulders like he

wants to pull me into a hug, but at the last minute, he seems to realize what he's doing. He pulls back, gives my shoulder a tight squeeze, and stands. "Let's get you out of here."

"I can do it," I say, but I wince as I unbuckle my seat belt and step into the street. The car is on a slant, halfway into a grassy ditch that lines the highway.

"Right," he says and steps back, burying his hands in his pockets as if it's taking everything he has not to touch me.

I reach up to my collarbone and hiss. The seat belt rubbed my skin raw and underneath, I feel the soft puffiness of a bruise beginning to form.

"Let me see." Finn's fingers move toward the collar of my shirt, but he waits for my nod before pulling it gently to the side to inspect. His fingers hover over my skin. "Hold on." He rummages through the back of the Porsche and returns with a first aid kit. "I'm sorry I only have alcohol wipes."

"I can handle it." I grit my teeth at the sting, but I refuse to make a sound. Finn is efficient, at least. After three quick swipes, he squeezes some Neosporin onto his finger and dabs it along my chafed skin. He's close enough that through the acrid smell of tire tread and car exhaust I can smell his skin and that familiar mix of woodsmoke and lavender. All I want is to bury my face in his chest, to let him pull me into that hug. I nearly give in to it, but a car zips by, and we break apart.

Once Finn is satisfied he's tended to all my bumps and scrapes, we inspect the damage to the car. "It looks like the front right tire blew." Finn points to the remains of shredded rubber hanging from the tire rim.

"I'm sorry. I'm not used to driving a car with the engine in the back. I should have just let you drive."

"Who's to say I would have handled it any better?" Finn asks. But I think back to how smoothly Finn moved between gears, how expertly he maneuvered the car, how he held my hand in his and shifted with the other. I wince again, but this time it's not in pain, it's in embarrassment. We might still have a blown tire if Finn was behind the wheel, but we probably wouldn't have careened off the side of the road.

"Do you have a spare tire?" I ask. "I can help change it."

"I do not."

"That's not very prepared of you, Mr. Boy Scout." It's a poor attempt at a joke, but after nearly killing us both, it's either make a joke or break down crying.

Finn shoots me an understanding look. "You're right. I did not prepare to have my car hijacked by a small elfin woman and run off the road." He smiles.

"Maybe next time you'll make better contingency plans."

"Next time, I will just tie you to the seat." He's still smiling, but now there's heat in his eyes. My skin prickles at the thought of Finn's hands around my wrists. With gallons of adrenaline coursing through me, all I want to do is reach for Finn and put all this nervous energy to good use. But as the shock from the crash fades, my walls begin to go back up. Our argument from moments before is still echoing in my ears. Finn calling me out on my passive-aggressive behavior, saying I micromanage everyone around me in order to avoid dealing with my own emotional shit. So I wrap my arms around myself instead.

Finn digs his phone out of the car and calls AAA. He makes a second call to Singer.

For the next thirty minutes, we stand at opposite ends of the car, waiting for the tow truck.

When it finally pulls up, the guy who climbs out looks like he's been towing cars since the Model T was invented, but he's spry enough to attach the winch to the Singer without any help. We grab our things out of the car and watch while the tow truck pulls the car from the ditch. There's a loud scrape, and Finn grimaces. It must be more than he can take, because he turns around and drags his hands through his hair again.

"Don't feel too bad, son. These roads are a mess," the tow truck driver says through his open window. Finn just nods. When the Porsche is out of the ditch and safely stored on the truck, Finn gives the address of the Singer-approved mechanic to the driver.

"I can give you guys a lift, but only as long as it's going back toward that repair shop in Flagstaff."

"That'd be great. Maybe there's a café or something nearby where we can hang while we figure out our next move." Finn seems relieved to have something to look at that isn't the scarred remains of the Singer—or me—and begins to navigate to the search app on his phone, looking for a Starbucks.

But we're in the middle of nowhere. And as I open my phone and look at the map, something dawns on me. Something that feels like a mix of dread and deep certainty. We're not *just* in the middle of nowhere. We're in the middle of a very specific nowhere. Just outside a town name I recognize from return address labels on birthday cards...

"Actually..." I hesitate. This is the last thing I want to offer up, but it's a logical solution to our problem. And more than that, it feels like fate. Maybe I'm just eager to prove Finn wrong about my supposed avoidance issues. Or maybe it's something more, like our talk last night broke open a wound that I can no longer avoid tending to. I remember Finn's words: *Parents have to love their kids. Kids get to choose if they love their parents.* And then I take a deep breath and tell him the truth: "I think my dad lives around here. We could wait it out at his place."

"You think?" Finn pauses and looks up at me.

I feel wobbly, and I'm not sure if it's from the injury just now or the choice inside my heart that seems to be making itself, whether I agree with it or not. "Let me call Liz and get his address." Because yeah, no, I don't actually know exactly where my dad's house is. I've never been to it in my life.

For starters, I haven't been invited.

Liz picks up on the third ring. "What's up, buttercup?" she asks brightly.

"I just got in a car wreck." I hate how small my voice sounds.

The playfulness in her voice disappears. "Oh my god, Em. Are you okay? What happened?" It's weird, hearing her concern—a total role reversal for us. It's almost always Liz calling *me* with some sort of disaster I need to walk her through.

"I'm fine. A tire blew, and I couldn't turn in to the skid like a normal car."

"Uh-huh." Liz knows and cares about cars as much as our mom does, which is to say, not at all.

"I'm also, kind of, maybe, near Dad."

There's an excited "Oh!" on the other end of the line, and then a heavy pause. "Wait. What are you doing in *Arizona*? Isn't Sybil getting married tomorrow?"

"Kind of. I don't know." I turn away from the road and look across the desert. "It's a long story."

"I bet. Hold on, let me check your location. I'm putting

you on speaker." There's another pause, as Liz navigates to her Find My Friends app. "You *are* very close to Dad," she confirms.

"Can you send me his address?"

"Sure, but you can always just call him to ask for it. Or maybe text. He's better with texting." While I've pretty much cut all contact with my dad, Liz keeps up with him semi-regularly. For her it's just as easy to have a relationship with Dad as it would be with any other adult who's vaguely in our orbit. Like Mom's coworkers we see at holiday parties, or our great-aunt Lilla, who always brings lemon squares to family reunions. She doesn't remember Dad as *Dad*. When he left, she was too young to have formed any memories of him as an actual parent. She doesn't remember the chili he used to make, or the way he'd let me sit on his lap to drive past the last few mailboxes leading up to our house, or his ridiculous attempts to braid hair. But I do. I have a bleeding space in the shape of a father, while Liz has an amorphous emptiness that expands and contracts. I don't think that it's necessarily easier for her, but I do think there are moments when she forgets that she even has a parent other than our mom. I never forget. I had a dad, who I loved more than anything, and he left. The idea of being cordial with him after how badly he hurt me seems impossible, so I just stay away. I'm not going to chase after my dad again. I've already, literally, been down that road before.

But now, I'm going to face him head-on. Finn says he thinks parents have no choice but to love their children, but he's clearly wrong. My dad made a choice, and it wasn't to love us unconditionally. And I deserve, at long last, to know why.

There's a ping, and a text from Liz comes through with the

address. When I pull it up in the map app, I'm shocked at how close we truly are. That feeling of fateful inevitability sweeps over me again.

Holding my phone out to the tow truck driver, I ask, "Can you take us here?"

He squints. "No problem, kids. Hop in the cab."

Finn and I cram in together with all our belongings, and I try not to let any part of my body touch his. I call my dad twice on the way there to let him know we're coming, but he doesn't pick up. My pulse starts to hammer in my neck as we get closer, every muscle in my body coiling and tense. It's a good thing I'm not the one driving now, because I'd probably be unable to stop myself from hitting the brakes and turning around. Anxiety crawls up my chest, into my throat.

The driver drops us off in front of a shabby house with a xeriscape front yard and a large collection of terra-cotta turtles arranged atop the crushed gray rock that covers most of the ground. There's a longhorn made of scrap metal tucked beside the front porch, but it's an old 3 Series BMW that convinces me we're in the right place.

I knock twice on the front door before a flash of navy catches my eye, and I freeze. Parked beside the Bimmer is my dad's old Wagoneer. The same car he drove away in nearly two decades ago.

23

FRIDAY AFTERNOON

(One day before the wedding)

THE DOOR SWINGS OPEN.

"Emma?" My dad manages a smile, but I'm still stuck in that moment. The moment twenty years ago when I watched the same truck pull out of our driveway and never come back. "Emmie Girl?"

I force myself back to the present, and to the man standing in front of me. It's the same dark auburn hair I see every time I look in the mirror, but his is streaked with gray. My father looks like a redheaded Matthew McConaughey, and he has the same gravelly South Texas twang. He puts his hand out in front of him, and I stare at it. Is he really trying to give me a handshake after not seeing me for half a decade? I look at his hand, then back to his face, and back to his hand. But while I'm deciding what to do, Finn reaches over my shoulder and shakes it, sparing all of us the awkwardness of a father trying to shake his daughter's hand instead of pulling her into a hug.

"Finn Hughes. Nice to meet you."

"Mike Townsend," my dad says, relieved. "Come on in." He steps out of the doorway to make room for us, but I can't pick up my feet to cross the threshold. The warmth from Finn's hand seeps through the thin cotton of my shirt, and it's enough of a steady presence that I'm able to take a deep breath and step inside.

"I almost didn't recognize you with that new haircut."

I've had this long bob since college.

"Wow." Dad just stares at me, perhaps trying to match the eight-year-old child he used to live with to this grown woman now standing in his doorway. "Well, this is quite a surprise."

For a moment, embarrassment washes over me. I haven't seen him since that football game at UT. Eight years ago. And even that was fleeting—unclear whether he'd really come to see me or the game.

"I tried to call," I say helplessly as I take in the house. It's sparse. There are a few posters of desert vistas along the walls in the living room and a framed Vince Young jersey, but no photographs. The furniture, all a cracked chocolate-brown leather, is pointed at a large television playing ESPN. I try to find anything that looks familiar, anything to indicate that there's at least some part of my dad's life with us that he wanted to remember. But there's nothing in the house that I recognize from my childhood. The homiest thing is the small woodburning oven in the corner that's currently cold. That's how I'd describe the whole place. *Cold.* My mom's house has art and photos on nearly every wall, and not a single piece of furniture matches. I feel a pang of nostalgia for the home I grew up in. Its cluttered chaos may have set my type A teeth on edge, but at least it was warm. Lived in. When I picture our cozy den, with its chunky throw blankets and stacks of magazines, I think, *Home*. Family. I survey Dad's nondescript living room again, thinking, *You left us for this?*

"Oh, was that you calling?" He moves into the kitchen. "I don't pick up numbers I don't recognize." His comment hits me in the gut. I swallow. "So what brings y'all to town? Can I get you something to drink?" But he's out of sight before we can answer either question.

"Oh, um, just a water would be great," I feebly toss out to him.

A cabinet slams shut, and there's the sound of the tap. He returns with water in a plastic cup, DALLAS COWBOYS SUPER BOWL CHAMPIONS 1996 emblazoned along the side. I try to place it in my memory. He must have had it when I was a kid before he left. Maybe I saw him drink out of it at some point, but the only plastic cups I remember are from Kuby's in Snider Plaza. My mom probably still has two dozen stashed away in her kitchen cabinet right now. I hadn't really thought about it until now, but I guess I've kind of divided my memories into "before" and "after." Things I associate with Dad, and therefore try to block out as much as possible, and things from my childhood after he left. Being here in the same space as him again feels like some kind of twisty time vortex, past and present, before and after, melding together in a way that makes my head ache.

Maybe coming here was a mistake. Just another example of my boneheaded stubbornness trying to prove a point. I should have just let the tow truck driver drop us off at some coffee shop where we could have arranged for a Lyft to the nearest airport. Go back to Malibu. Tell everyone the truth. Tap in the Rains, let them try to track their daughter down. After all, isn't that what parents are supposed to do? Take care of their children?

"So," Dad says, clapping his hands together. "I was just about to make a grilled cheese for some late lunch. Would y'all want one too?"

I'm about to refuse, when Finn says, "Sure."

I shoot him a look.

"I'm hungry," he mouths, but I just shake my head and follow my dad.

"You like mustard on yours, right, Emmie?" He lights up like he's remembered something about me.

"Um, no mustard. I'm a purist."

"Ah, okay."

"I'll take some mustard," Finn says.

"Good man." In a matter of minutes, our sandwiches are sizzling on the griddle. "So, what brings you two to the neighborhood?" he asks, as if our popping by is a casual occurrence.

"We were on our way to Albuquerque," I say vaguely. "And then we had a small car accident."

"Oh, man, Emmie Girl. I'm so sorry to hear that. What kind of car is it? I might be able to help with it." My dad slides the sandwiches onto three plates, and hands me my mustard-free one. The kitchen is tiny, so we carry our plates back out to the living room and sit on the brown leather furniture and eat with our plates in our laps.

"It's a Singer."

"A Porsche 911 reimagined by Singer. Technically," Finn clarifies.

My dad's eyebrows rise nearly to his hairline, and he lets out a whistle. "A man with a Singer, eh?" He gives me a playful punch on the shoulder. "Nice catch, Emmie Girl. You've gotta hold on to this one." Before I can correct him, he turns to Finn. "Those Porsches can be tough to drive." But he fixes Finn with a pitying look like anyone with half a brain could figure it out. "Should have let Emmie drive it. She's a natural."

I wait for Finn to clarify, to absolve himself of this insult to his driving abilities, but he just shrugs and continues to eat his grilled cheese. It's almost like he's covering for me, which makes my skin prickle. Why should he? I screwed up. I should take ownership of it. Finn's words from right before the crash come back to me. *Well, maybe your life would be a little better if you were a little more willing to make mistakes.*

"Actually, I was driving when we had the wreck."

"Oh." Dad's face drops the slightest bit. "Well...tough with those engines in the back, you know."

We sit in silence, chewing our grilled cheese sandwiches, and I'm struck by the surrealness of it all. It feels like some bizarre dream: Finn Hughes sitting across from my estranged father in Flagstaff, Arizona.

Finn points toward to my dad's commemorative UT cup. He seems to have a nearly endless supply. "Been a rough go for Cowboys and Longhorn fans."

"Don't I know it," Dad says, and takes a long drink.

"Most valuable franchises in their respective leagues but can't seem to turn it into a championship."

"You're telling me." He's animated with Finn in a way he isn't with me, as if sports is safer ground. "Did you go to Texas too?"

"No, I was in North Carolina."

"UNC?"

"Duke."

"Good basketball team." My dad takes another bite of his sandwich, and I want to scream. "More of a football guy myself."

"Me too."

It's the most banal conversation I've ever heard. My father hasn't seen me in eight years, and he'd rather talk to Finn about Duke basketball?

"Dad, I think I would like some mustard after all," I practically shout. "Could you grab me some?" The second he's up from the table, I lean over to Finn and hiss, "What are you doing?"

"Me?" Finn's eyebrows shoot upward.

I assume an exaggeratedly deep voice, mocking Finn's own. "Oh yeah, gotta love that Tar Heel basketball!"

"We are the Blue Devils," Finn corrects. "And I'm just trying to be polite to this asshole who abandoned you. You think I want to be making small talk with him? I'm just following your lead here."

I swallow a bite of grilled cheese, processing Finn's words. He's right. I am in the driver's seat here. This is one situation where I *should* be taking control. It's unfair for me to expect Finn to just intuitively know that watching him sit here and be friendly to my dad is killing me.

"I don't even know what to say to him," I sigh. "But I think

I need to try to connect with him about everything, you know? Not just chitchat."

"I think you're right." Finn nods.

When my dad reenters the room, I say, "We need to head out to the tow yard to see what the damage is on the car. Dad, would you be able to drive me over to take a look?" I glance at Finn, hoping he'll be okay with this plan for me and my dad to get some alone time.

"That'd be great," Finn says, wiping his hands on a paper towel. "I've got some work I need to catch up on. I can just hang here."

"Are you sure?" It's funny to think that after two days of trying to keep me out of the driver's seat, Finn is now going to let me be the one to take inventory of the damage.

"I trust you. Singer's going to get it on a flatbed back to California. I just want to make sure we've logged all the damage in case something happens during the shipment."

My dad gets in the BMW instead of the Wagoneer, and I breathe a sigh of relief. The drive to the mechanic is short. Dad flips through the radio channels, landing on a country station, and "Callin' Baton Rouge" fills the coupe. I try to figure out how to start a conversation, but we're pulling into the parking lot before I manage to find a way to break the silence.

The Porsche is front and center of the mechanic's shop. I take a few pictures of the major damage and a short video as I circle the car.

"It's really not that bad," my dad says, giving the roof a couple of loving taps. "Just a little bit of body damage." He circles to the other side of the car. "And obviously the tire." He squats down to inspect it further. "You and I could fix it right up, Emmie Girl." Warmth suffuses me, and I think back to all the times when I was a kid that I'd join him in the garage and watch him work on his Jeep.

"I don't know that I'm up to a Singer-level restoration," I say.

"You could be. I remember how nice that Bronco of yours ended up."

The Bronco had been my college car; I'd fixed it up all on my own. Dad had seen it when he came to visit that one time junior year. I remember him kicking the tires and nodding approvingly. He'd asked me all about the engine, the body, where I'd taken it for the paint job. But all I wanted was for him to ask me about my classes, my junior design project, my friends, my senior year plans, and what I hoped to do after graduation. He didn't seem to want to get into any of that. Cars were always the language that my father felt the most comfortable speaking, and as a kid, I'd always striven to gain my own fluency, proud that we had something in common. But as I got older, I realized that a shared love of sleek new rides and classic old engines wasn't enough to sustain an entire father-daughter relationship. That more than anything, a father-daughter relationship is just based on *being there*.

"I could have used your help fixing up the Bronco," I say to him now, trying to keep the edge out of my voice. "Could have used your help with a lot of things throughout the years, actually." My tone is still even, but I'm trying to get my dad to see how much his absence affected me. To finally have this conversation that we've put off for two decades.

"Nah, you didn't need your old man." Dad waves me off with his hand. "Your mom had things handled."

Yeah, well maybe she shouldn't have had to, I think. Rage blazes to life inside me. I've learned to bottle up my own hurt, but for him to pretend like he didn't royally screw Mom over is more than I can handle. Dad doesn't seem to notice the shift in my mood.

We confirm with the mechanic that Singer is sending a flatbed to pick up the car tomorrow morning. After that, there's really not much else for us to do.

We get back in the BMW, and I can't help giving some oxygen to the anger I have banked inside me. "Is Kimberly driving the Wagoneer these days? I didn't see another car."

"Who?" Dad asks. Then recognition hits him. He scratches behind his right ear. "I, uh, no. Kim ended up moving back to Dallas years ago. She's not really a desert girl. She never liked that I dragged her out here."

This update leaves me with a cold realization. For years, I'd had the specter of "Kimberly from marketing" to blame for dragging my dad away, but apparently I had it all wrong.

I pick through all the other ways my childhood could have turned out. My father could have been with Kimberly, but still in Dallas, still in my life. People leave marriages all the time without leaving their kids. Liz and I could have shared a room at his house. We could have switched off Thanksgiving and Christmas. Sure, it would have sucked. We would have wished our parents were still together, but I still would've had a dad. He could've been there when I broke my arm on Willow's trampoline, when I won state in debate, when I graduated from high school. My mom could have had a life outside of us. Maybe if she'd had a weekend free a month, she would've found someone. Instead, she spent twenty years of her life working or taking care of us with no downtime and no help. Thinking again about everything my mom went through obliterates any of the tactfulness I have left.

"So then why did you leave?" It's a straightforward question. I try to keep the anger out of my voice, but it creeps in.

"I always wanted to live out in the country. I couldn't breathe in the city." He's answering my question as if I asked why he relocated to Arizona, not why he abandoned his family. "Your mom would always brush me off when I said I wanted to move to the desert. We didn't quite see eye to eye on—well, on a lot of things."

He's almost fifty years old, and he's still making excuses.

Scraps of memory from the "before" half of my childhood begin to flood my mind. I remember lying in bed, listening to the sounds of an argument drifting up the stairs. Mom shouting, Dad not saying much. I can hear the pleading in Mom's voice—telling Dad they could work past this. That you didn't just walk out when things got hard. That you didn't do that to your children. Admiration at my mom's strength washes over me now. She was determined to try to make her marriage work even after my father cheated, but it wasn't enough. She couldn't force him to stay.

As I look out the window, we pass a playground filled with kids, their parents clumped beneath whatever shade they can find. I realize that my dad already had both me and Liz when he was my age. I can't imagine the responsibility of having a kid, much less two, but I know with every fiber of my being that I wouldn't leave them. Especially when someone was willing to forgive him for his infidelity. My mom was willing to look past a massive mistake. I can't fathom giving someone that amount of grace.

My voice is low with anger. "Mom wanted to work it out, and you still left. What the fuck is wrong with you?" It's a nuclear response, but I can't believe he was so self-centered.

"I was never a good husband—" Dad starts to give another excuse.

"You were a good *dad*!" The words leave my mouth in a hiss. "Your kids didn't just disappear when you crossed the state line. We were still there. We still needed a father. You abandoned us."

My tone finally seems to register with him, but he doesn't look over at me. I don't know what I expected from him. An apology? Some regrets? At the very least an acknowledgment of the pain he caused. But I'm getting none of those. He's sitting there, just as silent as he was back in our kitchen all those years ago when Mom was pleading with him.

His hands tighten on the steering wheel, and he keeps his eyes trained on the road. "It wasn't working out. So, I made the decision for us. I removed myself from the situation. It seems like y'all came out okay without me." He nods decisively as if the conversation is over. "I knew what was best for everyone."

A sick recognition twists in my stomach at his words. My anger shifts into something else. Shame. *I knew what was best for everyone.*

We sit in silence for the rest of the drive home.

When we pull into the driveway, my dad mutters something about needing to chop more wood for the stove if Finn and I are going to spend the night on the pullout, so I jump at the excuse to do something with myself. I can't stand sitting still in this discomfort for a second longer.

"I'll do it," I say, opening the door before he's even pulled to a stop and slamming it behind me. I have so much pent-up energy from my one-sided fight with Dad that I'm itching to burn through it all. Normally, I'd run until my brain turned off and the fatigue in my body broke down all my feelings into simple square blocks that I could compartmentalize somewhere in the back of my brain. But the only shoes I have are the stilettos I bought in Vegas and the flip-flops I'd slipped on to go to the spa.

"Great," Dad says. "Woodpile's around back. So's the ax."

In the scrubby little backyard, I can hear the faint sound of running water coming from the open bathroom window. Finn must be in the shower, and I'm grateful that at least I don't have to make any excuses to him too. I can't believe I thought this eleventh-hour plan to finally get closure with my dad—to break down the wall between us and have him actually *hear* me—would make me feel better. All I feel is sadness and anger and regret swirling around inside me. And worst of all is the realization that even with the miles of distance my dad forced between us, I still grew up just like him. Someone who thinks she knows better than everyone else. Someone who tries to control uncomfortable situations instead of letting herself feel. Who leaves before she can get left. Who ends up all alone.

I grab the ax and place the first log on the stump. Swinging the ax behind me, I stare at the wood…but what I see is the back of the Wagoneer. What I see is That Day.

The memory of my dad driving away.

We were all gathered outside the house, standing still as statues like it was some sort of ceremony. Dad had squeezed my shoulder like he was prepping me for a softball game, not a fatherless childhood. *Be good, Emmie Girl* was all he said.

I heave the ax behind me and smash it through the first piece of wood. *Thwack.* I swung so hard, the ax is embedded in the chopping block. My palm stings as I twist it free with a crack.

For years I've been angry that he couldn't even give me a hug goodbye. If he had, I would have clung onto him hard enough that he couldn't leave, but he twisted away from reach, nodding once toward my mom holding Liz on her hip. She didn't say anything. She didn't cry, but I could feel the anger coming off her in waves as he flung his duffel bag into the back seat of the Wagoneer, and I could sense this wasn't normal. I wanted to believe my dad was just leaving for a few days, like on one of the business trips he'd occasionally taken before. But there was something so sudden, yet so definite, in every movement. In the tone of their arguing earlier that day. In the stoic look on my mom's face. He waved to me one last time through the windshield and crunched out of the driveway to the end of our cul-de-sac.

Now, in Dad's backyard, the June sun is directly above the fence, beating into my face like it has a pulse. *Thwack.* The next log splits easily, but there's a twinge in my lower back. I ignore it and reach for the next log. The memories are harder to ignore.

In my mind's eye, I can see the Wagoneer pulling away. The stillness that had come over me That Day broke, and I bolted after the truck, waving my arms and screaming, "Dad!

Daddy! Daddy!" I heard my mom call for me, but I put on an extra burst of speed as the truck turned left, tearing down our little street toward the main road, where Dad's truck was almost out of sight. I would have kept running except that my flip-flop caught on the edge of a pothole and I slammed into the ground. My screams cut off as I sucked in air trying to regain the wind that had gotten knocked out of me.

Thwack. My breath now is getting shorter as I work up a sweat. It beads at my brow and drips into my eyes. The skin on my hands burns as I wipe away the liquid. They're raw from the rough handle of the ax. I put another log on the chopping block.

After I fell, my mom was beside me in an instant, Liz still clinging to her side. She wrapped us both in a hug. "It's going to be okay, girls. We've got each other."

There's a familiar ringing in my ears, but I push past it. *Thwack.*

Liz, only a toddler, also sensed that something was wrong, and she started crying. My breath was returning to normal, and all I wanted to do was go back to screaming for my dad. But Liz's cries ratcheted up even further, and I realized that only one of us could cry. One of us needed to find the pacifier and keep Liz calm while Mom cooked dinner. One of us needed to be strong. Good. Quiet. I stuffed down my scream and let my mother lead me back to the porch.

Thwack.

"Let's go inside, baby."

"No, I'm going to wait for Daddy to come back." It made no sense; he'd packed a bag. He wasn't coming back, certainly not right away. But I was stuck on this irrational hope that he'd simply forgotten we had plans. He'd remember, and turn around. "We're supposed to go to a movie," I explained to her. We'd been past the theater together and spontaneously got the tickets for the new Disney movie. For That Day at 5:00 p.m. I pulled the ticket out of my pocket. I had told a friend we were going to see it.

Thwack.

I pulled my little scraped-up knees into my chest and rested my chin between them. My eyes never left the end of our block. My mom hadn't cried when my dad drove away, but now she let out a small sob.

She bent down to my level. "Baby, he's not going to make the movie."

Thwack. The ringing in my ears is louder now, and blood rushes to my face, pulsing along with the heat of the sun, as my vision shrinks.

"He will."

"I'd go with you, but someone's got to watch Liz."

Thwack.

"I'm going with *him*!" I shouted. Maybe the louder I said it, the more power I'd have to make it true.

She sat beside me for almost half an hour, but Liz began to fuss again.

"Baby, I need to go inside to change Lizzie's diaper. Do you want to come in with me?"

I shook my head no. It took everything in my eight-year-old body not to throw myself on the lawn, kicking and screaming.

"He's coming back," I insisted.

Except he didn't. He could have loved and been loved, but he was so determined he knew what was best for everyone that he ended up completely alone.

Thwack.

Thwack.

Thwack.

The ax misses the log and skids off the stump. I release it and jump back to keep it from hitting my shins. My eyes are blurry with tears and sweat. I drop the ax, my breath ragged, and sink to the ground, pulling my knees to my chest, assuming the same posture I'd taken as a little girl on That Day. It's like the truth has only hit me now, nearly twenty years too late: *He's not coming back.*

Suddenly, there's a hand on my shoulder. Finn. It's as if he's materialized from thin air—I didn't even hear him come outside. I couldn't hear anything over the din of my memories. My ears are still ringing.

His fingers brush away a lock of hair that's fallen loose. "It's okay, Em. I'm here." But the wave of anxiety doesn't ebb. It keeps rising higher and higher. Finn pulls my face into his hands. "Emma"—his voice is calm, but firm—"we're going to do three things, okay?"

I nod.

"What are three things you can see?"

I take a gulp of air. Finn's face is a lifeline right now. I don't want to look away. "Um, your eyes," I say shakily. "A green ceramic frog." I drag my gaze back to him. "Your eyes."

He waits a beat for me to continue. "Okay, I'll give you 'your eyes' twice since I do have two. Now three things you can hear." His hands drop from my cheek to my shoulders.

"I can hear a dog barking, traffic, and a flag flapping."

"Good job. And, finally, three things you can touch."

"The ground." I press my fingers to the rough concrete

beneath me. "Wood." My hand grazes the handle of the ax lying harmlessly beside me. I still feel deflated, but thanks to Finn, I'm more in control. I muster a watery smile and tap his nose. "Pretty." He quirks a smile back at me, and I know he remembers that night by the pool. The night of our first kiss.

I lean toward him, and he pulls me into a hug. Resting my cheek on his shoulder, I take a deep breath in. His skin is warm and damp from the shower. He smells more like Irish Spring than lavender and woodsmoke, but beneath the smell of soap, he still smells like Finn.

"I'm so sorry, Emma," Finn says, his arms tightening around me. "I can't imagine how hard it is, being here with your dad after all this time. Do you want to leave? I can book us some hotel rooms."

"No, we can stay. I feel better now."

"Do you want to talk about it?"

"Not right now." Right now, I just want to stay right where I am, my head tucked beneath his chin with my ear pressed to his heart. Where everything I can see and hear and touch is Finn.

24

EARLY SATURDAY MORNING

(Wedding day)

"EMMA, WE'VE GOTTA GET up."

I wake up to the smell of clean laundry and coffee. It's still dark out, but Finn is dressed and ready for the day. Last night I ate pizza in a daze, totally drained from the confrontation with my dad and the anxiety attack I'd had afterward. After we ate—and I showered off the sweat and grime from chopping wood—Finn and I decided to wait until the morning to get back on the road. I think Finn could tell that I was still fragile and not up for an airport scramble back to LA just yet. He herded me to bed, tucking me in on the pullout sofa. In the middle of the night, I woke briefly to see Finn sprawled across my dad's recliner, his jacket tucked around him like a blanket, the soft glow from some old black-and-white sitcom dancing across his face.

He's much too chipper for someone who hasn't slept in a bed since Wednesday. "Too early," I mumble, pulling an orange fleece blanket back up over my head.

"Come on," he says, nudging my foot under the blanket. "Rise and shine."

"I can't rise when there's no shine," I say, pointing to the dark window. But I get up anyway and stretch my arms over my head. Then I notice a small pile of clothes—freshly clean and neatly folded. "Did you wash these?" Something trembles to life in my chest. No one has done my laundry for me in nearly two decades. As soon as I was old enough to take over that chore from my mom, I did. I think back to my wish at the fountain in Vegas. *I just want someone to take care of me the way I take care of everyone else.*

"I found my way to an express cycle." Finn shrugs. "I figured your dad wouldn't mind." He pulls the fleece blanket from the bed and starts casually folding it like the gesture doesn't mean anything. I swallow down the lump that has formed in my throat. Everything still feels raw, and I know I've only just begun to process the tangled web of emotions seeing Dad again has brought to the surface. But as I watch Finn carefully line up the blanket's edges, I realize maybe I don't have to do it alone.

"Do you think your dad has enough UT gear?" Finn moves on to the fitted sheet and pops it free of the thin mattress. "Maybe he'll let you borrow some. Freshen up your design aesthetic a bit."

He's looking at me expectantly, so I blink past my epiphany

and muster a reply, "Yeah, the man is a fanatic. You know, the last time I saw him before today was at a college football game. Honestly, I think at least fifty percent of why he even bothered to come was the chance to walk around his old alma mater." Finn offers me a soft, sad smile. "I mean, I enjoyed my time in college as much as the next person, but I'd like to think I have more to look forward to in life." A pang of sadness strikes through me, as I look around Dad's living room, these UT details the only personality in sight. Maybe college *was* as good as it got for my dad. Is there anything sadder than holding on to a piece of your past instead of living your life in the present? I wince as an image of the worn movie ticket I keep tucked in my wallet flashes through my mind.

"Come on." Finn jingles a set of keys in front of me. "I think there's somewhere we should go. Meet me in the kitchen when you're ready."

I pull on my clean clothes—all signs of coffee spillage now gone from my tank and sports bra—and find some mouthwash in the medicine cabinet for a quick swish, then head into the kitchen, where my dad's drinking coffee out of a UT mug. Finn hands me a Styrofoam cup with black coffee.

"I've got to head into work early, but it was nice seeing y'all," Dad says. "Come back anytime. And just drop the Wagoneer keys off in the mailbox whenever you make it back."

"You're letting us take the Jeep?" I ask.

Dad walks with us to the front porch. "Of course. And I've got your number saved in my phone now, so I'll text you to make sure the Porsche gets taken care of."

"I…Thanks, Dad." Part of me is tempted to bring up our conversation from yesterday. I start flipping through the different points I could bring up, the arguments I could make, but I stop myself. I don't want to hold on so tightly to the things that hurt me anymore. I don't want to be stuck in the past. So instead of launching into a heated debate, I just say, "And you know, you can text me other times too. Like you do with Liz. It'd be nice to know what you were up to."

He nods once and reaches out to pat my shoulder, then pulls me into a hug. I return his hug, a couple of tears leaking out as I do, and then, after a few seconds, I let him go.

"Y'all drive safe."

"Yessir." Finn shakes my dad's hand again and climbs into the Wagoneer. It rumbles to life. I take a deep breath and climb into the truck. The last time I was in it, my feet didn't reach the floorboard. And it occurs to me that my dad *did* keep something from his time with us. He kept this truck. The truck we spent hours and hours working on.

Finn looks over at me and smiles. "You're okay if I drive?"

"I'm okay if you drive." I smile back. "Besides, I don't know our mystery destination."

We're both quiet as Finn takes us further and further away from the city. The sky lightens from navy to a French blue, but the sun still hasn't risen. I expect us to turn in toward the airport, but we keep heading north. I'm itching to know where we're headed, but I try to just relax into the unknown, closing my eyes and just letting myself feel the rumble of the Wagoneer.

After a few moments, I'm the one to break the easy silence. "I fought with my dad yesterday. Or more like, I yelled and he just sat there."

Finn raises his eyebrows. "I thought there might have been

something to set you off." He looks over at me. "Did it make you feel better?"

"A little bit. He was just so selfish when he left us, and all I wanted was for him to admit to it. To admit that he screwed us over. To admit that he hurt me. To admit to anything. I don't know what I wanted. Maybe for him to say he was as miserable without us as we were without him."

Finn shoots me a look as he pulls onto an exit ramp.

"What?" I ask.

"I mean, did you see the man's house?" Finn asks. "Does he really need to tell you he's miserable?"

"I guess you're right."

"And I knew you as a kid. You weren't miserable. You were fearless. You sparkled."

"I sparkled?" I can't help the smile that comes to my lips. "Sybil's the one that sparkles. I'm just the one trying to point her in a safe direction."

"Maybe." Finn smiles back at me. "It's always been hard for me to see anyone else when you're around." My heart rate speeds up, and I'm about to ask him what he means, but he continues. "All you could do is tell him where you stand and what your feelings are. At least then you know that you've done everything you could. After that, it's up to him to make the next move."

"My dad?"

Finn furrows his brows at me. "Yeah, who else?"

"Right." I survey the road for clues about where we're headed, but can't come up with anything. "Where are we going?"

"You'll see." I'm tempted to pull up my phone and track us, but I decide to trust Finn.

Half an hour later, we pass a large sign. "Are we going to the Grand Canyon?"

Finn grins over at me. "We were so close," he says. "Seemed like a waste not to."

Finn flashes his national parks pass, because of course he has one, and the park ranger waves us through. It's early enough that the grounds are still quiet. We're all alone as we walk toward the edge of the canyon. The sun peeks over the horizon, and the first rays of dawn cut across walls carved by the Colorado River. Reds and oranges glow all around us, and the canyon seems fathomless, stretching out in all directions.

It feels like the perfect place to make peace. To accept that the version of Dad I thought I might have doesn't—and will never—exist. I pull the movie ticket from my wallet. The once slick paper has gone soft with age, and half is clouded light pink from when my blush compact broke apart in my purse in eighth grade.

"He was supposed to take me to a movie the day he left," I explain to Finn. "I don't know why I've even held on to it. But I'm done holding on to the dream of what kind of father I was supposed to have. I just feel like I've been holding on to this awful day for the last twenty years. I wanted to just scream after his truck until my lungs gave out, but I couldn't. I had to keep it together for Mom and Liz, you know? Like if I just keep moving, keep working, keep achieving, then maybe I can outrun what happened."

Finn doesn't say anything, he just pulls me into a hug. I let myself lean into him for a few moments. Then I pull away, but I grab his hand. The ticket snaps once in the wind, slipping from my fingers. I let it go. It sails upward for a moment and hangs above us briefly before it's whipped away into the canyon and out of sight.

I exhale, feeling lighter than I have since I was a kid.

And then, I don't know what comes over me, but I let out a giant scream into the abyss. I pour out everything I've kept inside since the day my dad left, every secret pain that I've held on to, releasing it all in an act of catharsis that makes my throat raw. And I feel a power coming over me as Finn, at my side, lets out an equally wild scream. More of a howl. I can hear in it, in both our voices, the hurt of things that happened outside of our control. I know, without having to ask, that the loss of his own father is a big part of that hurt. Our shouting is so loud and so long that it startles a giant bird into flight. The bird swoops above us once, twice.

We stand silently as it continues on its way, heaving for breath, our hands entwined. As the bird flies off, I think, *This is goodbye*. Except what I feel is not the feeling of goodbye at all. The bird isn't leaving, I realize—it's *flying*. And what I feel is not sadness, not anymore. What I feel is hope.

After a moment, Finn gently tugs my hand, leading me toward a hiking path marked the Trail of Time.

"Emma, I wanted to tell you something." His voice is serious, and my heart instantly begins to shield itself, bracing for some terrible truth that's going to ruin everything, but I push down my defenses. I need to be better at trusting Finn. He's not that teenage guy who left me standing with a corsage all those years ago. The Finn Hughes I know today is the guy who rubs my back and grounds me through an anxiety attack. The guy who supports me with his friendship even after I've shut him down romantically. The guy who saves me from falling off a kayak. Who encourages me to chase my dreams and believes in my talent. Who opens up to me about the darker moments of his past over candlelit dinners and tells me I look beautiful. He's changed, and so have I. And when people show you who they are, you should believe them.

"I know you're upset about my not telling you the whole story about Sybil." He stops to lean against the informational placards that line the path. "On that voicemail yesterday, I was talking about something that happened that day—the day I stood you up for prom. And if it was up to me, I'd tell you all about it. But it's Sybil's story to share. I just can't break her confidence. She's trusted me to keep her secret all these years, and I can't betray her. It's important to me that when someone trusts me with something personal and true, I stick to my word and protect that."

I take both of his hands in my own. "I understand. Thank you for telling me. I'm glad that Sybil had you when I wasn't there for her."

"I don't think it's that you weren't there for her. I think sometimes we just need different people at different times in our life." He pushes off the sign, and we keep walking.

I almost want to laugh. All this time I've been telling myself Finn isn't trustworthy. A big part of that started on prom night, when he stood me up and didn't explain why. And yet, what if that night was proof he is the most trustworthy person I know? I just didn't have the full story. And I hadn't asked.

"There's one more thing." Finn has stuffed his hands into his pockets, and he looks nervous. "I've been talking to my real estate agent, Christine—"

"Christine is your *real estate agent*?"

"Yeah, Christine Gilchrist. She's a friend of my parents."

"So you weren't setting up a date?" I hope that the teasing tone of my voice masks my relief.

"I don't think Christine would have me. She's been happily married for four decades to my dad's best friend. They were like a second set of parents to me after Dad died. Anyway, she's working on the paperwork for my mom to sell the house. To me."

I gasp. "Are you serious?"

Finn nods. "I'd been thinking about it ever since my mom said she wanted to move. It's such a great house, and I'd been looking at coming back to Dallas anyway. Plus, with the sale of my company, I could afford to make her a good offer."

"So the Dilbeck won't get torn down?" I ask breathlessly.

"It will not get torn down."

I squeal and throw my arms around him. "Oh my god, Finn. That's such great news." I release him reluctantly. "What made you finally decide to buy it?"

He shrugs. "You asked me to." Like it was as simple as that. Like all I ever had to do was ask, and I could have everything I ever wanted.

ON OUR WAY BACK to the car, the shops are just opening, and I duck inside to grab a postcard. Maybe I'll send it to my dad when I'm back in New York. Little things to reopen the lines of communication. I can't control who my dad is, but I can control my own actions. And who knows. Maybe, if I give him a chance, I'll see that my dad has changed too. Or, rather, that maybe I've let myself grow blind to the good parts of him that were always there, unable to see past the one mistake he made that hurt me so badly. After all, he opened his home to me when I really needed it, even though I hadn't reached out to him in years. He let us take his beloved Wagoneer, no questions asked.

Just like with Finn, I can forgive him for the past without letting it define our future.

Finn is waiting for me when I get back to the car. "I got something for you." He places a white quartz figurine in my palm. It's the shape of a bear, and I can't stop the laugh that escapes from me.

"I'll treasure it forever," I say sarcastically.

Finn grins at me, then says in a softer voice, "The woman who sold it to me says it symbolizes protection and healing." I curl my fingers around the carved stone and bring it to my heart.

Healing. I could use some of that. So I say again, this time more earnestly, "I'll treasure it forever."

"I don't know..." Finn says skeptically. "This coming from the girl who just let a supposedly beloved memento go flying straight into the Grand Canyon."

"Hey!" I smack his arm with a grin. "That was an accident!"

Finn's about to retort, when suddenly my phone buzzes in my back pocket, interrupting us. "Oh my god," I say, looking at the screen. "It's Sybil."

25

SATURDAY MORNING

(Wedding day)

"Sybil! Are you okay?"

"Ma'am?" A man's voice comes through the speaker.

"Who is this? Where's Sybil?" I can't keep the panic out of my voice. Finn's arm is around me in an instant, and I put the call on speaker so he can hear.

"Ma'am. Calm down. I'm Rick. I'm just a Lyft driver. This number was the emergency contact." I'd forced Sybil to add me to her phone's emergency settings when we'd moved to New York in case something happened to her, and it seems like she never changed it.

"Is she okay? Please, let me talk to her."

"I don't know, ma'am. I just found this phone in my back

seat. She must have left it charging back there. I recognize the photo on her home screen. I picked her up from the airport Thursday afternoon."

"The airport? What airport?"

"Harry Reid," he says. "Las Vegas. I dropped her off at Caesars Palace around, oh, I don't know, three p.m.?"

I think of us tracking Sybil's phone, it pinging back and forth all down the Strip. It wasn't Sybil herself, it was just her phone in the back of the car. But wait—how did her tracker start traveling toward Albuquerque? Rick the Lyft driver has an answer for that too.

"I did a bunch of Vegas rides on Thursday night, and then I had to go check on my mom's cats while she's traveling. She lives out in Santa Fe. I'm actually headed back to Vegas now to do some more runs. If you want your friend's phone back, maybe we could meet up."

My heart is pounding. The prospect of Sybil going out to Albuquerque to meet up with her problem ex-boyfriend Liam was worrisome enough, but now I realize we have *no* idea where she is. She could be hurt or in danger. Finn senses that I'm starting to spiral and places a calming hand over mine. "If we get her phone, we can see if there's any clues on there. Maybe we can find out why she was going to Vegas, or who she might have been meeting up with."

I nod. "Are you anywhere near Flagstaff?" I ask Rick. "Can you meet us? I'll text you an address."

"Sure, give me an hour or so."

There's a Toyota Corolla idling in front of my dad's house when we get there. A Latino man in his fifties in a red Diamondbacks hat steps out of the car.

"Hey, you're on the home screen too!" He hands me the phone without hesitation.

I look down at the phone in my hands, and the four of us stare up at me: Willow, Nikki, Sybil, and me at golden hour with the Pacific Ocean in the background from three days ago in Malibu. It's a photo we took moments before I went on my tequila shot crusade, and I realize that she must have set it as her phone background that night.

"I can't thank you enough for this," I say as Finn comes up beside me.

"No problem. I know my daughter would lose her mind if she lost her phone. You girls are about her age."

I'm about to pump the Lyft driver for more information, anything he can remember about his brief interaction with Sybil, when I get a text from Nikki:

Sybil is on her way here.

I immediately call Nikki, but it goes straight to voicemail. So, I resort to what I do best: hammer until I strike a nail.

Nik

Nik

Nikki

NICOLE MARIE

Finally, a response comes through.

I can't talk right now. Shit is going down. But Sybil is safe. Just get back to Malibu ASAP!!!

I turn to Finn. "Nikki says Sybil's back. We need to get to LA right now. Rick, can you take us to the airport?" I'm already pulling the back door of his Corolla open.

"Sure thing. Hop in." Finn throws our bags in the back of the car, and Rick floors it to the Flagstaff airport.

Finn books our flights on his phone, and I don't even let myself think what the last-minute fares must be costing him, while I keep calling Nikki until she picks up. "Sweet Jesus, Emma, I was going to call you as soon as I was free!"

"What is going on? Tell me everything. Is the wedding still happening?"

"There's nothing to tell right now. I don't know if the wedding is going to happen. All I know is Sybil called and told her parents that she was on her way back. Mrs. Rain just came by to tell us. Do you think you'll make it back in time?"

"Yes," I say firmly. Given all the travel snafus I've experienced over the past two days, I shouldn't be so confident, but there's no way I'd miss Sybil walking down the aisle. "I'll be there."

The flight back to LA is a whirlwind—but I'm amazed that there is not even a flutter of anxiety in my chest. No need for the 3-3-3 technique. I guess the chaos and catharsis of the past few days have been enough to drain my body of nervous energy for the time being. And having Finn sitting beside me, holding my hand during takeoff, doesn't hurt either. Before the plane begins its final descent, I spend several minutes in the tiny lavatory, putting my Vegas makeup to use and trying to get all my hair to go in mostly the same direction. After we land, we spend another hour in traffic to get to Malibu. That's when the nerves set in. What will I be walking into? Is Sybil really okay? Where has she been the last two days? I'm practically vibrating as we pull up to the resort. Finn grabs my hand and pulls me to him, dropping a soft kiss on my cheek. "It's going to be okay," he says. I let out a deep breath, and I believe him.

"You're right." We head to our separate rooms.

Willow waves me down as I'm scanning my key card in front of my door. She's already wearing her champagne silk bridesmaid's dress. "How's Sybil?" I ask.

She ignores my question. "Did Finn Hughes just kiss you?"

"Maybe."

She looks at me expectantly, waiting for me to elaborate, one hand on her hip, the other on her pregnant belly, her lips a perfect French red. She really is stunning. "Listen, Wills, I'm sorry I always nag you about the cigarette thing. I know you're an adult, and you can make your own decisions about your body."

Narrowing her eyes at me, she asks, "What the hell happened on that road trip, Em?"

I don't know how to sum up everything that's happened in the last few days with my dad, with Finn, with me, so I just throw my hands up and offer her a watery smile.

"Oh, sweetie." She tries to pull me into a hug, but mostly I end up bent over her stomach with my face resting in her cleavage while she rubs small circles on my back.

"Willow." My voice is muffled. "I can't breathe through your boobs."

She releases me with a laugh. "Another benefit of pregnancy: giant boobs. Put that in the pro column. Though, the fact that they're always sore is definitely one for the con column." A sharp movement ripples the satin of Willow's gown, and she cradles her belly.

"Did the baby—"

"Just kick?" Willow's smile widens. "They must want to say hi to their aunt Emma." I loop my arm through Willow's, and the DO NOT DISTURB sign swings as I open the door to a room that is exactly as I left it. "You can nag me about cigarettes as much as you want," Willow adds, settling onto the little couch in the cottage's living room as I race to my suitcase to slip out of my shorts, tank, and sports bra, shimmying into a strapless bra instead. "I know you only harp on it because you're worried about me. Besides, I've been reading a lot about it, and I think I might be more of a psilocybin woman these days."

Reaching for my shoes, I try to make sense of Willow's words. "Psilocybin...like...shrooms?" I pause, one high heel shoe dangling from my fingers. It takes everything in me, but I force the words out. "If...that's what...makes you happy."

"I'm just messing with you, Em." Willow cackles from the couch. "The hardest thing I'll be on for the foreseeable future is acetaminophen." I giggle as I throw on my own champagne bridesmaid's dress and rejoin Willow in the living room. She studies my face and gently smooths down a bit of haltered neckline. "Wow. Finn Hughes really did a number on you. I like it."

A soft smile comes to my lips. "I like it too." More than that. *I love it.* My breath hitches, and I realize I have to talk to Finn. But first, I need to see Sybil. On impulse, I pull open the closet, and Sybil's wedding gown is gone. Sighing in relief, I throw my heels on, and Willow and I book it out of the cottage.

It's a perfect Southern California afternoon. The sun is shining golden, and a breeze is blowing sea air up into the mountains. It's only been a few moments that I've been away from Finn, but I already miss him so much I imagine the faint scent of woodsmoke and lavender. Except, I'm not actually imagining it. Because as I turn down the path toward Nikki's cabin, I spot Finn just a few yards ahead of me. He's managed to put on his tux, and I'm struck all over again by how handsome he is. "Stop, Emma. I just need one minute."

"Oh no. Is Sybil gone again?"

"No, this isn't about Sybil. You look beautiful, by the way."

Willow gives me a wink and keeps waddling toward Nikki's room.

Finn takes my hand and pulls me closer to him. "I wanted to talk to you. I know you might have a few regrets about how—"

Before he can continue, I put my fingers to his lips. Because the truth is, I don't regret what happened with Finn two nights ago in the hammock (and on the hood of his car the next morning). I don't regret what happened on my rooftop years back. Or really, any single moment between us—I've only ever wanted *more* of them. My only regrets are the things I didn't say, mistakes I didn't let myself make. I know now that all my bitterness and frustration with Finn over the years was compounded by other wounds—ones I'm only now realizing need healing. It wasn't about prom, or a kiss in the pool, or a rooftop hookup, or an ex-girlfriend rearing her gorgeous head. It was about Finn and me—wanting to trust each other, but not fully trusting ourselves enough to go there.

I can finally admit to myself that I love him. I've loved him for a long time, and even if he doesn't love me back, I owe it to Finn to give him all the facts so he can make his own decision. I take a deep breath and look up at him, feeling the old nervous energy overtake me. I look up into Finn's whiskey-brown eyes and pull my fingers from his lips, slipping my hands into his. "So, there's something I need to tell you too."

Finn smiles back at me. "Okay, shoot."

Where to start? Maybe if I think of it in debate terms…"I know you've been up-front about not wanting to be in a relationship," I say tentatively, like an opening statement, "but I would put forth the argument that maybe you should reconsider. Being in a relationship, that is. And furthermore, I think it should be with me."

Finn's smile grows. But my heart is suspended in the air, and I don't know if it's going to take flight or smash to the ground.

"Hmm," he says, "do you have any evidentiary support for this argument?"

"We get along, mostly. You can keep up with my quips—not an easy feat, by the way. You're not horribly unattractive, and I, of course, am gorgeous," I rattle off, ignoring Finn's eye roll. "Plus, we have pretty amazing sex. I wasn't lying about your prowess," I add, and Finn barks out a laugh that can only be described as giddy. "And there's the fact that I haven't been able to shake you for the better part of a decade, so I might as well accept that you're going to be a permanent fixture in my life, Finn Hughes."

"So you're resigning yourself to me, after all this time?" Finn says. I can't tell if the joke is another way of just playing along with me, or if there's hurt there, or something more.

"Well, yeah, but there's one last point I need to make," I say, putting on my serious, about-to-crush-a-debate face.

"I'm ready for it."

"Are you?" I tease.

He looks at me. "I'm ready," he says. And in that moment, I hear my cue. He's ready. He's ready for whatever is next. And so am I.

"My closing argument is that, when all is said and done..." The sun shines over the sea, ringing Finn's head in light, and I have to squint as I say it, my eyes tearing from the brightness. "I love you."

For a second, I feel as if I've stepped backward off the Santa Monica Mountains, that I'm free-falling into the Pacific. And then Finn's voice brings me back to the present with a soft laugh. "Damn" is all he says.

"'Damn'? I say I love you and you say '*damn*'?!" I smack him on the chest, and he laughs.

"I'm just…processing," he says.

"Processing? What do you need to process?"

"Well…" He looks down. "It's been a helluva long weekend, and we're both tired and—"

"Are you saying you don't believe me?"

He looks back up, straight into my eyes. "I want to believe you, Emma. More than anything. I'm just…scared."

At this, I burst into laughter. "Well, Finn, that makes two of us."

"Yeah, I guess it does," he whispers. His half grin sends sparks through me, and then he's leaning down toward me, and his lips open against mine, and I'm flying.

After a few minutes, Finn pulls back slightly, but I keep my hand on his cheek. "Are you sure? Because I…" *Ask him, Emma. Just ask him.* "I need to know how you feel. I need to know what you really want." I need more, deserve more, than a simple *I guess*.

"Emma, you have to know that I've wanted to be with you since I was sixteen."

"What?" I say dumbly.

He blushes and turns to kiss the palm of my hand. I can't help smiling when he says, "I'd get drunk with Sybil and tell her how you were out of my league."

"Sybil *knew*? Wait, what would she say? I can't believe she didn't tell me." My hand moves from Finn's cheek to his neck. I can't stop touching him.

"She mostly agreed that as long as I didn't have the balls to tell you how I felt, then you *were* out of my league. She did yell at me about showing up to Vail with Pilar."

"Good." I laugh and run a hand under both of my eyes again.

He smiles at me. "I'm sorry. I was an ass. I couldn't believe you'd broken up with that guy for me. Or that you would care enough to make it work long distance. And I panicked and got back with Pilar because that felt safe. There was always going to be an escape route with her. I knew it wasn't going to be anything permanent, so it lessened the pressure."

Keeping everything close to the vest hasn't worked so far, so I take the last step. Looking up into Finn's warm brown eyes, I say, "Look, if you're not in a relationship place right now, I respect that. I'd rather just know the truth up-front. I don't want us to keep hurting each other with misunderstandings."

"Emma," Finn says, tucking hair behind my ear, "when I said the other day that I wasn't looking for a relationship, I did mean it—or I thought I did. It just seemed easier, you know? If you have no commitments, you have no one to disappoint." There's uncertainty written all over his face, so I reach out and squeeze his hand. "But for the past three days, I've been trying to make sense of *this*. Seeing you again. All the old feelings that came right back up, as if they'd never gone anywhere." I nod, knowing exactly what he means. "I knew I screwed things up between us last time," Finn continues. "That I'd be crazy to think I deserved another chance with you, no matter how much I might want one..." Then, after a pause, Finn looks back at me, the slightest hint of a smirk forming on his lips. "You made that pretty clear the first night. What was it you said? 'Absolutely not my type. Never has been, never will be'?"

"That may have been *slightly* hyperbolic," I admit with a cringe.

Finn gives me a soft smile. "Well, it sounded pretty fair to me, considering."

My heart clenches. Finn did hurt me with the way he handled the Pilar situation, but I know now it was just a mistake, born out of the same insecurities that had me keeping Finn at arm's length. I hate that he's spent years thinking I was some unattainable figure on a pedestal that he wasn't worthy of pursuing. Because the truth is, Finn is more than deserving of being with whoever he wants. And not just because he's successful, smart, and frickin' gorgeous, but because he has one of the strongest moral codes of anyone I know—he always has; I just couldn't see it at the time. Looking back now, it's so obvious. He's kept Sybil's secrets for nearly a decade. He stopped us from going too far the night on the rooftop when I was still with Preston. And he's never promised me more than he knew he could deliver. I want to tell him all this, to make sure he knows he's a good man, to—

"But the thing is"—Finn interrupts my racing thoughts, his mouth curling into grin again—"I always did like a challenge." I pull my hand from his to give him a playful smack on the arm, but then he recaptures my hand and presses it to his heart. "And proving myself worthy of your love sounds like the best challenge yet." My heart swells at that; I can practically feel it threatening to burst through my rib cage.

"You don't have to prove a damn thing." I barely get the

words out before his lips crash to mine. They stay there for several moments until I pull back for air. "But seriously," I say as the ocean breeze ruffles the skirt of my bridesmaid's dress, "I know it will be hard, but I care enough to try to make this work."

"I do too."

Now I'm the one who's giddy. "Wait, really? Really, really?"

Finn laughs. "Yeah, really, Emma. I guess what I'm trying to say is, I love you too."

And those words take my breath away.

But only for a minute. "Took you long enough," I say, smiling so hard it hurts my face.

"Only eleven and a half years," he says. And then we're kissing again, and I let myself finally melt into the moment, into him, into the inevitability of it all. The inevitability of *us*.

"What are we going to do about the continent in between us?" I ask.

"I'll move to New York. Or you'll move to California. Or we'll both move back to Texas or Paris or Morocco. Whatever you want to do. I'm a free agent these days. But if you're going to design that house for me, I'll need you to be nearby. In case I have an emergency question about drapes or tiles."

"We certainly can't allow for any tile emergencies. I think I can manage to make myself available to you."

He presses his lips to mine. It's a kiss that feels like a beginning.

26

SATURDAY AFTERNOON

(Wedding day)

I HALF EXPECT HER not to be there when I open the door to Nikki's room.

But there she is, in all her white-gown glory.

"Sybil!" I wrap her in a hug so tight she lets out a small squeak. "Are you okay?"

"I'm okay, Mama Bear," she wheezes out, patting me on the back. "You can release me. I'm not going anywhere."

Those words. *I'm not going anywhere.* They hit me right in the chest. Because until now, I think I really believed that the reason I was so determined to find Sybil was so she could marry Jamie and have her happily ever after with him. Because that was what was *supposed* to happen. Because I was in charge of helping make sure that's what happens. Only now, the obvious truth makes it hard for me not to let tears burst down over my freshly made-up face. It was never about Sybil and Jamie. It was always about Sybil and me.

And now, I know exactly what to say in my maid of honor speech. It's a love note to the friend who has always come back, who has never left me, not really. Who has, even in her wildest or flightiest moments, shown what loyalty really is.

"I'm so glad to hear that. I love you, babe," I tell her, willing myself not to cry. I pull back to give her a once-over. Her hair is in a messy braid, and there are dark circles under her eyes peeking through her fabulous makeup job, but she seems at peace. The crackling current that had radiated off her during our failed bachelorette party has been replaced by smooth calm. Nikki and Willow, meanwhile, both look how I feel—exhausted but buoyed by adrenaline.

"Oh, and maybe you want your phone back, too, Sybs," I add, handing it to her.

"Thanks." Sybil takes the phone and tucks it into a small beaded bag on the vanity, then crosses the room and perches beside Willow on the bed. "I can't believe I left it in the back of the car. God, I'm such an airhead."

"You might have one or two missed calls from us," I say, coming to join the two of them.

"Or, like, six dozen," Nikki adds.

This gets a watery chuckle from Sybil. "I'm so sorry I scared you all, going off the grid like that. I just...I needed to figure some things out on my own."

"And...have you?" Willow asks tentatively.

Sybil gives a nod, reaching out to squeeze Willow's hand. "Yeah, I think I have."

Nikki comes to sit beside me, leaning her head on my shoulder and linking her arm through Sybil's. For a moment we stay like that, the Core Four, reunited once again.

"You know, I think this calls for a toast," I say, my voice thick with emotion.

Nikki shoots me a grin. "There's no tequila."

"I say we give tequila a break for a bit." Willow rocks to one side and then levers herself off the bed. "Maybe champagne instead." She heads for the small fridge on the other side of the room and pulls out a dark green bottle. Popping the cork and pouring the fizzy drink into the plastic cups stamped with SYBIL & JAMIE that we all got in our welcome bag. I smile at my friends and take a breath as I raise my glass.

"As maid of honor, I want to raise a toast to Sybil." The girls dutifully raise their glasses to meet mine. I know that, later, at the reception, I'll be telling the guests about my best friend, Sybil. About our shared childhood, our wilding around Europe, our fourth-floor NYC walk-up. The fun stories. The classic Sybil stories. The times she brought an extra lunch to school when she knew my mom wouldn't have the time to make me one. The many, many times she was there with open arms when I was at my lowest.

But right now calls for something else. I meet Sybil's hazel eyes. "Sybs, whatever you're dealing with, I need you to know that I love you no matter what. And if you don't want to get married, I support you completely. Same as if you do want to get married." I gesture to Nikki and Willow. "We all do. We're here for you. Whatever you need. No conditions." I raise my cup again. "To Sybil, the bravest woman I know when it comes to love. To the hope that we're all as fearless when it comes to sharing our hearts."

Nikki, Willow, and I take a small sip, but Sybil downs her glass, and we all give her a look. "What? Sometimes I need a little help with the fearlessness." She shrugs. "Okay, time to talk to Jamie."

Before she heads out the door, Sybil pulls me aside. "Is it true you and Finn went on a wild-goose chase to track me down? As in, the two of you *together*?"

"Your sources are correct."

"I never thought I'd see the day." Sybil shakes her head. "Well, I may have ruined my wedding and destroyed all my future hopes of happiness, but at least I got the two of you to be civil to one another again," she adds with a sad smile, her Disney princess eyes brimming with tears.

"Oh, Sybs." I hug her to me.

"Emma, I've already apologized to everyone else about a million times since I got back, but I need to tell you how sorry I am. I shouldn't have bailed without telling anyone. I just got so in my head. I needed to be alone, to get away from...everything."

I want to know where she went, what she's been doing for the past two days, what sent her running in the first place. But I swallow my questions. I need to give Sybil space to breathe. To figure things out on her own.

But the thing about having a best friend for the better part of two decades is that sometimes, they can see right through you.

"I know you're dying to ask where I've been."

"Who, me?" I say with feigned innocence. "I'm not dying

to ask anything. I actually suffer from a clinical lack of curiosity, so—"

"I'm not ready to talk about it just yet," Sybil says, cutting me off, "but I promise, as soon as I am, you're my first call." She pulls away and clasps my hands to hers. "I still can't believe you drove halfway across the country to find me."

Now it's my turn to tear up. "Sybs, you're my family. I knew you needed me, and I will always be there when you need me." I give her hands a squeeze and brush away a tear. "That said, I can admit, I was a bit...*single-minded* in trying to track you down. But I'm turning over a new leaf where I don't spend all my energy trying to control the people I love. So, honestly, if you want to take off again right now, that's cool. I'll even drive you this time."

Sybil laughs, but then her expression turns serious. "I need to tell you about what happened the day of prom." She looks away, like she doesn't want to make eye contact with me, but then she squares her shoulders and looks me straight in the face. "What really happened with Liam. I've always felt like this secret is the reason why you and Finn were never able to get things figured out. There was never anything romantic between us—Finn and me—you know that, right?"

"I do."

"Okay, good." She takes a deep breath then says, "The day of prom something...happened to me, like...medically." I can tell she's struggling to get the words out, so I nod encouragingly even though I'm not quite following. It seems like she's still not ready to give me all the details, and I'm trying to respect that. "Anyway," Sybil continues, "it was bad, and I couldn't go to Liam about it, or my parents. So I went to get some professional help, and Finn was there. He was so supportive, like the big brother

I never had, like…a knight in shining cargo shorts." This gets a chuckle from me. "He found out I had no ride home, so he let me take his car since he was there with his parents. I made him swear not to tell anyone about seeing me at the hospital."

"But why?" The words tumble from my mouth before I can stop them. "Why couldn't you tell me, Sybs?" I ask in a small voice.

"Emma," Sybil says. "You've always been so on top of everything. You're so confident and capable. You never let boy drama get to you. If I had told you how fucked-up things really were with Liam…I just knew you'd be disappointed in me."

"I wouldn't have!" I protest.

"Well, you definitely would have run through walls trying to fix it." She nails me with a hard stare, and I have to nod. She's right. "You've always looked out for me, Emma. Always kept me in line. And I'm so grateful for it, but maybe…" Sybil takes another deep breath. "Maybe I need to learn to keep myself in line. To handle my own shit for once, you know?"

I nod again. I wouldn't trade my friendship with Sybil for the world, but I think we've both realized this weekend that some of our dynamics haven't been the healthiest. It still hurts a little to loosen my grip, to let Sybil fend for herself and not swoop in to save the day. But it's only natural for friendships to grow and change with time. And I know our friendship is strong enough to take it.

"Well, if I'm not going to be dealing with *your* shit anymore"—I roll my eyes playfully—"then I guess I'll have some more time to deal with my own. Like, you know, my budding romance with one Finn Hughes."

"Your *what*?!" Sybil lights up.

"I'll tell you about it later. I think somewhere around here there's a groom missing his bride. I love you so much, Sybs. No matter what."

"I love you, too, Em." She squeezes my arm and walks down the path toward Jamie's bungalow.

I don't know what Sybil is going to say—or what Jamie will say back to her. I don't know if thirty minutes from now will see me walking down the aisle and holding Sybil's bouquet during the vows, or if we'll end up back on the road with a true runaway bride. And I remind myself it's okay that she doesn't know what she's about to do, that none of us knows what will come next. All we can do is step bravely into our lives, and trust that we'll be okay—even if we make mistakes. I don't know if my dad will text me—if we'll repair our relationship or build a new one. I don't know how my review at work will go, either, but I have a pretty good idea that something major needs to change. It's time I finally admit what it is that *I* want. Even if it means breaking out on my own.

As for Finn? I don't know if things with him will last, but I'm willing to give forever a shot. And for the first time in a while, I really like our chances.

After all, we always did make a great team.

I watch as Sybil reaches Jamie's door, and the last of the setting sun lights up around her in a halo. She takes a deep breath, then gives two soft knocks. There's a pause, and then the creak of a door opening. Sybil moves through the doorway into her future, whatever it holds.

EPILOGUE

Six Months Later

After I got back to New York, I took that Monday meeting with my boss. I tried one last time to advocate for myself, but when it was clear that I wouldn't be able to grow any further at Maywell, I put in my two-week notice. I spent the summer working on a spec portfolio, and taking networking meetings, and by August, I'd packed up my tiny one-bedroom and shipped everything back to Texas. Finn flew out to NYC to meet up with me, and we shared a much more leisurely drive through the eastern half of the country on our journey back to Dallas. It was blessedly uneventful: no runaway brides, no car wrecks, no screaming into abysses to release decades-old childhood trauma. We stopped a couple of nights to see Willow and the new baby, but otherwise, it was just me, Finn, and a rented cherry-red Mercedes convertible.

When we finally made it to Dallas, I put most of my stuff in storage and lived with my mom to save up some money. The first night we were back, my heart flip-flopped in my chest when Finn showed up on my porch with a bouquet of bright yellow butterfly ranunculus. My mom pushed us together on the stairway and forced us to take a picture. It wasn't quite the prom photo we missed out on (I was in jean shorts and a flowy white blouse, while Finn was in his "performance fabric" chinos and plain gray T-shirt), since we were just headed for tacos and margs. In it, I'm looking up at Finn and he's looking down at me, and we can't keep the smiles off our faces. It's been the background of my phone ever since.

Finn, as promised, was Emma Townsend Design's first client, and he gave me nearly free rein to redesign his house (though he did nix my plan to tent the entire dining room in striped blue and green silk after several rounds of debate). His mom, when she moved into her new condo, was my second client. Friends from high school and college started reaching out about design help, and soon, I was able to put together a solid book of business—not enough to buy a Singer of my own (Finn's, thankfully, made a full recovery), but enough that I was able to buy an original powder-blue Mustang. Right now, it's parked in front the Dilbeck while I confer with the photographer who spent the day documenting all the work we've done on the house. Mostly I'm just glad we were able to get all my boxes unpacked and out of the way before the cameras showed up. When I told Sybil earlier this fall that Finn and I had decided to take that next step in our relationship, she shrieked through the phone for a solid minute.

"Oh my god! Moving in together after just four months of dating? That's rather reckless of you, missy. Who do you think you are, me?"

I laughed. "No competition there, I assure you." Sybil's fateful wedding weekend had ended in a way that truly *none* of us had expected, and we were all still reeling from it—but that was another story. I was more focused on *my own* for once. "What can I say," I sighed. "When you know, you know."

NOW, THE PHOTOGRAPHER AND I say our goodbyes, and Finn joins me in the living room. My hand lingers on a giant electric-blue vase, which is currently resting on my vintage Italian roulette table. Because yes, that needed to find its forever home here. I turn to him. "We don't have to keep this vase, by the way. It was just for the staging photos."

"Do you like it?" he asks.

"I love it. The color is perfect in this room."

"Then we're keeping it." The warm, fluttery feeling that hasn't left me since our kiss in Malibu rises to the surface.

I start rifling through the fridge, checking to see whether we have enough leftovers to cobble together dinner, or if we need to order in, when Finn calls out to me.

"Hey, Em? Can you take a look at something in the den for me?"

"Sure." I follow Finn to the back of the house, but he motions me ahead once we reach the den.

Finn's voice comes from behind me. "Do you think that painting above the fireplace is straight?"

I reach up ready to readjust the piece hanging above the mantel but drop my hand almost immediately. "Hmm, I do actually. I—"

There's a soft sound behind me, and I turn to see Finn with one knee on the floor, holding a small red velvet box in his hand.

"Wh-what are you doing?" Finn and I have talked about getting married, and in my head, I knew this was coming. But I'm still not prepared for the adrenaline that spikes through me. I want to think of something else to say, but the only thought in my brain is a ticker tape of *It's happening. It's happening. It's happening.*

"Something that I've been wanting to do for a long time." He's smiling at me, but there's a thread of nerves running through his voice as he asks, "Emma Mae Townsend, I am not a perfect man, but when I'm with you, I feel like I could be. I know we've made mistakes along the way, but I am just glad that all the mistakes I've made in my life have led me back to you. Would you do me the honor of marrying me?"

This is one of the most important moments in my life, and I try to remember every detail. The way the evening sunlight filters through the sheer curtains onto the wood floors. The smell of the lavender candle I burned earlier this afternoon lingering in the air. The nervous smile on Finn's face. "Emma, please say something."

His words break me out of my sensory trance. "Yes. Yes, of course I'll marry you." I have never felt so certain of anything.

I throw my arms around him, and he lets out a laugh as he falls against the armrest of an overstuffed leather chair. Pulling me onto his lap, he slips the ring on my finger.

"I do have to have one objection to your proposal, however. A critique, really." The diamond sparkles in the light as I brush my fingers across Finn's face. Once again trying to memorize everything about this moment.

Laughing, he says, "Of course you do." He catches my hand and presses a kiss to my wrist.

"I think you *are* absolutely perfect." Finn's smile widens, and then his lips are on mine, and I know I'm home.

ACKNOWLEDGMENTS

I FIRST WANT TO thank the "core four" that made this story come to life: Lexa Hillyer, Jenna Brickley, Emily Larrabee, and Madeleine Colavita. I could not have done this without y'all! Lexa, thank you for believing in me from the beginning. Jenna, your attention to detail helped make this story so special. And Emily, you are a superstar. I am inspired by your ability to take all of our ideas and expand them into a new multiverse for our characters to live and love in. Collaborating with you all was a gift. Thank you for caring so much for this project.

Madeleine, thank you for believing in *Mistakes We Never Made* and joining our efforts to make this an epic summer read. Your willingness to be so hands-on and your overall passion for the project made you the perfect addition to our group of badass women creating and collaborating together. I am so thankful for you and the rest of the team at Forever: Grace Fischetti, Tareth Mitch, Daniela Medina, Angelina Krahn, Estelle Hallick, Alli Rosenthal, and Marie Mundaca.

I also want to give a big shout-out to Kaitlyn Kall for the gorgeous cover art. You really captured the tone of the book, and I'm in love with it!!!

Thank you as well to Stephen Barbara at Inkwell Management and my agents Gwen Beal and Albert Lee at United Talent Agency for working so hard to make our dream of this project a reality. Also, to Max Stubblefield and Jamie Youngentob: Thank you for making it ALL happen—I am incredibly grateful for you both!

To my amazing team at Align PR: Nicole Perez, Taylor Rodriguez, and Paige Alvarez, thank you for working so hard to help promote this book and create wonderful opportunities for me to connect with readers everywhere.

Thank you, to both the new readers and the die-hard fans, who've opened your heart to this book and rooted for Emma and Finn to work it out. It feels amazing to share my love of love stories with you all.

I'm so grateful to my family and friends who've been along for this ride. And last but not least, thank you, Adam, for being there for me, no matter what. I've made my share of mistakes on my own personal journey—but I have to say, falling in love with you was a pretty great move on my part. Love you, Babe.

ABOUT THE AUTHOR

Hannah Brown is a television personality, lifestyle expert, podcast host, and *New York Times* bestselling author of *God Bless This Mess*. After winning Miss Alabama USA in 2018, she went on to star on season fifteen of ABC's hit reality series *The Bachelorette*, win season twenty-eight of *Dancing with the Stars*, and compete on FOX's *Special Forces: World's Toughest Test*, where she ended up being one of two women who completed the course and outlasted the other sixteen contestants, most of whom were professional athletes.

Brown's authenticity and charismatic personality have captivated her millions of followers, and she continues to inspire and empower others by advocating for mental health awareness and emphasizing the importance of self-love.

Born and raised in Tuscaloosa, Alabama, Brown currently resides in Nashville, Tennessee.